MW01710871

Breathless

COLE GIBSEN

www.crescentmoonpress.com

Breathless
Cole Gibsen

ISBN: 978-1-937254-27-8
E-ISBN: 978-1-937254-28-5

Cover Art: Jeannie Ruesch
Editor: Rochelle French
Layout/Typesetting: jimandzetta.com

Crescent Moon Press
1385 Highway 35
Box 269
Middletown, NJ 07748

Crescent Moon Press electronic publication/print publication: March 2012 www.crescentmoonpress.com

Dedication

To my mother, who always found money for a book even in the hardest of times.

Chapter 1

Only three more hours until my curfew. Three long hours of biting my tongue and pretending I wanted to be on the boat when, really, I wanted to be anywhere but here.

Marty Sherwood, my horrible mistake of a date, ran his hands along the edge of my swimsuit, pulling me from my thoughts and making my body grow rigid. Before he could shove his fingers underneath the elastic, I quickly crossed my legs.

He laughed, resting his hand on my thigh. “God, Edith, when I asked you out I had no idea you emo-types were so uptight.” His lingering touch, along with the smell of his breath—a combination of beer and cigarettes—filled my stomach with something sour.

I shrank back against the side of the speedboat and brushed away the dark hair that the wind was whipping across my eyes. “I’m not uptight,” I yelled over the roar of the motor. “I’m cold.” But that was a lie. The truth was, the only thing keeping me from diving off the boat was the growing distance between me and the shore.

He shrugged. “Sure. I still think you’d have more fun if you’d drink a beer.”

Actually, I’d have more fun letting a dentist pull out all my teeth. Only two hours and fifty-two minutes to go . . .

Russell Talbert twisted in the captain’s seat to look back at me. “I’ve got some weed if that’s more your thing.”

Huh. High school quarterback *and* a pothead? Shocker.

I shook my head and wrapped my arms around the plain black Speedo clinging to my body, desperately wishing I hadn't abandoned my jeans in Marty's trunk.

Marty dropped his hand from my leg and huffed. "I can tell you're going to be a *lot* of fun."

"Well, if she doesn't want to smoke, I do." Gabrielle glared at me from behind sunglasses the same bubblegum pink color as her swimsuit.

I marveled at the fact I'd managed to end up on a boat with the kind of girl who color-coordinated her sunglasses to her outfit.

"Where's your hitter, Russell?" Gabrielle asked.

"Atta girl!" Russell took his hand off the wheel to swat at her butt. "In the bag with the beer. Inside the side pocket."

Gabrielle raised her pointed nose in the air and trotted past me. She was the captain of our school's equestrian team and played the part well. I wondered if the bouncing walk was something she picked up after riding all those horses. But—if the rumors of her reputation were true—horses weren't the only things she rode regularly. She grabbed a red duffel bag off a bench and rummaged through it. "Here it is!" she said, pulling out a small wooden box and a plastic bag of weed. She stood and tucked her streaming blond hair behind her ears. "Who wants to pack?"

"Give it here." Marty reached his hand out.

Gabrielle smirked at me as she handed him the box. "Maybe we can find you a box of razor blades if that's more your thing?"

Right. Because I wear black I'm automatically a cutter. I sucked in a gulp of salty air and held it until my boiling anger reduced to a simmer. When I felt I could safely answer her without saying something that would get me in trouble, I still had to force the words through clenched teeth. "I'm fine, thanks." But, truthfully, if she had a box of razor blades, I wouldn't turn them down. I could tape them to my swimsuit and maybe then Marty would stop trying to feel me up.

Gabrielle shrugged. "Whatever." She turned to Russell. "We're far enough from the shore, and I don't see the Coast Guard. I think it's safe to light up."

Russell nodded and eased the boat to a halt, then killed the engine. He left his seat behind the wheel and crossed the boat, kicking several beer cans out of his way before sitting beside Gabrielle.

I pretended to study the distant shore of Florida's Destin Beach, where we'd come from, as Marty ground the metal pipe against the weed in his palm. I pulled my legs up onto the narrow plastic bench and hugged my knees against my chest. If only Sir could see me now. My stepdad would totally have a heart attack, but it would serve him right.

Before the move to Eglin Air Force Base, Sir had made it clear that when we arrived, I was to do things differently than I had at the last base. I wasn't to stay in my room scribbling emo poetry in my notebooks. I was to make friends and sign up for extracurricular activities. I wasn't to be caught with the obituary section of his paper again. And I didn't even want to know what would happen if I disobeyed. So when Martin Sherwood, son of Lieutenant Colonel Sherwood, had asked me out, I'd agreed solely to make Sir happy.

If I wasn't so miserable, I might have found the irony funny.

"Marty says you're a military brat," Gabrielle's shrill voice shattered what little serenity the sound of the waves brought me.

"Air Force," I said. "We were last stationed at Scott Air Force Base in Illinois."

"Meaning that since you just got here, there's no chance you'll be moving anytime soon?" Her smile was sweet, but it didn't mask the venom on her tongue.

"I don't think so." As long as I played by Sir's rules and didn't give him a reason to send me off to military school, that is. If I could make it until graduation, then I'd go off to college. I'd finally able to live my own life. There wasn't anything I wouldn't do to make that happen—even if it meant getting pawed at by Marty and hanging out with his pothead friends.

"Oh." Gabrielle didn't bother to hide the disappointment in her voice. "How long have you been going to our school, anyway?"

I shrugged. "About a month."

"That's weird. All that time and I've never noticed you."

I knew she meant it as an insult, but I was comforted that she hadn't noticed me. Wearing black kept me off the radar of people like Gabrielle. Which was exactly why I wore it—to keep people away. Well, that, and to remember what I'd lost. Death sets you apart from other people. It marks you. And when people sense that you've been scarred by death, they don't want to be friends anymore. I found that if I kept them away in the first place, getting through high school became a lot easier.

Gabrielle flipped a lock of hair behind her shoulder. "How did *you* find her, Marty?" Her tone made it more of an accusation.

Marty finished dragging on the pipe and coughed several times before answering. "Edith sits in front of me in Chem." He passed the pipe to Russell, then threw his arm around me. "You know I can't resist fresh meat."

Two hours and twenty-eight minutes to go. I twisted my head toward the Gulf, letting the ocean breeze push away the smell of Marty's sweat. *You can do this, Edith.* Two hours was nothing. I'd be home, alone in my room, before I knew it. I'd never have to hang out with these people again. Sir would be appeased because I'd done what he asked and tried to make friends. How was I

~ ☾ ~

supposed to know when I'd agreed to this date that these people were all losers? I placed my hand on my throat and nervously fingered the strand of pearls I wore.

Gabrielle twitched her head like a falcon watching the movements of a mouse. "What's with the necklace? Isn't it a little old-fashioned?"

"My aunt . . ." The sound of a motor growled and I let the sentence hang in the air. Gabrielle twisted on the bench, no longer interested in what I had to say.

"Shit!" Russell cried, tossing the metal pipe into his bag. "Is it the Guard?"

Gabrielle squealed and clasped her hands together. "No! It's Scott!"

I had no idea who Scott was, but if Gabrielle was thrilled, his arrival probably meant that the day's suck meter was about to move a few notches higher. The red boat that stopped next to us was easily twice as big and occupied by girls I recognized from the cheerleading squad, along with a half-dozen football players.

A bronze-skinned, lanky boy raised a beer as he leaned over the side. "Hey Russell! Did your piece-of-crap finally bite it?" Several oil-slicked girls tittered from the bow.

Russell stood up and chucked an empty beer can into the waves. "You wish, Scott. This baby could shred your boat any day."

Scott crossed his arms. "Is that so?"

Marty dropped his arm from my shoulders and rose to his feet. Scott snorted. "Come off it."

While I was thankful for the reprieve of Marty's hands, the tension mounting between the two boats buzzed along my skin like an electric current.

"That's funny, that's what your mom said last night," Russell replied.

Gabrielle wrapped her arms around Russell's neck and threw her head back, laughing. Russell snaked an arm around her waist and hiked her tightly against his hip. She giggled louder, along with the occupants of Scott's boat.

Scott's jaw tightened. "Screw you, Russell."

"Weren't you listening? Your mom already took care of it."

Scott's cheeks burned red until his whole face was flushed. "If you're so certain your raft can take me on, how about you prove it?"

"Right on!" Marty shouted. "Russell, let's smoke him."

My stomach tightened as I mentally calculated all of the beers Russell had downed. "Marty," I stood and tugged on his arm. "I don't think that is such a good idea."

Gabrielle turned to me, the smile dying on her face. "Oh my God, Edith, do you have to be such a baby?"

"I'm not a baby." Despite my best efforts, I found myself squirming under the intensity of her glare. "I just . . . don't feel good. Probably a little seasick or something. I think I need to go home."

"Nah. You'll be fine. After we do this, I'll take you home." Marty pinched my butt, making me gasp and tumble back onto the bench.

Gabrielle rolled her eyes. "Seriously lame."

Oh, God. Oh, God. I searched the horizon for help. The waves burned orange as the sun made its descent into the water. The approaching night meant there were few boats remaining on the water and no sign of the Coast Guard.

Russell released Gabrielle and took his seat behind the wheel, then turned the key and revved the engine. "Let's do this!"

Gabrielle clapped her hands. The rest of the squad cheered along.

Marty laughed as he slid onto the bench next to me. "This is going to be great."

~ ☾ ~

I was trapped—like a caged animal. My heart hammered inside my chest. Not a soft mass of tissue, but an iron wrecking ball determined to collapse my ribs. There was no escape. No stopping them. I dug my nails into the seat cushion, certain I was damaging the vinyl but not caring.

"Are you scared?" Marty's sour breath stung the inside of my nostrils.

I turned away, sucking in my bottom lip to keep it from trembling. I would not let them see me cry.

"Don't worry." He pulled me against him, his sweat sticking our skin together like paste. "I'll protect you."

My stomach lurched, and I tasted bile on the back of my tongue.

Scott took his place behind the wheel and revved the boat's motor. The growl was deafening. Russell stood up and pointed to a distant buoy, then jerked his hand back to Destin Beach. Scott nodded.

The red boat jumped forward, and Russell, mouthing a curse, jerked the throttle full-speed. We flew through the water, and the speed flattened me against the back of my seat, leaving me gasping for the breath that was lodged in my throat.

Marty shouted wildly as Russell inched us closer to the stern of the red boat. When we were bow-to-bow, Gabrielle climbed up on the side bench, and, holding on to the rail, began to dance. The football players on the red boat clustered around their rail and encouraged her with shouts and whistles.

I pulled my windblown hair back with both hands as I watched the approaching buoy grow larger ahead of us. If we made the turn at the speed we were travelling, there was no way Gabrielle could keep her footing. I looked to Marty for help, but he continued to hoot like an idiot. Russell, oblivious, stared straight ahead.

I swallowed past the lump of fear wedged in my throat. "Gabrielle!"

~ ☾ ~

Her eyes never left her crowd of admirers.

"Do you want to dance, too?" Marty pulled me to my feet by my wrists. "Show 'em what you got."

He released me and I wavered, widening my stance to steady my balance in the jumping boat. Inch by inch, I shuffled toward Gabrielle, sliding my hands along the side rail, watching the buoy draw nearer. We only had seconds before Russell would make the turn that would bring us back to the beach. I had to get Gabrielle down before she fell overboard.

When Gabrielle was within reach, I slid my fingers around her ankle. She snapped her head around to face my direction, then shot me a seething look. "Please sit," I begged.

She kicked her foot free of my grip and turned back to face the other boat, giving me a smug look over her shoulder before she released her grip from the rail and lifted her bikini top, continuing to thrust her hips.

We were at the buoy. "Gabrielle!" I shouted. This time I wrapped both my hands around her ankle.

"Get off me!" she shrieked. She gripped the rail and kicked out again. Her foot cracked into my jaw just as Russell jerked on the wheel, twisting the boat in the opposite direction. The blow sent me sprawling to the floor. I looked up in time to see Gabrielle's wide-eyed gaze lock with my own a millisecond before the force of the turn threw her into the air.

I screamed.

Russell turned toward me. After he'd noticed that Gabrielle was no longer with us, he let go of the wheel.

"Russell! No!" Marty yelled.

But it was too late.

We had been closest to the buoy when both boats made the turn to take us back to the beach. But when Russell let go of the wheel, our boat veered left and drove us straight into the side of Scott's boat. The crunch of splintering fiberglass was loud enough to drown out my screams and the screams of everyone around me. The force of the impact ricocheted our boat into the air before it disappeared beneath my feet.

I could fly.

Or at least it felt like I could in the seconds I was airborne. Then gravity plucked me from the sky and hurtled me into the ocean. Colder-than-expected water greeted me and held me under. I fought the urge to scream, knowing I would drown if I did. I kicked hard, reaching for the surface. Still underwater, I opened my eyes, but immediately wished I hadn't. The sun's orange glow seemed impossibly far away. Fire replaced the air in my lungs. My vision blurred and I ground my teeth to keep my lips from parting. Finally, my head broke the water, and I cried out in what was more of a shout than a gasp of air. I rubbed my stinging eyes. I was alive . . . but for how long? When would help come? Would I be able to tread water until it did?

I fought to stay afloat, pulled down by the weight of my terror—a heavy knot wedged inside my gut. My arms flailed and my breaths came in short, ragged bursts. If I didn't get a grip soon, I was going to be dead in seconds. I forced myself to slow my breathing and pull in air as if I were sucking through a straw. With each breath, the tightness in my chest eased and the spots cleared from my vision. *A panicked soldier is a dead soldier, he just doesn't know it yet*—isn't that what Sir always said?

The sound of crying broke my thoughts. I searched for the source but couldn't see past the splintered fiberglass, coolers, and vinyl seat cushions that floated around me. I swam forward, grabbed onto a cushion, and clutched it to my chest, giving my legs a reprieve. The buoy, which had been close enough to touch when we began our turn, was now yards away, an oddly-angled body draped over the bottom rung. I recognized the pink bikini bottoms as the one Gabrielle had been wearing.

~ ☾ ~

My stomach lurched and I jerked my head away, feeling the tightness beneath my ribs return. "It's okay. I'm okay," I muttered over and over.

The unseen crier began to wail.

I shook my head in an effort to clear my mind of the sound. "It's okay. I'm okay." Hysteria twisted my words into a yelp.

There was a splash and someone screamed. I twisted in the direction of the sound only to come face to face with an orange and white cooler.

I heard Scott's yell of "Oh God!" followed by another splash. He screamed, then shouted, "Shark!"

An icy ball of fear plunged into my stomach, threatening to drag me under the surface with its weight. I stretched my arm behind me and pushed back in the water, away from the screams. Before I had completed two full strokes, something cold and slippery brushed along my calf.

I froze, too afraid to breath.

A girl screamed behind me. "Scott, no! Scott!"

I heard a gasp for air followed by more thrashing in the water.

I closed my eyes and tried to focus. Surely I had imagined the brush against my leg. My fear was getting the best of me. The smart thing to do was swim like mad in direction of the shore . . . wherever that was.

But then I felt it again—another brush against my leg, hard enough to make me bob in the water.

My jaw trembled so violently that it chattered my teeth. I was going to die.

What would Sir do if he were in this situation? My stepdad had served eight tours in Iraq. He'd survived landmines and ambushes. There was no way he would let some fish get the best of him. No, he would wrestle the beast like it was nothing more than a guppy.

But I was nothing like Sir, or the son he longed for.

Something bumped me, knocking me underwater. I

came up sputtering. So pathetic. What would Sir say if he could see me now?

Soldiers don't cry, they act!

I swallowed down a quivering breath and nodded. I needed to act.

The sun was setting to my left, which meant I needed to swim straight to get back to shore.

Are you waiting for a printed invitation? the voice of my stepdad demanded.

"No, sir!" I shouted before taking a deep breath and diving headlong into the ocean.

~ ☾ ~

Chapter 2

The first tug at my ankle only startled me. The second shot needle-like ribbons of pain up the entire length of my leg. I tried to scream but was pulled under the waves. Saltwater flooded my mouth. A glittering fish tail the length of my body passed before my eyes as I thrashed my way back to the surface.

I broke through the water and gasped, only to be jerked back under.

Fight! Sir's voice thundered in my head.

Despite the saltwater burning my eyes and blurring my vision, I could see them. I couldn't make out what they were, but at least five large shapes swarmed around me.

I doubted even Sir could withstand such a fight.

Something nudged my back. I twisted around, only to find nothing there. Fear amplified my pulse into deafening waves inside my head. Another bump, but this time something cold slid around my leg and wrenched me further down. I fought the scream that rose in my throat and clawed for the surface, but whatever held me felt like an anchor. Sinking deeper, I watched, helpless, as the orange glow of the sun melted into the inky blue of the oceans depths.

I am going to die.

The realization drained the fight from my body. My muscles burned in relief. *Soon, now. A couple of minutes at most, and it will all be over.*

I couldn't believe death was actually happening. My death. I'd often fantasized what it would be like to die.

To me, death wasn't the hooded skeletal figure come to drag you, screaming, into the abyss. Death was an out. An escape from late nights spent studying under the blankets to earn my meager slightly-above-average grades. An end to the Air Force Academy applications strategically placed on my breakfast plate. And if I was gone, I could be with my brother instead of here. Where I was hated because I'd let him die.

But now, as certain death loomed in front of me, I was unable to remember a single line of poetry I'd written for just this moment. Gone were the words to well-memorized prayers. Instead, the only thought running through my mind was this: *I hope it doesn't hurt.*

I closed my eyes and waited. Had it even been a minute? Seconds felt like hours. My heart beat wildly, echoing inside of my head like footsteps in a cavern.

When I thought I might go crazy with anticipation, my ankle was released and what felt like a row of razor blades cut into the side of my neck, popping my aunt's pearls free from their strand. Reflexively, I opened my eyes and brought my hands to my neck, pressing a couple of pearls into my stinging wounds. Blood clouded my vision with a red haze.

I gasped, which I immediately regretted, as my mouth flooded with water. The raw flesh of my neck burned white-hot from the ocean's salt. I wished death didn't have to hurt so much or that it would go faster. My vision began to blacken around the edges, but the unconsciousness I desperately hoped for wouldn't come.

I considered inhaling the water in my throat—that would speed up the process considerably. And yet, I couldn't bring myself to do it.

You're weak! Sir's voice roared in my head.

I nodded in agreement. I couldn't kill myself. I could only lie still and let something do it for me.

Just then, my head was jerked roughly by something

pulling my hair, and I found myself looking into the eyes of a girl not much older than me. An angel? I quickly abandoned that notion when a corner of her mouth pulled up into a cruel smile. Her jet-black eyes never blinked. She was definitely more demon than angel. Did that mean I was going to hell?

I held my hand up to clear the blood clouding the water and she pulled back, hissing, the sound as clearly heard underwater as if I had been standing on the shore. Her midnight-blue hair swirled around her like a cloak. She was beautiful in her hate.

My heart pounded out a frantic warning that reverberated throughout my body. This was not what I wanted. The creature in front of me was not sent to set me free, but rather to devour me whole. Her bottomless eyes promised to savor every moment of my lingering pain.

I had to get away. I kicked for the surface, but she reached out and wrapped cold fingers around my throat.

My need for air was excruciating. With the last of my energy, I pried my hands around her slender fingers, which in turn, dug into my skin.

Her twisted smile was the last thing I saw before my world went black.

~ ☾ ~

Chapter 3

My throat felt like it had been scoured with steel wool. Each cough wracked my body with agony, forcing tears from my closed eyes. I shook my head slowly from side to side, hoping to calm the ocean waves crashing inside of my head. There wasn't a place on my body that didn't ache.

Someone exhaled sharply, then said, "She's breathing." The male voice was warm and thick, like honey. I couldn't be sure, but I thought I detected a note of relief.

What was going on? Had I been rescued? I tried to lift my arm but my body felt foreign and useless. Moving wasn't an option, and even though I knew the tide brushed against my feet, the water seemed miles away from where I was.

"Rest," he whispered to me.

Rest? I would have laughed if I was able. It wasn't like I could do anything else but lay there. I tried to open my eyes but I was unable to fight the velvet warmth of unconsciousness that pressed against me. Maybe I was dying, after all.

I heard a sound of female disgust. "Can't you see how badly injured the thing is? It would be cruel of us to leave it in this condition. Allow me put it out of its misery." Hers was the voice of an eerie lullaby, and I cowered inside my lifeless shell.

Were they actually talking about killing me? What kind of rescuers were they? I tried to ask them but only managed a low, cracking groan. I sensed movement and knew that one of them had shifted closer.

"Absolutely not." His voice swirled in my head like satin.

"But she saw me! You know the danger in that!"

"I do. I see you every day and it's made my life hell."

She hissed, and it was the same sound I'd heard under the water from the blue-haired demon. "The king is not going to be happy with you."

"And how would that be different from any other day?"

"Bastin! You curse us all with your short-sightedness! These creatures are weak and stupid. They destroy everything they do not understand, and that makes them more dangerous than any foreign army we've ever faced. How can—"

"Luna." The voice was no longer caramel-coated but now a jagged, tangible force.

Bastin. His name was Bastin.

"That is enough!" he continued. "Do you need to be reminded of your rank?"

"Remind *me*? Evidently, I know my duty better than you."

I felt the slight breeze of a swift movement and heard the girl gasp.

"Please do not confuse your rank with *my* authority," Bastin growled.

The one he called Luna made a choking noise.

"Perhaps," he continued, "you would like to spend some recon time with the humans. A week maybe. You could scout for purifiers and hopefully would come back with a better respect for your superiors."

"No!" Luna's cry came out as a garbled whisper. "You would do that? After all I've done for you—all the purifiers I obtained today?"

"From that one there?"

Even teetering on the edge of unconsciousness I felt the weight of their gaze settle upon me.

~ ☾ ~

"Yes," Luna answered.

"Interesting," he murmured. A finger slid across my forehead and pushed my wet bangs from my closed eyes. "I wonder . . ." Bastin let his words hang in the air.

"Well, if you're not going to let me kill it, *Your Majesty*," the bitterness in Luna's voice was unmistakable, "I suggest we get back. Its kind will soon swarm this area like the parasites they are."

My lungs burned, the feeling growing until it exploded up my throat and wracked my body with a series of violent coughs. When it subsided, I rubbed the back of my hand into my stinging eyes and wedged my lids open.

Even in the dark, I could see the moon reflecting blue orbs against the two sets of onyx eyes that stared back at me.

Icy fear sank into my bones and froze the marrow within. I thought I was paralyzed in my terror, but a sharp pain below my neck brought my eyes down to the shredded skin around my chest. Among the crumpled crimson, I saw a flash of silver and was certain I was seeing my own collarbone. The shock was enough to send me spiraling back into the black depths of unconsciousness. But not before I heard the sound of two large splashes.

~ ☾ ~

Chapter 4

The low grumble breached through my black haven and pulled me painfully into consciousness. I had been around Sir long enough to know the difference between a casual clearing of the throat and an unspoken order. I opened my eyes and blinked several times to clear the blurriness from my vision. When the stark white walls of the room came into focus, I discovered that I wasn't in my bed, but a hospital room.

"Michael, maybe we should let her get her bearings together?" my mother asked from the foot of my bed.

I flinched at the look Sir shot her from where he stood in the doorway. She seemed to shrink before my eyes. I wasn't the only one expected to obey orders.

I watched as Sir turned away from her and marched to the side of my bed. I averted my gaze from the muscles that flexed in his jaw. Instead, I studied the reflections the florescent lights made on his bald head.

"Do you know where you are?" he asked.

I twisted my hands into the stiff sheets to keep from jumping out of the bed and fleeing, my IV in tow. "The hospital?"

"Very good," he answered, his voice thick with sarcasm. "Now would you care to tell me how you got here?"

That was the last thing I wanted to do. As I thought about the possible answers, I wondered which would get me shipped off to military school faster: the fact that I was riding in a boat with kids who were drinking and smoking weed? Or that while I was in the ocean, a girl with blue hair had clawed at my throat and tried to strangle me?

I bit my lip and looked past him, hoping that a doctor might come to my rescue. But help didn't come, and I knew my mother, who stood a safe distance away twisting her hands together, would be useless.

"Answer the question, Ed." His eyes blazed, exposing the tiny red veins that surrounded his crystal-blue irises.

I didn't know if it was the cold IV fluid leaking into my veins or fear of the man before me, but I began to tremble. I tried not to feel ashamed—those eyes had broken stronger soldiers than me. The only difference was that most of those men had grown to love and respect the sergeant. "I don't know, sir."

He arched a thin brown eyebrow. "You don't know? You have deep lacerations along your neck and collarbone, scratches along your legs, and you have no idea how they got there?"

I shook my head.

Sir narrowed his eyes. "*Excuse* me?"

"No, sir." It was barely a whisper. "The last thing I remember is riding in the boat with Lieutenant Colonel Sherwood's son. I don't know what happened."

His jaw flexed. "I'll tell you what happened," he snarled, leaning into me.

I sank as deep into the bed as the rock-hard mattress would allow.

"Kids died, Ed."

Bile crept up the back of my throat.

"Lieutenant Colonel Sherwood's boy has a punctured lung and a skull fracture."

I looked to my mom for help, but her eyes never left the wedding band that she twisted around and around her finger.

"And, apparently," Sir continued, "some shark found you too much trouble to eat."

I looked down at the bloody gauze wrapped around

my chest and shoulder and cringed. Funny how things hurt so much worse when you paid attention to them. "I think I'm going to be sick," I whispered.

Sir leaned down so that only inches separated our noses. "You will speak up when addressing me."

The throbbing in my neck and shoulder intensified by the second. The pain made my vision teeter. Sir's face rippled like a lake disturbed by a thrown pebble. I closed my eyes and swallowed the excess saliva in my mouth. "I said, I think I'm going to be—" but I had run out of time.

Sir barely had a chance to blink, let alone move, before the onslaught of saltwater and my partially digested lunch spewed from my throat. As I continued to heave, Sir scrambled backwards, his teeth grinding as he used his fingers to clear the vomit from his eyes.

I wanted to apologize, to tell him that I'd tried to warn him, but I couldn't talk around the choked cries brought on by my stomach's contractions—even after it was completely purged.

"Oh, honey." My mother moved toward me but was stopped by Sir's outstretched arm.

"Carol."

Mom glanced at me—a bold move on her part—and before she looked away, I watched the sadness in her eyes smooth into the blank mask that she had perfected long ago. "Michael?" she asked.

"I'm going to find a bathroom and clean myself off," Sir said, seething. "I need you to go find a nurse, doctor, or whoever runs this monkey operation they call a hospital, and get the rest of Ed's tests run. Then maybe we can get some goddamn release papers. I don't want to stay here longer than what is absolutely necessary."

My mother opened her mouth, but a disapproving look from Sir had her snapping it shut just as quickly. "Yes, Michael," she said, then turned on her heels and left the room.

"Now," Sir said as he swiveled his head back in my

direction, "this is not over, Ed. Kids are dead. Sherwood's boy was seriously injured. I will have answers from you. Do I make myself clear?"

I nodded weakly. Using the bed sheet, I wiped at a line of saliva that dripped off my chin. After Sir left and I pushed my soiled sheets to the foot of the bed, I gave in to the grief pulling at my heart. I curled into a ball and cried. Kids were dead? I sucked on my lip to keep from releasing the desperate wail lodged in my throat. Why couldn't I have been so lucky?

~ ☾ ~

Chapter 5

Much to the protest of the ER doctor, Sir had me released from the hospital and home shortly thereafter. I breathed a sigh of relief when we pulled up to our two-story rental in neighboring Valparaiso. This place was only temporary, as Sir was fond of reminding me, until a house—if that's what you called the tiny duplexes they shoved us in—on the Air Force Base opened up. I prayed every night that nothing would.

I loved living among civilians, away from the Stepford life that was base living. Here there was no prerecorded horn blaring through loudspeakers to wake you up in the morning. In the afternoon, there was no *Star Spangled Banner* forcing you to stop what you were doing, even if it was driving, so you could pledge your allegiance. And, lastly, there was no *Taps* to signal the end of your day. No, in Valparaiso, there was nothing to announce the coming and going of my day other than the songs of the bullfrogs in the nearby bayou and the sun and the moon themselves.

I pushed open the door of Sir's 4x4 and, even after a month of living in Florida, was no less surprised by the forceful impact of the humidity. Right away I could feel my lacerations burn with the sweat that beaded along my skin.

Sir stood at the front of the 4x4, watching me. "Do you need help?"

I shook my head. I knew a test when I saw one. "No, sir."

He nodded once and strode up the sidewalk and into

the house without a backward glance.

Mom was instantly at my side, pulling me against her as she led me into the house. "You know your father is only acting like this because he's upset."

Father. If I could have chewed up the word and spit it on the sidewalk I would have. My real dad took off when I was an infant. When I was three, Mom met Sir and they were married in a courthouse after only a few months of dating. Sir was rigid from the beginning, but the birth of my brother seemed to soften him a bit. There were fewer orders and I was allowed to call him "Dad." When my brother was alive we were a family. Practically happy.

Now it was all gone and Sir blamed me.

I leaned into my mother's arms, inhaling the fragrance of English roses, her favorite perfume. Something deep inside of me loosened, like a stray thread on a sweater had been tugged, and I worried that I was on the verge of unraveling.

Mom gave me a hard kiss on the top of my head. "So scary . . ." She shuddered. "I don't want to think about it."

That was good because just placing one foot in front of the other took all my concentration. Sir had retreated to his room upstairs, so Mom led me quietly to the back of the house and into my bedroom. The previous tenants painted the master bedroom pink—a color that gave Sir aneurysms—and because Sir was convinced we would be moving any day now and because painting a rental was a waste of time and money, he and Mom occupied one the smaller bedrooms.

Even as tired and miserable as I felt, as soon as I stepped into my flamingo-colored room, I smiled. I didn't even like pink—though the fact that it worked as Sir repellant gave it bonus points—it was just the first time in my life that I lived in a room with color of any kind. Base housing was very strict about keeping the walls eggshell-white.

Mom walked me to my full-sized bed and gently eased me onto it. "Do you want to sleep in those?" She motioned to the pale green scrubs the hospital gave me.

"Not really."

"Didn't think so." She shuffled through my drawers until she found an oversized T-shirt. "Would you like some help getting dressed?"

"No," I said automatically. I didn't ask for help. Ever. Years of Sir demanding to know if my arms were broken had cured me of that.

Something clouded Mom's face—regret? I couldn't be sure because it was gone as soon as it came. She pushed her shoulders back. "Don't be silly, Edith. I'm going to help you."

"Yes, ma'am."

She stiffened.

"Mom," I corrected.

She made a sound like a choking sigh and approached me. Carefully, she pulled both of my arms out of the scrub top and slid it over my head. She looked at me and hissed. "You're bleeding through your bandages. I'm going to have to change those, too."

I fought the urge to cross my arms over my bare chest, reminding myself that Mom had seen me naked before, and looked at my shoulder. Sure enough, a large patch of crimson had bloomed, like an angry rose, onto the gauze.

Mom left my room and returned moments later with our first aid kit. She worked fast, removing the soiled bandages and exchanging them with fresh gauze and tape. I was careful not to watch. Somehow it hurt less that way. After she packed the supplies away back in their small plastic container, she stared at me—much to my discomfort—in an almost trance-like way.

I hugged my arms across my body. "Mom?"

She didn't move, and when she spoke, sounded far

away, like she had fallen deep into herself. "I was wondering . . ."

When her voice trailed away I made a nervous grab for my T-shirt. "You were wondering?" I prompted, pulling the shirt over my head.

She shook her head and appeared to come back to herself. "I'm sorry."

I shrugged, but the pain that seared across my shoulder made me immediately regret that action. "That's okay. What was it?"

Mom tucked a stray lock of brown hair behind her ear and bit her lip. "Does it hurt much?"

I could only blink at her. What kind of question was that? I thought of a dozen smartass replies—*I don't know, how about I jab a fork into your neck and you tell me*—but I wasn't that kind of girl. In fact, I wondered if I was any kind of girl at all. I went to school, participated in the required after-school activities, did my homework, ate what was placed in front of me, and spoke when spoken to. No, there was no teenage-girl here; I was an empty shell housing only the remains of my spirit, long broken from squeezing inside of molds that didn't fit.

Absently, I touched my bandaged shoulder and winced at the biting shards of pain that exploded under my fingertips. Yes, Mom, it hurt—and I relished each agonizing second. The pain reminded me I could still feel—something I thought I had lost a long time ago.

***

Late that night, I lay in bed and watched the shadows cast by the moon dance across my ceiling. One of the benefits of having the master bedroom was the sliding glass door that opened to the outdoors. I liked to keep the vertical blinds pushed to the side so I could invite the moon in, the light unobstructed.

Tonight, however, I didn't find the dancing shapes, usually a beautiful kaleidoscope, to be comforting. Tonight, the shadows of branches from the tree outside my window reached for me like claws from my ceiling. I tried to shrink deeper into my bed and pulled my covers up to my chin as the reaching fingers appeared to peel from the walls and inch their way closer.

Afraid of shadows? Sir's voice thundered inside my head. *You're pathetic.*

I shivered, despite the warmth of the March night, and clenched my eyes shut. Maybe I was pathetic. After all, there were no such things as monsters. I closed my eyes and willed myself to fall asleep.

The wind shifted, and I heard movement in the yard. "Only the trees," I whispered to no one.

A twig snapped outside the window behind my headboard, the sudden sound forcing a whimper from my throat. I rolled onto my good shoulder, away from the door, and slowly opened my eyes.

A human-sized shadow stood motionless against my wall.

I quickly snapped my eyes shut and swallowed the scream that lay just inside my lips. All I needed was to give Sir one more reason to ship me off to military school—seeing shadows come to life would certainly do just that. It had to be a hallucination—a side-effect of my pain medication.

I opened my eyes to be sure. The shadow remained.

"This is not happening," I whispered. Then louder, "You're not real."

As if sensing my disbelief, the shadowy figure raised its arm; the soft thump of its hand against the glass seemed to jar my bones loose from my skin. I struggled to swallow against the lump of fear stuck in my throat. Whatever was going on, it couldn't be real—it wasn't possible. My imagination had to be playing tricks on me.

The shadow cocked its head, waiting.

~ ☾ ~

"Go away." My lips trembled, distorting my words. I tried again, louder. "Go away." And when it didn't move, I added, "Please."

The hand dropped. The squeal of skin sliding against glass clenched the muscles in my chest and made me shiver. How could a figment of my imagination make so much noise? Slowly, as if waiting for me to change my mind, whomever—or whatever—it was took several steps back, then hesitated.

"Go," I whispered, hoping my voice could be heard above the hammering of my heart that seemed to echo against the walls of my room.

The figure appeared to nod, then shrank from view until its form was absorbed by the darkness of my room. Even then, I couldn't bring myself to look outside for fear that I would see the black eyes whose gaze I'd felt pressed against me.

"I'm losing my mind," I said out loud, which made me giggle. Talking to myself was just another symptom of insanity. Or a brain way overdosed on pain meds.

Something rustled through the grass outside the door and I nearly choked on what was left of my laughter. The brief lull had allowed me to gather the little courage I possessed, and, with more difficulty than I'd expected, I pushed up on my elbows and looked outside. Empty darkness greeted me.

I settled back against my pillow and sighed. The night was eerily silent; even the bullfrogs had stopped their serenades. I shivered and hugged my covers tighter. My only hope was that sleep would come and take me out from under the watching eyes of the stranger still lurking in the night. God, pain meds were wild.

~ ☾ ~

Chapter 6

The morning sun barged into my room like an unwanted guest. I rubbed my gritty eyes with the back of my hand and yawned. I had a brief but deliriously happy moment, right before I became fully awake, where I convinced myself that the previous day was nothing more but a horrible nightmare. Then I tried to sit up. My aching shoulder brought the painful reality crashing down on me.

Quietly sobbing, I fell into my pillow as a flood of images of yesterday's accident pushed through my mind. I could still hear their screams. I rolled my head back and forth against my pillow in the hopes that I could loosen the terrified cries that gripped my mind with razor-edged talons.

Sir said kids had died. The image of Gabrielle's bikini-clad body strung from the buoy surfaced, forcing tears through my tightly clenched lashes. Had she survived? She wasn't my pick for Humanitarian of the Year, but being a bitch didn't mean you deserved to have your life cut off at sixteen. If it did, half of the girls I knew would be dead.

I started to push myself up out of my bed when a knock sounded outside my door. "Yes?" I quickly dabbed at the tears in my eyes with the corner of my blanket.

The door opened, and my mother tentatively stuck her head in. "You're up!" Her smile brightened. "I've been checking on you all morning. I didn't have the heart to wake you." She ducked out of the doorway and reappeared, holding a tray with a bowl of something steaming. It smelled like chicken soup.

My stomach roared to life. "Soup for breakfast?" I asked, then yawned.

"It's not breakfast, silly." Mom set the tray over my lap and adjusted my pillows so I could sit up. "It's now past noon," she said as I picked up the spoon.

I dropped the spoon against the bowl. The tinkle of metal against porcelain sent stabs of anxious energy through my nerve endings. "Sir?" If he was around, there would be hell to pay for sleeping the morning away.

She waved away the question. "He knew you needed your rest, so he thought it best not to wake you when he left for work."

I picked the spoon back up and dug out a carrot from the pool of broth. Why did Mom always talk about Sir as if he was someone else? It was almost as if by saying those things she could trick herself into believing Sir cared, when it was far more likely he was more concerned about the shine of his boots than the wellbeing of his stepdaughter.

Mom smoothed a lock of my bed-mangled hair behind my ear. "How did you sleep, honey?"

The image of the shadowed figure beckoning me from outside appeared in my mind. I froze with the spoon halfway through my lips, a piece of celery pressed against the roof of my mouth. A lump knotted in my throat and I struggled not to choke on it when I finally managed to swallow.

Mom frowned. "Do I need to call the doctor?"

I shook my head. "I had some pretty bad nightmares, that's all."

She chewed on her lip for a moment before she clasped her hands and smiled. "We haven't done Dog of the Day yet!"

Happy about the change of subject, I swallowed

another bite of soup and watched her grab the daily calendar of dog breeds from my desk. She carried it to my bed and sat next to me, careful not to disturb the soup.

Dog of the Day was something Mom and I had started at the beginning of the year after she'd found the calendar on a sales rack at the book store. I'd wanted a dog for as long as I could remember, but Sir didn't allow pets. So Mom had bought me the calendar, which detailed a different dog breed for every day of the year. She'd explained I could use the calendar as research to find the perfect dog, so when I had my own place I'd know exactly what kind of dog to get. So far I'd yet to discover the perfect breed.

"Let's see." Mom tore off yesterday's dog—the Shetland Sheepdog—and set the paper aside. "Today's dog is the Chow Chow." She showed me a picture of something that looked more like the lion from *The Wizard of Oz* than a dog.

"He's so cute!" I grinned.

Mom nodded. "He sure is. It says here that the Chow Chow originated from Mongolia. They were bred for hunting but may also have been used for fighting. Here, listen: 'The Chow Chow is loyal and affectionate only to those it bonds with and may not take well to newcomers. If not from a good breeding line, the Chow Chow may be dominant and aggressive.'"

Disappointed, I spooned more broth into my mouth. The Chow Chow was definitely not *The One*. "It sounds like a dog version of Sir."

Mom stood. "Because it's loyal?"

"Mmm-hmm." I rolled my eyes when she turned to place the calendar back on my desk.

She walked back to the side of my bed. "So how about it, Edi-girl? Is the Chow Chow the dog for you?"

"Nope." I pushed the bowl away and Mom removed the tray. "Maybe tomorrow's dog."

~ ☾ ~

She nodded. “Maybe tomorrow.” She was almost to my bedroom door when she stopped abruptly, her focus narrowing in on the glass sliding door. “Edith.” She tsked. “You know how hard I work to keep this place clean for your father.”

Of course I did. Every Sunday the two of us spent the day scrubbing and dusting to keep the house clean enough to pass a white glove-inspection, which incidentally, Sir only performed once a year. I followed her gaze to the floor in front of the door, thinking that I might have tracked some grass or sand in from outside, but the carpet remained bare.

She set the tray on my dresser, walked to the door, and inspected the glass. That’s when I saw it—a handprint in the exact location where the shadowy figure had pressed its palm to the glass last night. It hadn’t been a dream after all.

My blood turned to mercury—heavy, thick—and threatening to rupture my veins. I wrapped my arms around my body and shuddered.

Mom tsked again and made her way back to my bedroom door. “I’ll get the glass cleaner. Just make sure you use the door handle, honey. Keep your hands off the glass.”

I nodded, trying to suppress the shivers that raised goose bumps along my arms.

“Good girl.” She opened my door and grabbed the tray from my dresser. “Be careful, okay?”

I hitched my blanket under my chin and nodded again. Now that I knew the late night visitor had been real, I had to figure out what he was doing in the back yard. Was he a burglar? Or worse, some type of perv? Neither one of those options was good. I only hoped that because I’d spotted him, he’d be too spooked to come back. Either way, Mom was right. I needed to be prepared.

~ ☾ ~

***

I spent the rest of the thumbing through a stack of old women's magazines that Mom had pulled from her collection, and trying to devise a plan should my night visitor return. So far, my only idea involved a trapping him with very large cardboard box propped open with a stick and a cupcake for bait. My reasoning was that everyone liked cupcakes—so perverts and monsters must, too.

It was safe to say the brainstorming wasn't going very well.

I heard Sir drive into the garage at five o'clock and stomp into the house. The muscles in my chest tightened around my ribs like barbed wire as I waited for him to appear, but he never did.

A half hour before I was supposed to go to sleep, I was balancing a spoon on my nose when my bedroom door squeaked open, causing me to gasp. The spoon fell from my nose and I juggled it for a few seconds before it slipped through my fingers and landed on the carpet.

Mom stepped into my room, then eyed me curiously as she retrieved the spoon from the floor and placed it on my dinner tray next to a plate of untouched sauerkraut and sausage. She narrowed her eyes as she scanned my plate. "Why didn't you eat anything?"

"Not hungry," I lied. The truth was I hated sauerkraut and sausage, but it was Sir's favorite, so it had become our Sunday night meal. Every night of the week had its own meal and I disliked all of them, except for Friday, which was pizza night. But Mom didn't have a clue because when I sat down at a table with Sir, I wordlessly ate what was in front of me in the time allotted, regardless of whether or not it was edible.

She set the tray on the floor and lowered herself next to me. After shifting several times, she began picking at a nonexistent piece of lint on my blue and gold comforter—the official colors of the United States Air Force and last year's Christmas present from Sir. "Tomorrow is Monday." She let the sentence hang in the air like a gavel held by a judge before a verdict was given.

"And?" I asked, awaiting my fate.

Mom smoothed out a crease in the blanket, careful to keep her hazel eyes locked on her fingers. She'd make a terrible poker player.

I sighed and leaned back against my pillow. "I'm going to school," I muttered.

A frown darkened her face as she patted my hand. "Your father and I discussed it, and we believe that the best thing for you to do is move past this boat accident."

"A good soldier knows that to look back is to move back," I quoted Sir.

"That's the spirit, honey." Mom gave me a quick squeeze before standing up. "One more thing." She reached into the pocket of her waist apron and withdrew her fist, slowly uncoiling her fingers to reveal two pearls, slightly yellowed with age.

When I realized my mom held the surviving stones of Aunt Margie's necklace, my heart swelled. Mom's sister, Aunt Margie, had given the family heirloom to me two summers ago when she'd visited us from her cabin in the Smoky Mountains. Unfortunately, Aunt Margie and Sir had gotten into a horrible argument about Sir's *attitude* (that's one way to put it), and Sir had not allowed her to visit since. We still emailed each other, but that didn't stop me from missing her. Wearing the pearls made me feel like Aunt Margie wasn't a thousand miles away. "Where did you find those?"

She took a deep breath, then set the pearls on my nightstand. "The doctor at the hospital gave them to me before we left. She found them inside your wound."

I fingered the bandage on my shoulder, my momentary burst of happiness shattered as I

~ ☾ ~

remembered how the needle-like claws of the blue-haired girl had dug into my collarbone. “Oh,” I murmured.

“Yes, well . . .” Mom reached back into her apron. “I also called the doctor. She prescribed medication for you.” This time when she uncurled her fingers, all that remained was a single blue pill.

“What is it?” I pulled the comforter under my chin. The scent of English roses wafted up from the section of fabric where my mom had sat.

“To help you sleep,” she answered, thrusting her hand closer.

I reached for the pill the way one might reach for tarantula. Sure, they didn’t *normally* bite, but the threat lay as close as the fangs resting against your palm. What would happen if the shadowy stranger came back for me tonight? Would I be too groggy to escape? Or would I sleep through his appearance? Actually, the last part didn’t sound too bad, so I slipped the pill onto my tongue and chased it down with a sip of water from the glass on my nightstand.

“Good girl,” Mom said. She bent down to kiss my forehead before she lifted the tray of discarded food from the floor and walked to door. She paused at the light switch, then flicked it off with her elbow. “Don’t let the bedbugs bite.”

***

I was roused from the depths of a dreamless sleep by a faint tap against the glass sliding door. Someone was outside.

My heart stirred, trying and failing to beat its way out of the cage created by the sleeping pill. It was a strange feeling, to know I should be afraid—that I *needed* the fear to pump adrenalin into my blood to ensure my survival—yet to not have my body cooperate. In fact, just waking up felt like pushing myself through a curtain of syrup. The harder I shoved, the deeper I sank.

The tapping continued.

I opened my eyes. Shadows danced on my ceiling, blurred by the weight still pressed against my eyelids. I balled my hands and rubbed at the grit matted in my lashes and tried again. Several blinks and I still couldn't see more than fuzzy shapes outlined by the moon.

The tapping became fevered, a sporadic rhythm that my pulse, a lazy river in my veins, should have matched. I moved my head to the side and saw the outline of a shadowy figure standing outside of my room, one palm pressed against the glass.

Great. I'm going to have to get the glass cleaner.

The thought was so ridiculous that I laughed, a sound that swirled around my head like water in a drain. A tiny voice inside my brain warned me that I shouldn't be laughing, that the appropriate response to a stranger outside my bedroom was to scream—a thought I found even funnier, so I laughed harder.

The figure stopped tapping and cocked his head.

I stopped giggling. "Sleeping pill," I explained to the stranger, my voice gurgled and thick. "It's affecting my brain. I can't think straight so . . . I really can't deal with you tonight. You should go."

His shoulders fell, as if disappointed. I almost felt bad that I couldn't be a more exciting murder victim. "Sorry." My tongue felt thick and fuzzy, like it'd been wrapped in gauze. "Try back tomorrow."

The shadow backed away from the door and melted into the night. I turned on my side and gave in to the blackness that poured over me like ink. Alone in my head, I swam through my dreams, looking for the pieces of myself that never came out in the waking world. Not much remained, but what did, I rolled in like a dog marking its scent.

Sleep was sacred—*my* time. Tomorrow, when the

alarm clock blared the white static of a nonexistent radio station, *my* time would be over and I would surrender myself to the authority of Sir's command. But for now, I could lie in the satin sheets of unconsciousness and simply *be.*

~ ☾ ~

Chapter 7

The hiss of static from my clock radio dragged me from sleep like a chunk of pineapple fished from the bottom of a gelatin mold. Slow and sludgy. My pounding head rolled against my pillow. I was going to need some serious caffeine to pull myself out of the lingering grasp of the sleeping pill.

Mom cracked open my door as soon as I switched the alarm off. Like always, she was dressed in her faded "Mom" pants—jeans with such a high waist they buttoned inches below her breasts. She had kept her makeup simple, as usual—a brush of blush and a dab of gloss but never any foundation. Her hair, the color of harvested wheat, was smoothed into a ponytail on the back of her head. Zero percent style, one hundred percent my mom.

"You have fifteen minutes until breakfast." She stepped in and closed the door soundlessly. "Just enough time for me to help you get dressed and for us to go over Dog of the Day."

I pulled myself up into a sitting position, then tried but failed at not wincing when a wave of pain rolled across my shoulder.

Mom's smile tightened at my pained expression. "I'll need to re-dress that as well." She jutted her chin at my shoulder before walking to my desk and ripping free the page with the Chow Chow, revealing today's date.

"Here we go." She lifted the calendar so I could see a photograph of a small, fuzzy grey dog with a white beard. "Today's dog is the Miniature Schnauzer."

"It looks like the doggy version of Gandalf the Grey," I said, identifying my favorite character from J.R.R. Tolkien's series.

Mom giggled at that. "It says here that the Miniature Schnauzer originates from Germany in the early twentieth century." She rattled off the definition: "'They were originally bred to hunt rats but make excellent companions. While they are affectionate toward their owners, they may be standoffish toward guests. Miniature Schnauzers have a tendency to be vocal.'"

As Mom placed the calendar back on my desk, I peeled the covers back, swung my legs to the ground, and curled my toes into the thick carpet. "Doesn't sound like the dog for me."

"No?" Mom pulled a pink plaid button-up shirt from my dresser along with a pair of jeans. She set them on my bed before helping me off with my shirt and removing the bandage on my shoulder.

I winced when she smeared on the antibiotic. "We don't have a rat problem." I didn't want to tell her that the real reason was that I'd been ordered around by Sir long enough. I didn't need a dog to take over when I moved out.

"Your wound looks pretty good." Mom smiled as she taped the fresh bandage into place. "I'll bet in a couple of weeks you'll be completely healed."

I nodded and allowed her to help me slip on the hideous pink top. Definitely not my style of clothing, but that was okay. I kept several spare shirts tucked inside my backpack and a few more in my locker at school. While she stood before me, buttoning my shirt, I looked over her shoulder at the sliding glass doors. That's when I saw it. Something roughly the size of my fist, looking very much like a rock, sat on the concrete step outside my bedroom.

My first thought was that a rock or chunk of bark had been blown into the yard and had somehow found its

~ ☾ ~

way onto the deck, but then I noticed a piece of twine wrapped around it and tied into a bow. Weird.

"Edith?"

"Huh?" I looked up at my mom to find her eyebrows knitted together in worry.

"Are you feeling okay? Maybe I could talk to your father—"

"No!" I forced a smile on my face. "I'm great. I just . . . zoned out a bit. I think that sleeping pill made me a little groggy."

Mom nodded, but her eyes said she wasn't so sure.

"I'm fine, really. Give me five minutes to brush my hair and find my shoes and I'll meet you at the table."

"Okay." She walked to the door but continued to throw me worried glances. "Just don't be late. You know how your father can be."

Father. Every time she said that word I had to swallow the bile that rose up my throat. Why couldn't she see that the man she thought she married didn't exist? She'd buried the reality beneath a mountain of excuses. I wondered what would happen when the excuses finally ran out.

I pushed the thought away as I shut my bedroom door, then dashed to the sliding glass door—I had my own problems to worry about. I stepped outside. The morning air slammed into me, thick and wet, like the steam rising above a pot of boiling water. I kneeled, and grabbed the object. I inspected it, discovering that it was neither a rock nor bark as I'd thought, but an oyster shell tied together with twine.

I sucked on my bottom lip, tasting the saltiness of the sweat that had beaded along my skin. The knot had been expertly tied, and it took me several minutes of picking and tugging before it came undone and the shell fell apart in my hands. Inside, instead of an oyster or a pearl, there was a round stone, unlike any I'd seen before. It was twice as large as the pearls on my nightstand and green, like the color of seaweed bending under the tide. Despite the morning's heat, the stone felt cool as I rolled it along my palm. The sun's light reflected shimmering gold flecks on its surface.

I wondered at the meaning. The oyster had been tied up like a present and left outside of my door. Was it a gift? And if it was, why had it been given, and who had given it? The shadowy stranger? Pressure built against my forehead, warning me that a headache was close at hand.

Sir's voice bellowed from outside my bedroom door. "Five minutes!"

I pocketed the strange stone, along with the twine, and scrambled into my room. I tossed my book bag over my shoulder and yelped at the pain that erupted. This injury was going to take some getting used to. After hastily running my fingers through my hair and snatching Aunt Margie's pearls from the nightstand, I left my room.

When I arrived in the kitchen, the lingering smell of bacon made my stomach growl. Sir pushed his plate away from him and stood. "You're late." He opened a nearby drawer, snagged a protein bar, and tossed it to me. "Breakfast is served. Now let's go."

Mom didn't say anything as she scrubbed the maple syrup from Sir's plate.

I shoved the bar in my backpack and tried not to groan. Tree bark had more flavor than one of Sir's protein bars.

Sir grabbed his keys that hung from a hook by the door. "Are you waiting for a written invitation?"

"No, sir." I followed him to the 4x4 and climbed inside. After buckling my seatbelt, I sat back against the stiff leather seat and tried to ignore the tightening inside my chest. Soon I would have to face the stares and whispers I knew waited for me at school. I was sure everyone had heard about the accident: it was high school, after all, and a person couldn't sneeze without half the school talking about what color the mucus was and whether or not it affected your social status. Only the cool kids had lime green snot. Sea-foam green was *so yesterday*.

Sir glanced at me. "Have you remembered anything else about the accident?"

I pulled my backpack against my chest like a shield. "No, sir."

"You will," he said, then turned on his favorite conservative radio show.

The weight of his words settled on my shoulders like a wall of cement. Last year we'd toured a military school. I couldn't help notice that most of the kids seemed even more lost than me. Lifeless clones marched across the too-green grass: glazed expressions lost to the spirits crushed within. Sir hadn't been serious about enrolling me at the time of the tour. Our visit was to serve as an example of what would happen if I stepped out of line. The tone of Sir's words let me know the threat remained. I, too, could belong to the ranks of uniformed kids whose souls were dug out like melon-balls, their hollowed-out shells filled with barked orders. How could I survive such a thing? A nagging voice inside my head told me I wouldn't.

Ten minutes later we passed the Valparaiso High School sign and pulled into the lot. My stomach lurched. Here I was about to enter the school's hallways, while several of the kids in the boating accident would never walk through the metal doors again. I bit my trembling lip. I'd never felt more alone.

Sir turned down the radio. "Be here at fifteen-hundred sharp. Got that?"

"Yes, sir." I stepped out of the 4x4, my backpack no longer a shield but an anchor that weighed down my footsteps, forcing me to endure the unwanted attention that much longer.

~ ☾ ~

Ahead of me, what looked to be a freshman boy exited his parents' car.

"Have a great day, Henry!" his father called. "Love you."

The boy said nothing as he darted away, blushing.

Longing, like a blue-flamed torch, burned through my body. Henry didn't know how lucky he was. If I were him I'd be so happy that I'd get a T-shirt with the words *My dad loves me* screen-printed on the front. But, unfortunately for me, I wasn't Henry and they didn't make T-shirts that said, *Yay! My stepdad hasn't killed me yet!*

I approached the stairs to the school and almost didn't notice the girls lounging by the doors until they ducked their heads and whispered in frantic hisses as I began my ascent. Even the bronze eagle in front on the school's entrance, a gift from the Class of 2006, seemed to watch my progress with unblinking interest.

My shoulders hunched, I pushed past the maroon doors and darted inside.

Where it was worse.

The halls were no longer the sea of teenage bodies into which I could blend and maintain anonymity. As I walked to my locker I felt like Moses, trekking across the parted Red Sea. To either side of me, students moved to stand against their lockers, wide-eyed and open-mouthed, as if I, too, had died in the accident and it was my reanimated body that roamed the halls. Or maybe it was the cloud of death, still clinging to me, that had them backing away. If that were the case, I wished I had a straw so I could suck it in. To end it all.

And how many of them would prefer my non-existence? How many of my peers would gladly exchange my life—the quiet, new girl who had no friends—for the lives of the football players and cheerleaders that had been lost? I couldn't blame them. They missed their friends. But at the same time, I knew the accident thrilled them. I could tell by the excited shivers of the students I walked past.

They might not voice it out loud, but people loved death. They loved it for the same reason people rushed outside to watch a gathering storm. It's exciting and mysterious—a puzzle waiting to be solved but lacking all the pieces. They yearned to stand before it and admire the beauty, the power, the actual hand of God—but not before painting lamb's blood over their doorways lest the angel of death visit *their* household.

It's not death they hate. It's the pain of being left behind.

I ducked my head and picked up the pace, keeping my eyes on the toes of my black ballet flats peeking out from the hem of my jeans as I hurried down the hall. I made it to my locker just as the intercom announced that first-period classes would be canceled for an assembly.

My throat went dry, my tongue thick so I had difficulty swallowing around it. This wouldn't be a rally for the football team, soccer team, or whatever sport was currently in season. With trembling hands, I pulled my books from my backpack and organized them on my locker shelf, ignoring the way my classmates' voices dropped to muted levels when they walked by me and picked up in volume the further away they got. Every now and then I could pick up a snippet of conversation.

"They say he might never wake up."

"I heard *she* was there."

"Bit by a shark."

"Who *is* she?"

"His body hasn't surfaced yet."

Oh God. Despite having ditched the protein bar, my mouth watered, warning me that I was going to throw up. I slammed my locker shut and ran into the bathroom, where I kneeled at the first toilet and heaved what felt like acid burning up my throat. When I finished, I stood on shaky legs and rinsed my mouth out with water from the sink. As I dried my face with a paper towel, I looked in the mirror and immediately regretted the action. The girl who stared back at me was one I barely recognized. Dark circles hung under my eyes and the color had drained from my lips, leaving them the same pasty color as my complexion.

The pink shirt only made it worse.

I slipped it over my head and exchanged it for a black v-neck T-shirt I'd stashed inside my bag. Sir had strictly forbidden me to wear black, telling me that when I did I looked like a Satan worshiper. Any other time, when Sir told me to do something, I did. But what Sir didn't realize, or what anyone else who called me emo didn't realize, was that wearing black wasn't a fashion statement. It was a tribute to my brother.

Two days after William had died, Sir called a charity and, despite Mom's begging, had them come in and take everything away that was William's. From his clothes to his toys and even his crib. Next, Sir pulled down the Noah's ark wallpaper border and painted the pastel blue walls white. All that was left was a white, empty room with brown carpet. He told us that we couldn't live in the past. A year later, when he caught Mom staring at a picture of William with tears in her eyes, that's when Sir demanded all the pictures be stripped from the walls. It wasn't enough that Sir had all traces of William stripped from our home, he wanted William erased from our memories, too.

But I wouldn't let that happen. After reading *The Scarlet Letter* during freshman year, I became fascinated with the idea of Hester Prynne bearing the mark of her shame in public. I felt that because I was responsible for William's death, I should have to suffer as well. I owed it to him not to forget. The black clothing and the heavy makeup kept the other students away from me, which I deserved. William certainly didn't have the chance to live life, have fun, and make friends, so I shouldn't either. The black was my scarlet letter.

When I'd finished changing, I pulled out a small bag filled with more forbidden paraphernalia, like eyeliner and lipstick. I applied thick lines around my eyes, finishing with a sweep of dark purple shadow and a brush of mascara. When I was finished, I felt better. No longer exposed.

As I zipped my makeup case, I heard voices outside the bathroom door and, not wanting to be seen, darted for the nearest stall and locked myself in.

"Peter told me he saw that Edith girl at her locker."

"No! The one from the accident?"

I peered through the crack of the stall to find two girls bent over the sinks, dabbing at their faces with various cosmetics. A twinge of jealously washed through me. Despite the fact that I worked hard to keep people at a distance, it didn't mean I didn't wonder what it would be like to gossip in the bathroom with someone while applying makeup—not that I ever *had* any good gossip.

The redheaded girl nodded. "That's the one. What kind of name is *Edith,* anyway?"

The second girl, who had her blond hair knotted into messy buns on both sides of her head, snorted. "I have no idea. Speaking of, Amanda told me that her boyfriend's sister went to visit Gabrielle in the hospital—she has a couple cracked ribs. Amanda said that Gabrielle says the whole accident was that girl Edith's fault."

I bit my lip to keep the cry of protest from leaving my mouth.

The redheaded girl snapped the top of her lipstick back on and leaned against the sink. "What happened?"

The blonde's pleasure at having the better gossip was evident by the twisted smirk reflected in the mirror. "Amanda's boyfriend's sister said that Gabrielle told her Edith tried to push her out of the boat. She was jealous because Gabrielle was dancing. I guess she stood and—"

~ ☾ ~

The blonde thrust her arms outward, then shrugged. "Russell lost control of the wheel when he saw what happened. That's why he crashed into Scott's boat."

"No!" The redhead gaped. "So she's, like, a murderer, then?"

"A total psycho. I don't know why the cops didn't arrest her." After the blonde finished blotting her lips on a paper towel, she crumpled it up and tossed it at the trashcan. It bounced off the rim and fell to the floor. Garbage. Like me.

"Come on," The redhead grabbed her friend by the shoulder and steered her to the door. "We don't want to be late for the assembly." The bathroom door swooshed as they exited.

My vision teetered and I sat down on the toilet to keep from falling over. Murderer. Psycho. The words echoed in my head like a gong. "They're wrong." I whispered, my voice quivering. The accident had been caused by Gabrielle and her need to thrust her hips like a five-dollar hooker. *I* had tried to *save* her.

But of course no one would see it that way. Who would believe Edith Small, a nobody, over Gabrielle Rederick, the pretty blond captain of the equestrian team? I already knew the answer to that. The more important question was, how long until that story infected the entire school? Or worse yet, how long until Sir found out?

Blood pounded inside my head in angry waves as I fumbled with the door lock. Once the door had opened, I stumbled from the stall on legs of rubber and managed to grab hold of the sink before I sank to my knees. I was about to cup some water to my mouth when a low rumble sounded from the wall behind the mirrors, causing the sink to tremble under my fingers.

"What the—" But my sentence was cut short by a low groan, followed by cracking porcelain and the sharp clang of a metal faucet as it shot across the room and ricocheted against the ceramic tile.

I screamed and covered my head as the remaining faucets broke free and shot across the bathroom, one missing my face by mere inches. Four geysers erupted from the uncovered pipes in streams that reached the ceiling. I scrambled backward only to slide on the wet floor and land on my butt.

I rolled onto my knees and waited for the breath to return to my lungs. My back arched, I hung my head and sucked in as much air as my constricted air passages allowed.

My eyes burned and I couldn't be sure if I was actually crying, soaked as my face was. I wished I could turn my body into liquid and escape down the rusted drain in the middle of the floor, along with the water raining down on me. It would take too much effort to get up and face my classmates. More effort than I had. Maybe I could lay here forever.

As if reading my mind, two hands wound themselves in the front of my shirt. The stranger's tone was an accusation that stung worse than the freezing water pelting my face.

"What the hell?"

~ ☾ ~

Chapter 8

The worst part of starting a new school was lunch. That was always the moment that defined my social standing for the rest of the year.

My first day at Valparaiso High had been no different. I stood in the lunch line pretending to focus on the nutritional guideline sticker on my fruit cup while I searched the room for an empty table. I didn't want to sit next to someone and force them into awkward conversation. The ideal spot had to have a buffer—a good two or three chairs away from other people—so I could read the obituaries in peace while I ate. I spotted a potential opening in the back of the room, a table occupied by a lone girl with skin the color of a cup of coffee filled halfway with cream and with purple dreadlocks cascading down her back—a girl whose name I'd learn later was Morgan Pratt. She sat, alternating her chopsticks from eating tools to drumsticks, while bobbing her head in time with the music on her iPod.

After paying for my food, I walked along the rows of tables, hunched under the weight of the curious eyes all around me. I could feel them taking me in, from my heavy eyeliner to my Cure T-shirt, forming their opinions and categorizing me into something that made sense to them.

"Check out the new emo chick," a girl whispered.

And just that fast, I was tagged and branded like another cow in the herd. I approached Morgan, struggling not to squirm under the continued stares of the students around me. Her eyes locked with mine, and before I could reach for the back of the metal chair, she pulled it against the table by looping the toe of a red stiletto around the bottom rung.

"What do you think you're doing?" She ripped the ear buds from her ears and pressed her shoulders back.

The nearby tables fell silent as students abandoned their conversations and shifted their bodies for optimum visibility.

"N-n-nothing." I felt the eagerness of the surrounding students as they leaned forward, waiting for a fight to break up an otherwise boring lunch.

"Who sent you?" Her eyes narrowed and she whipped her head around the room. She scanned the tables of kids whose smiles shriveled like month-old bananas. "Which one of you was it?" She zeroed in on a group of whispering girls who wore matching maroon ribbons in their hair. "Gabrielle?"

A blonde with frosted pink lip gloss rolled her eyes and flipped her ponytail behind her shoulder. "Look, Morgan, I don't know who lit the fuse on your tampon, but your obsession with me is getting old and a little creepy. I already told you that I'm not into chicks."

Morgan's hands began to tremble and she quickly balled them into fists. "I think the bleach has gone to your brain, Gabi. You clearly don't understand the definition of lesbian. It means I like *human* girls. Your family tree, however, is nothing more than a rest stop for dogs."

A hiss reverberated against the cafeteria walls as the entire room sucked in a collective breath. I clutched my fruit cup to my chest and took a step backward, wishing I could become a chameleon and fade into the white concrete walls.

A pulsing vein appeared on Gabrielle's temple as she pushed back her tray and stood. "The only reason you're a lesbian is because no guy will touch you."

Morgan threw her iPod into her backpack and zipped

it shut. "And the only reason you're a whore is because every guy here already has." She slipped her arm through the strap and pushed away from the table. "Stop sending your little minions over to screw with me." She scanned the room. "Everybody, just leave me the fuck alone." With that she threw back her shoulders and marched from the room.

"Freak!" Gabrielle called after her, eliciting giggles from the girls around her. She smiled smugly and sat back down, never once looking in my direction.

That day, I had ducked my head and tucked my fruit cup close to my body. Alone, I had slunk away in the opposite direction as Morgan, where I'd found a bathroom to enjoy my lunch in peace.

The same bathroom where I now found myself sprawled on the floor, an angry Morgan Pratt hovering over me.

***

"What the hell?" Morgan repeated. She reached out an arm, which I gladly took. She shielded her eyes from the spraying water with one arm and hoisted me up with the other. "What happened in here?"

"I have no idea," I answered. "The floor started shaking and before I could get out, the sinks exploded."

She looped fingers adorned with thick plastic rings around my wrist and pulled me toward the door. "Don't just stand there. Move. Before my hair dye starts to run." This week her hair was a mix of black and pink dreads, tied into a high ponytail with a black ribbon.

I nodded and followed her out of the bathroom, bracing myself for the looks I was sure to receive due to my sopping wet appearance. Instead, an empty hallway greeted me.

My heart sank into my knees. "The assembly," I muttered. My shoes made squishy protests as I shifted my weight back and forth. Wet footprints led from the bathroom to where I stood. "I can't go in there like this!" Water trailed down my arms like silvery veins and hung from my fingertips in fat beads.

Morgan laughed. "That's for sure."

A sob worked its way up my throat but I swallowed it before it could escape. "It's bad enough half the school thinks I'm responsible for the boat accident. But this—" I shook water from my hands.

"Wait a sec." Morgan's eyes, sparkling with glitter, bulged from their sockets. "You mean to tell me *you're* Edith Small?"

My body trembled, a precursor to the breakdown that was sure to come. "I don't—I don't want to talk about it." She opened her mouth but I cut her off before she had a chance to speak. "I appreciate your help in the bathroom but we're late for the assembly." My shoes squeaked in protest as I spun on my heels and sloshed down the hallway in the direction of the auditorium.

"Smalls! Hold up!" Heavy footsteps descended upon me, then I was twisted around by my elbow. A flash of metal appeared between her lips as Morgan played with the barbell implanted in her tongue. "You're going the wrong way. If you don't want to make a scene, you'd be better off using my private entrance." She jutted her chin toward the door at the opposite end of the hallway.

I frowned. "But that door leads outside."

She laughed, looping her arm through mine and pulling me in the direction of the door. "You want to go to an assembly? Great. Let's assemble. Who says we have to do it with the rest of the school?"

My mind reeled even as my feet followed her lead. "But—but that would be skipping."

Morgan snorted. "Nothing gets by you, does it, Smalls?"

Sir's voice spoke inside my head. *Skipping school? You're practically begging to enlist in the military academy.*

My steps slowed. “I don’t know, Morgan. We could get in trouble.” I couldn’t do anything that would jeopardize my chance to at going away to a college that didn’t require uniforms.

“Not likely.” Morgan reached out and pushed the metal bar, swinging the door wide. The sun’s rays spilled across my chilled skin like warm fingers urging me forward. “I’m pretty sure the teachers are expecting you to be all traumatized and messed up. This boat accident is your get-out-of-jail-free-card.”

I stumbled as the memory of the crash resurfaced in my mind. “People died,” I whispered.

She shrugged and continued to pull me down the sidewalk. “It’s natural selection, Smalls. Dumbasses are going to die. There’s nothing you can do to stop it. It’s the Darwinian way.”

I thought about that. Could it really be that simple? Marty, Russell, and Gabrielle had all been drinking and smoking pot before the boat race. Did their stupidity absolve me from any blame? Or could I have done something more to prevent the accident? My head pounded under the weight of my thoughts and I pressed two fingers into my temple to ease them away. “Aren’t *you* worried about getting in trouble?”

“Me?” Morgan appeared to hold back a laugh. “In case you haven’t noticed, I make teachers uncomfortable.” She gestured to herself and her short plaid skirt dripping at the side with several chains. “They tend to look the other way when I don’t show up for class.” When I didn’t answer, she stopped short in front of the turnoff leading away from our school. “Look, I’m not kidnapping you. I’m trying to do you a favor. For all I care, you can turn back and go to the assembly looking like a drowned—” She bit off her words when I inhaled sharply, then waved her hand in dismissal. “Whatever. Or you can come with me. Whatever you think you know about me—you don't. I'm not going to smoke dope, shoot up, or any other dumb shit. My drug of choice is caffeine. Preferably in the form of a vanilla latte. It's your choice, Smalls. Free country and all that jazz."

I swallowed as I considered my options. There was no denying that Sir would be watching me closer than before—I walked a frayed rope on stilts made of scissors. But on the other hand, I was dripping wet and another pair of accusing eyes would be all it took to send me over the edge. It was true I didn't quite understand Morgan or her reasons for asking me to tag along, but ever since the moment she'd pulled me up from the bathroom floor, the ever building pressure in my chest loosened. And that was enough. "I'm in."

A smile tugged at Morgan's lips. "There's only one rule if you're going to hang out with me. You are not, under any circumstances, allowed to tell anyone I'm straight-edge. I've got a reputation to maintain. If anyone asks, make something up. Tell them I took you behind a Dumpster and snorted lines of coke between shots of tequila. Got it?"

"Got it." I smiled.

She grinned back. "Be careful, Smalls. It looks like you don't smile much and I don't want you to hurt yourself." She looped her arm back through mine and hummed the *Star Spangled Banner* as we hurried down the street.

***

I glanced at the digital clock hanging from Morgan's backpack and picked up my pace. Somehow, I'd lost track of time and spent nearly the entire school day at a graffiti-covered booth in the back of a coffee house with Morgan. We'd sipped lattes, painted our nails black, and talked about everything from emo bands to the perfect smudge-proof eyeliner. And yet, all that time, Morgan was nice enough to not bring up the boat accident, even though I saw her eyes wander to the edge of my shirt collar where a corner of gauze lay exposed. When I brought up our first meeting in the lunch room she was clearly surprised, not realizing the trembling girl with the fruit cup had been me. She'd gone on to tell me how Gabrielle—or Hagrielle as Morgan called her—found it hilarious to send girls over to flirt with her and gauge her reaction. Her outburst had been the result of those assaults.

I locked my eyes on the brick building still a block away, as if by sheer will I could teleport myself inside its walls.

"Wait up, Smalls!" Morgan cried, balancing a Styrofoam cup of coffee as she ran in her lime green heels to catch up to me. "Where's the fire? I told you that the teachers won't give you any trouble."

"It's not the teachers I'm worried about," I panted, accelerating my jog to a sprint.

"Yeah, well," she grumbled behind me. "I don't like doing anything that accelerates my heart rate." She giggled. "Well, *almost* anything."

I ignored her and kept running but, after making the turn down the school's drive, I saw that my efforts had been for nothing.

Amid the students streaming around his parked 4x4, Sir stood, leaning against the hood, his arms crossed and a scowl etched on his face.

Morgan slammed into my back when I screeched to a halt, spilling half her latte on the sidewalk. "Smalls!" she groaned.

But I didn't respond. I was too busy fighting to stay standing despite the fact that my heart bounced around my chest like a hornet in a glass jar.

After shaking off the coffee off her hands, Morgan looked up. "Smalls?" She took a tentative step forward.

~ ☾ ~

"What's up?"

Dread stole the words from my tongue, and I was helpless to do anymore than nod in Sir's direction.

She followed my gaze. "Is that your old man?"

I nodded.

Her brow folded under her scowl. "Ugh. I know the type." She looked around and gave my elbow a tug away from the curb into the parking lot. "Come on. I don't think he's spotted us yet. There's still time."

I shook my head. Even from a distance I could see the muscles in Sir's jaw tighten as he ground his teeth. "I'm in enough trouble. Running away is only going to make things worse."

"Run away?" Morgan feigned hurt but she couldn't mask the mischief that ran through her eyes. "Really, Smalls. I would have thought that after today you would give me more credit."

"But if we're not going to run away, what are we going to do?"

She smiled. "I have a plan." She motioned me to follow and waded into the parked cars.

"Military school, here I come," I muttered.

Chapter 9

"Smalls, get down!" Morgan hissed as she crouched behind a rusted Taurus.

I darted between two parked cars and knelt next to her. "I still don't understand what we're doing."

She sighed dramatically. "I'm saving your ass. *Again.*" She stood up and peered over the car's hood in Sir's direction. "God, Smalls, he looks like a complete tool. How do you stand it?" She looked over at me, and whatever she saw made the smile fall from her face. "Follow me."

I crouched behind her, bobbing and weaving through the maze of cars until we came up to a fire-hydrant-red sports car.

"Here!" She motioned me over with a wave of her hand.

I crouched beside her. "Whose car is this?"

She opened the door, reached across the seat, and rummaged through the glove box. "Mine."

I didn't bother hiding my surprise. "Are you kidding me? It's brand new."

"Present from Daddy." She grimaced on the last word as if it left a bitter taste in her mouth. "Anyway, I found the answer to your prayers!" Morgan withdrew her hand from the glove box and uncurled her fingers to reveal the prize within.

"An inhaler?" My heart sank. This was her big plan?

Morgan huffed. "You're not seeing the bigger picture here, Smalls."

I waited.

~ ☾ ~

She crossed her arms. “We don’t have time for me to explain. Do you trust me?”

“Yes.” The speed of my reply surprised not only me but Morgan, who blinked several times before responding.

“Good. Now let’s go meet Pops.”

“M-m-meet Sir? I don’t think that’s such a good idea.” Much to Morgan’s amusement, I pulled the pink plaid shirt from my backpack and buttoned it over the black v-neck. Next, I dug the heel of my palms into my eyes to rub off any of the makeup that remained after my incident in the bathroom. I wouldn’t have time to remove the nail polish. I could only hope that Sir wouldn’t notice. “Look, I’m not saying that I’m ashamed to be with you or anything, but obviously you stand out. Sir’s not one to appreciate non-conformity.”

Morgan rolled her eyes. “You said you trusted me, now come on!”

I followed her through the rows of cars. Inside my chest, the sense of dread built into a painful crescendo. Still leaning against the hood, Sir’s frown deepened as he glanced at his watch.

I wondered what the military uniform would look like that I’d be required to wear at my soon-to-be new school.

As if sensing my arrival, Sir glanced over his shoulder. His eyes darted from me to Morgan and back to me. I could almost feel the anger rolling off of him like waves of heat from sun-drenched blacktop. He stepped around the hood and folded his arms as we approached.

“Where have you been?” Sir’s voice was a jackhammer on cement. “I told you to meet me here at fifteen hundred hours sharp. And why are you coming from the parking lot?”

I forced myself not to shrink back. “I—I—” But before I could answer, Morgan was in front of me, taking the full weight of the sergeant's stare with her chin lifted and shoulders back.

"I'm afraid it's my fault, Mr. Small."

Sir's eyes narrowed, registering the pink-haired girl before him and making his own conclusions. "*Master* Sergeant Small," he corrected her.

"Sure." Morgan waved her hand in the air as if Sir's rank were of little importance.

Sir made a choking noise and curled his fingers into fists. "Explain yourself," he said to her.

"Edith saved me." Morgan held the inhaler up for inspection. "I was in the bathroom when I found myself having an asthma attack. I accidentally left my inhaler in my car, and if Edith hadn't been there to help me to the parking lot, I don't know what I would have done." She smiled sweetly.

"Regardless—" Sir began, but Morgan cut him off, drawing a shocked expression from him.

"I know my father will be so grateful. He'll insist that your family comes over for dinner."

"Your father?" Sir blinked, as if trying to understand how he'd lost control.

"Sure." Morgan shrugged. "He's the base commander for Eglin Air Force Base. Lieutenant Colonel Pratt. I'm his daughter, Morgan." She held her hand out and grinned a thousand-watt smile.

I couldn't have been more shocked if I'd licked a nine-volt battery. The base commander's *daughter*? And I wasn't the only one stunned.

Sir's eyes clouded over and his Adam's apple bobbed in his throat like a fishing lure. "Lieutenant Colonel Pratt is your father?"

Morgan snatched his hand dangling at his side and pumped it twice. "Like I said, I'm awfully grateful. Edith saved my life. I'll have Daddy call you with dinner plans." She winked at me. "Oh, and if it's all right with you, maybe Edith can stay over. For a sleepover?"

~ ☾ ~

I fought off the grin that pulled at the corners of my mouth. I'd never seen Sir bested before. And the fact that it happened by a seventeen-year-old girl with pink hair made it that much more awesome.

Sir opened his mouth but nothing came out. He cleared his throat and tried again, his voice a pitch higher than normal. "We'd be honored. My wife will bring a casserole."

"Great!" Morgan gave me another wink and skipped away into the parking lot.

Sir blinked several more times before he turned to me and growled, "Car. Now."

I scrambled in, keeping my head low. After buckling the seatbelt, I propped my backpack on my lap so I could hide not only my painted nails but also the smile I wore the entire way home.

***

That evening Sir and I sat in uncomfortable silence at the kitchen table. It was nice to see that some things were back to normal. Mom slipped her hands into a pair of frayed potholders and lifted the casserole onto the table.

Tuna noodle.

I sighed.

"I just don't understand it." She set the dish on the counter and dug the spoon into the crust. "I'd noticed the kitchen faucet leaking while I made breakfast, but when you two left this morning, it stopped. I thought maybe I didn't have it all the way closed, but look, it's started up again."

Sir and I glanced at the sink, and sure enough, water trickled down like a thin silver ribbon.

Sir turned his attention back to his plate and the casserole that Mom heaped upon it. "Call the plumber tomorrow." He picked up his fork and speared a noodle.

~ ☾ ~

"And then call the landlord and tell them that whatever the plumber charges we're taking it out of the rent. There's no way we're going to pay for a repair on a house that's not ours. And I'm not going to pay extra on a water bill while we wait for the landlord to take his sweet time getting the repair done."

After dishing her own plate, Mom sat. "You're right, of course." She unfolded her napkin across her lap and looked at me. "How was school today, honey?"

Before I could say anything, Sir answered, "She was hanging out with some delinquent in the parking lot. Get this, Carol, the girl had *pink hair,* and she's the base commander's *daughter*. His daughter! How's the guy supposed to command an entire base consisting of thousands of soldiers when he obviously has no control over a seventeen-year-old girl?"

Mom smiled. "You made a friend?"

Sir shoveled another forkful of tuna noodle into his mouth. "You should have seen her." He shook his head angrily. "Not only did she have pink hair, but it was all knotted up in those dreadlock things. Can you imagine the infestation of insects living on her head? I don't understand how any base commander can allow his daughter to present herself that way. Ridiculous."

"She's nice," I said.

Sir snorted. "Really? You want to know what kind of girl paints her nails black? I'll tell you: a drug user or a Satan worshiper. And I don't have the time or the patience to deal with either." He stared at my hands as if knowing that I'd spent the last fifteen minutes in the bathroom removing the polish.

No longer hungry, I lowered my gaze to the table and I pushed my food into a high pile so it looked like less was on my plate.

"I'll tell you another thing," he continued. "If her father had any sense he'd send her to a good military school. They'd whip her into shape in not time. That's what I'd do." He paused, giving me time to take in the masked threat before he sat back in his chair. "Anyway, we're invited to their house for dinner. I want you to make a casserole, Carol, but not the ham casserole that you made last month. Disgusting."

Mom twirled her fork on her plate. "I saw the recipe on Rachel Ray and thought—"

"No," Sir said, "you didn't think."

Mom nodded. We ate the rest of our dinner in silence.

***

I stood at the door in my bedroom watching the horizon darken from purple to black, like a bruise settling into its true color hours after the strike.

The handprint remained. I exhaled, the fog from my breath rolling across the glass where it touched the palm of the print and quickly retreated. I should have wiped it away before Mom noticed, but I couldn't bring myself to do it. Something about it felt important.

I was afraid.

If I wiped the print away, the stranger might not come back. Stupid, because I didn't even know what he wanted. Of all the things he could be—thief, pervert, or worse—all that mattered was what he was. *My secret.* And in a world where I was constantly reminded how I could lose everything in a moment, I just wanted something to belong only to me.

I placed my hand inside the print. The fingers were just long enough that, if they curled, they could swallow my hand entirely.

A voice growled from outside my bedroom startling me from my thoughts. "Lights out in five!" A typical Sir goodnight.

I peeled my cheek off the glass, leaving an oily imprint of my own. Luckily, Mom had already come and gone, changing my bandages and trying to pump more information out of me on my new friend. I stuck to the story Morgan had concocted, insisting I had helped the wheezing girl from the bathroom to her car where I'd heroically retrieved the inhaler. Mom had smiled and kissed the top of my head. I hated lying to her, but it was nothing she wasn't used to.

I turned away from the door and climbed into bed, trailing my fingers along the nightstand and over the two remaining pearls and the strange green stone. I'd removed the stone from my jeans pocket over an hour ago. The pearls were room temperature, but the green stone still held a chill that tickled the tips of my fingers like an electric current.

Strange.

I climbed under my heavily starched sheets. They remained stiff and unforgiving as I struggled to fold them around my body. How long would I have to wait tonight? It wasn't a question about whether or not he would show. I knew—my body hummed in anticipation.

The digital clock on my nightstand ticked off another minute as I watched. The flashing colon beat a hypnotic rhythm, pulsing in time with my heart.

Flash. Thump. Flash. Thump.

Minutes passed. Then hours. I wiped my sweating palms along the sheets. My throat was dry and I wished for a glass of water.

Flash. Thump. Flash. Thump.

The sound of my own heartbeat grew to a deafening level, echoing in my room until I was sure it would shake the walls around me.

I almost didn't hear the tapping.

At first, I thought the wind had brushed the tree branches against the window. But then the shadow spilled across my lap like an overturned bottle of ink, and I knew.

He was here.

~ ☾ ~

Chapter 10

I sat up, gasping. The stranger stumbled back a step.

A quick glance at the clock told me it was two AM. Suddenly, this was no longer the brilliant idea I'd thought it to be. I couldn't face the shadowy figure alone in the dark! What if he was here to kill me?

The fine hair on the back of my neck raised as my hands began to tremble. *Stupid, stupid Edith.*

The stranger took two cautious steps forward and tapped on the glass pane again.

I whimpered before shrinking back against the headboard and raising the covers to my chin.

He spoke, his voice muffled, yet oddly familiar. "On my word, you are safe with me."

His voice was low and smooth, like a bow drawn across the strings of a cello. I knew I'd heard it before . . . but where? The covers slipped from my chin and pooled around my waist. I narrowed my eyes, hoping that would allow me to make out the distorted shape behind the glass. It didn't. Curiosity pierced me like a fishing hook and pulled me forward. Slowly, I peeled my comforter back and slipped my bare feet onto the floor. Not feeling particularly stable, I curled my toes into the carpet for support.

I took a step forward then stopped. What was I doing?

As if sensing my doubt, the stranger stepped away from the door and held his arms wide, indicating his willingness to give me space.

His gesture worked to unwind the locks on my bones

and pull them into movement. One step. Then another. The closer I came to the door, the more difficult it was to breathe until I stood before the glass gasping for air.

"What do you want?" I whispered.

The stranger had backed into the shadow cast by the house, yet I could see something glinting silver in the moonlight. A weapon?

"To talk."

I knew that voice, thick like a pool of chocolate syrup. It was the voice of the boy from the beach. The one who'd pulled me from the ocean. Bastin.

Before I knew what I was doing, I flicked open the lock. A cool breeze greeted me, fluttering the hair across my face. I tucked the ends behind my ears.

"Thank you," he said, still hidden in the shadows.

I said nothing, only stepped outside, slid the door shut, and leaned against it.

Bastin stayed hidden a moment longer, as if deciding. Finally, he stepped out of the shadows, and I was glad that I'd shut the door. Otherwise, the cry that tore from my throat would have certainly woken Sir.

The boy that stood before me was unlike any I'd ever seen. He wore only a pair of beaten up cut-off jeans. A curtain of silver hair cascaded over one shoulder, ending at his knees. Only it wasn't the same silver-grey like the roots of my mom's hair before her monthly dye job. His hair was the shining metallic of tinsel on a Christmas tree. But unlike tinsel, when he tossed his head, it swayed like a silk curtain down his back.

"Please don't be frightened," he said.

I tried to answer him but my words tangled into a gurgle. I coughed to loosen the knot and tried again. "I'm sorry, but your hair—" My words trailed off as he took a step forward and the shadows were peeled back from his face.

His eyes held only night.

Two black orbs gazed at me. He licked his lips and

blinked repeatedly, an action too impossibly fast to be human. I clung to the door handle, trying to think, trying to make sense of what I saw. The hair couldn't be real—probably a wig. And his eyes . . . maybe he had a medical condition? Or really freaky contact lenses?

The boy took another step forward and blinked another inhuman blink. "I'm sorry for startling you tonight and the nights before. I—" He tilted his head toward the sky as if the right answer might fall from the moon itself. "I needed to talk to you. I wouldn't have put you through all the stress if it hadn't been important." He lowered his head and directed his onyx eyes at me.

"Important?" I focused my attention on the sharp lines along his jaw, afraid that if I kept staring at his eyes I might fall in and drown.

"Yes." He swept his gaze around the yard. "Are we safe here?"

I wanted to laugh at the absurdity of his question. Had I ever been safe a second of my life? "Probably not," I answered. "There's a chance that Sir might find us."

He cocked his head. "Sir?"

"My stepdad." The words tasted sour on my tongue. "He's a master sergeant and pretty strict."

He nodded. "Come with me?" He held his hand out and I marveled how the moon bathed his pale skin in a blue glow.

I shook my head. "I can't do that."

"Why not?"

There had to be a good reason for not wandering off in the night with a strange boy, but for whatever reason, my mind refused to conjure one up. Absently, I began to pick at the gauze that stuck out from the edge of my nightshirt.

His eyes swept along my injured shoulder and his face turned hard. The muscles along his jaw flexed. "I am sorry Luna injured you. I wouldn't have allowed it, but her orders came directly from the king."

~ ☾ ~

My head swam in a sea of confusion. "Luna?"

"The one who hurt your shoulder."

Fear, like the rustling of scales, tickled along my skin as I remembered the girl who smiled as she watched me drown. Instinctively, I brought my hand to my throat. "She broke my necklace."

He frowned. "We have to hunt for the old power spheres. It's a rare thing when a human brings them into our waters. It was too much for her to resist."

A dull ache pulsed inside my head and I pressed my fingers into my temples to keep the throbbing at bay. "Nothing you've said makes any sense."

"I know." He held his hand out to me. "If you come with me—to a place where we can talk safely—then I can explain everything.

I stared at his reaching fingers and hesitated. His skin was so pale that it seemed to glow in the moonlight. There were a million reasons I shouldn't go with him; he didn't *look* like a normal teenager, he didn't *talk* like a normal teenager, and his friend almost ripped my throat out. Not to mention, if I got caught, I'd be on the first bus to military school. And then it would be goodbye to college and the freedom I desperately craved.

But there was something else. In front of me, the boy's fingers wavered in the air, waiting to take hold of my own. A knot formed in my chest and I struggled to breathe around it. I'd never held hands with a boy before.

Before my boating trip with Marty Sherwood, I'd never been on a date. It wasn't that nobody had asked me out, it was just that the high school boys I'd met, with little more on their brains than sex and football, held little appeal to me.

Until now.

My hand trembled as I reached out. *Remember what happened the last time you went out with a boy?* a voice inside my head warned. The safe thing to do would be to run back inside, lock my door, and pretend this whole night never happened. Only, that was what I'd been doing every single day since my brother's death—and look where that got me.

The coolness of his skin startled me. My breath hitched in my throat when his fingers wove into mine. There was no backing out now.

~ ☾ ~

Chapter 11

"Thanks for coming with me."

I couldn't answer, could only stare at our fingers knit together so tightly that they resembled a peony closed to the dark. It was strange that instead of clasping hands, he'd chosen to slip his fingers through mine. It was more intimate and—I realized when he pulled me forward—a more difficult grip to slip out of.

He smiled once before leading me to the back of the yard and down a thin animal path that twisted beyond the overgrown vegetation and led to the bayou.

"It means a lot that you trust me," he said over his shoulder.

Did I trust him? There had to be some reason I felt compelled to follow him as he led me behind peeling privacy fences and over fallen trees. The path grew narrower. The long grass on either side scratched along my bare feet and ankles until we emerged from the trees. A sun-bleached dock rocked on the water before us, a dozen crab traps roped off its side. I wrinkled my nose as a breeze carried the smell of rotted fish from the shore. Why had the boy brought me here?

He climbed on the dock, which swayed lightly under his weight. Before he could pull me beside him, I dug my toe under the edge of the dock and ripped my hand from his grip.

He turned, frowning. "Is something wrong?"

The closest house was nothing more than a pinprick of light down the shore. There was no boat, and as far as I could tell, no one else around. Ribbons of fear tightened around my chest. I shouldn't have come.

The boy cocked his head to the side. It was too dark to see his eyelids close, but I could tell he blinked by the disappearance and reappearance of the moon in his eyes. "You think I'm going to hurt you?" he asked.

My fingers brushed the edge of my bandage. "Your friend did. Maybe you're here to finish the job?"

"Why would you think that?"

I shrugged. Death was always on my mind. After it devoured my brother, it consumed me—grinding me against its razor teeth, and yet, always refusing to swallow. I was obsessed. I wrote poems about it. I listened to music about it. I read the obituaries to see if there was a way to die I hadn't discovered. No wonder being taken to a remote location by a stranger didn't exactly give me the warm fuzzies.

Bastin's lips pressed into a straight line. "I understand," he said. "You have every right to not trust me. I just wanted to talk with you and . . . I feel better by the water. It's soothing." When I still didn't move, he nodded to the shore. "We can sit on the grass if you'd like."

"I'd like," I answered. Land seemed a safer bet, even though my other decisions tonight hadn't exactly had caution in mind.

He hopped off the dock and I followed him to the edge of the beach. I sat down on a patch of grass that had folded under its own weight. He sat beside me, his long legs crossed at the ankles.

I'm not sure how long we sat that way, staring at each other. Seconds? Minutes? An hour? His eyes hypnotized me with their disappearing, reappearing moons.

Finally, he spoke. "I've never talked with a girl before."

That made me sad. But I had to admit, the freaky wig and contacts were a little off-putting. I wondered if he wore them to hide an illness, or if he just had a bizarre sense of fashion. "If it makes you feel better, I don't talk to boys much, either."

He smiled. "My name is Bastin. What's yours?"

"Edith."

Bastin sounded out my name in two long syllables as if drinking it from a straw. "Eeeeh-Dith." He smiled again, this time flashing deep dimples in both cheeks, which brought about a strange tickling sensation in the pit of my stomach. "Very unusual name."

"Old-fashioned, you mean."

Bastin frowned. "I don't understand."

I shrugged. "Only little old ladies are named Edith."

He blinked.

"You can blink really fast."

His laugh wrapped around me, clinging to my skin like taffy. "I guess I can."

I waited but he didn't elaborate. We sat in silence for another minute before I prodded, "So you wanted to talk to me?"

He picked a piece of grass from the sand and wrapped it around his finger. "I wanted to make sure you received my gift."

It took me a minute before I remembered the oyster shell outside my room. "Oh, you mean the green stone!"

His pulled the piece of grass from his finger and snapped it in two. "Yes. I feel bad that Luna took your necklace and wanted to give you something in turn."

The blue-haired girl again. "Why *did* she attack me?"

He snorted. "She wasn't supposed to, but as captain of the guard she takes certain . . . liberties." His jaw flexed as if he had trouble getting the last word off of his tongue.

"The guard? Like the Coast Guard?"

"No." Bastin continued to pull apart the blade of grass until it was nothing but green slivers in his lap. "My father's guard."

I huffed. "You're still not making any sense."

~ ☾ ~

Bastin stared at the shredded grass, as if he were avoiding my gaze. "My father. The king."

I laughed. Obviously his sense of humor was as weird as his sense of style. But I didn't mind. It had been a long time since I laughed. It felt good. "If your father is a king that would make you—"

"A prince," he answered.

"Of course." I giggled again. Was this his crazy idea of a pickup line? "Very funny."

He looked up at me. There was no trace of humor on his face. "Not really. In fact, my father would have my tail if he knew I'd told you."

"Tail?" I sobered. Apparently there was more wrong with him than I'd imagined. "Are you talking, like, extra vertebrae or webbed toes?"

He doubled over with laughter, which only confused me more. When he finished, he wiped his eyes with the back of his hands and stared at the moisture he'd found there. "Huh, that's strange."

"Understatement of the year," I said.

If he'd heard me, he pretended he didn't. "Sorry, I went off topic." He brushed his hands on his jeans. "What I'd meant by tail," he gestured toward his legs, "was, you know, an actual tail."

I took a deep breath and let it out in a slow hiss. Either he had a warped sense of humor, or he had a mental illness. The more we talked, the more convinced I became it was the latter. Didn't people develop schizophrenia in their late teens? "You don't have a tail. You have legs."

"*Now* I do. Because of the moon."

There was another explanation that made sense. "Are you on drugs? Or have you been drinking?"

He turned a thoughtful expression to the moon. "The surface is ruled by the sun. Everything here requires it for life. From your plants to your animals to"— he blinked onyx eyes at me—"you. But the ocean is

~ ☾ ~

different. We are ruled by the moon. The moon controls the tides and allows us to walk the land."

"Hold up." I held up a hand to stop him. "You mean to tell me that you live in the ocean?"

"Yes." He pulled another piece of grass from the sand.

I opened my mouth to tell him where he could shove the load of crap he'd just fed me, only the words didn't come. Instead, I found myself with my eyes closed, inhaling the scent of him carried by the ocean's breeze. He smelled of salt and surf, his scent stronger than the sand at my feet, stronger than the water yards away. And if the moon had a smell, surely the dark fragrance that rolled off of him was the closest thing to it.

His voice grew cautious. "You're quiet." It was more a question than a statement.

I opened my eyes, surprised all over again by the hair cascading down his shoulder like a silver cloak. My head reeled. Last week, if someone told me that mermaids existed, I would have laughed in their face. Now, I wasn't so sure.

"Can I?" I reached a hand out to his hair.

He nodded and closed his eyes.

Tentatively, I brushed my fingers along the ends of his hair. I'd never seen anything like it. Despite having the reflective quality of tinfoil, the strands felt like silk against my skin.

Bastin sat motionless as I continued to study his hair. Feeling bolder, I grasped hold of the tendril in front of his ear and tugged. Bastin winced, but the hair remained rooted in place.

Definitely not a wig.

"Oh my God!" I dropped the lock of hair and scooted away from him. "I don't believe it."

Bastin opened his eyes and rubbed his head with his palm. "Then what was that for?"

"No . . . it's just . . . I don't . . ." My thoughts jumbled together so fast I couldn't hold on to a single one. I looked at him. "This is crazy, right?"

He smiled at me. "Very."

I stared at him for another moment, not ready to believe what my eyes and hands had proved to be real. But what other explanation was there? Every nerve under my skin screamed with the truth of it. "What happens if I do believe in you?" I asked.

He leaned closer. "What do you want to happen?"

A hundred butterflies with wings of ice fluttered inside my chest. Even if I knew how to answer that question, I couldn't have because I'd forgotten how to talk.

Bastin opened his mouth to say more, but a nearby splash killed the words on his tongue. He was on his feet in an instant, scanning the water.

He was too tall to see over so I peered under his elbow. "What is it?"

He frowned. "Our time has run out. I have to go."

I was surprised by the disappointment flooding through me. "I should go, too. If Sir finds me missing I'll be in a ton of trouble."

Bastin's eyes didn't leave the water. "I'm sorry I am not able to walk you back."

"That's okay." It wasn't like it was a date or anything. In fact, I didn't think the rules of etiquette applied to nighttime visits from ocean-dwelling strangers. I quickly dusted the sand from my nightgown before turning toward the path.

"Edith?"

I froze. "Yes?"

"Could I see you again? Tomorrow?"

A warmth crept from the pit of my stomach, up my neck, where it burned hot in my cheeks. I'd risked so much by sneaking from my room tonight. To continue to do so would be stupid, and yet I couldn't bring myself to say no.

"Yes," I answered.

~ ☾ ~

"Good." I didn't need look over my shoulder to see the smile on Bastin's face—I could hear it in his voice. "Tomorrow, then."

I resumed walking down the path toward my house and my room, hoping my footsteps didn't sear the ground as I burned my way through the night.

~ ☾ ~

Chapter 12

Morgan flopped down next to me at the cafeteria table. The chains hanging from her pink skirt clanged sharply against the metal chair. "How's it going, Smalls?"

"It's . . . definitely going." Surprised to have a lunch companion, I folded the copy of the obituaries I'd smuggled from the library and tucked it into my backpack. It was nothing I hadn't seen before, anyway. Just the usual heart attacks, drunk drivers, and cancer.

Morgan ripped opened a cheese-and-cracker lunch kit. "Did the old man lay into you?"

"No." And I was so sure that I'd get busted. The fact that I didn't must have thrown the planets out of alignment. Sir's favorite pastime was breathing down my neck. He lived to watch my every move, just waiting for me to step out of line. And, aside from my school bathroom makeovers, I never did—until yesterday.

When I'd returned to my bedroom after my night with Bastin, I'd been woozy with fear and adrenaline. I'd lain in bed until the sun came up, alive with an electricity that jolted every nerve in my body. Which was why I couldn't wait to do it again. Tonight. The anticipation of the high was almost as exciting as getting to see Bastin again.

Almost.

Morgan snapped her fingers in front of my face, dissolving the image of Bastin's onyx eyes and moon-drenched skin. "Earth to Smalls! Snap out of your emo trance and tell me what happened."

"Sorry." I took a bite of my apple and spoke between crunches. "Sir's been too distracted by the plumbing to get after me. The kitchen sink started leaking yesterday, and this morning I couldn't shut the water off after my shower."

She laughed. "What is it with you and busted pipes already?"

I shrugged. "It's weird, right? Anyway, thanks for saving me yesterday. If Sir found out I'd skipped class, I'd be on a bus to military school right now."

"Another Sergeant Shithead." She rolled her eyes. "I know the type." She waved her hand dismissively. "But whatever. Friday's going to be great. My old man is always giving me a hard time about not having friends. This will get him off my back."

My heart sank. Was that all I was to her? A way to get her dad off her back? I knew deep down I didn't deserve to have friends. But that didn't mean I didn't want them.

Morgan, as if reading my thoughts, punched my arm lightly. "And it's an added bonus that you're the one person in this school I don't find unbearable."

"Thanks?"

She laughed and I laughed with her.

"You two are unbelievable," a voice from behind me said.

A lump of apple wedged in my throat as the fruit fell from my fingertips and spun a lazy circle on the lunch table. Morgan's expression went dark.

I almost didn't recognize the girl standing behind me with her arms crossed and a brace fastened around her neck. Her normally bronze-colored skin had paled to a grayish hue and dark circles pulled at her eyes. Two girls wearing jodhpurs and riding boots stood behind her mirroring her outraged expression.

Morgan clicked her tongue ring against her teeth. "What the hell do you want, Hagrielle?"

Gabrielle's face flushed. "My boyfriend is dead." Her

voice broke into a sob and her eyes shimmered with unshed tears. “I know you don’t know how to act like a normal human being, Morgan, so it’s not surprising that you’re acting like the Bitch Queen that you are. But you, *Edith*.” Her eyes bore into mine. “*You* were there. For reasons I will never understand, Marty liked you. He’s in the hospital and here you are laughing, acting like nothing happened. I heard you haven’t even visited him.”

My jaw throbbed from how hard I pressed my teeth together. But what could I say? Gabrielle was right. I’d been so caught up in my own world I’d forgotten how the accident had affected more people than just me. No longer able to meet her gaze, I grabbed the apple off the table and picked at a bruise on its skin with my fingernail. Just because Gabrielle wasn’t the nicest person around didn’t mean that she didn’t have feelings.

The cafeteria had gone silent, the entire room clinging to her every word as she continued. “I mean, the whole thing was your fault and you know it. It’s your fault Marty’s hurt and Russell’s dead. You owe their parents an apology.” She took a moment to choke back a sob. “With the way you’re acting, I’m starting to think you did it on purpose. Maybe Morgan told you to do it. Is that why you pushed me?”

I stood up before I realized what I was doing. “That’s a lie! I didn’t push you from the boat. I tried to save you!”

The tears welling in Gabrielle’s eyes broke free in thick streams. “Edith Small, you’re either a liar or you’re crazy.”

My hands rolled into fists as waves of heat boiled the blood running through my veins.

“I loved Russell and you took him from me,” she spat. “You ruined my life and I’m going to make sure you don’t get away with it. People will learn the truth.” With that she turned on her heels and stormed away. Her friends swarmed behind her, embracing her as she fled.

The room erupted in a buzz of hushed whispers. It didn't matter that everything Gabrielle said was a lie. What mattered was, from the stone-eyed glares I was already receiving, people believed her.

Morgan grabbed my wrist and pulled me down into my chair. "What a psycho bitch," she muttered. "Don't let her get to you, Edith. She's crazy."

I swallowed past the lump that formed in my throat. "If this gets back to my stepdad, I'm a goner for sure." Everything I'd done to make Sir happy—always making sure to say the right words and do the right things for a chance to break free from Sir's hold when high school ended—would all be nothing. All because of a stupid date, with a stupid guy, on a stupid boat.

Morgan shook her head. "Not going to happen."

My appetite gone, I twisted the stem off the apple and set it in the middle of the table. Unfortunately, I couldn't agree. Given the sound of the hushed whispers filling the cafeteria, the rumor that I'd tried to kill Gabrielle was already in motion. This was high school, not a monastery. There was no question the rumor would spread. The real question was, would it spread far enough to reach Sir?

~ ☾ ~

Chapter 13

Morgan followed me from the lunch room and leaned against the lockers as I pulled my books for next period. "I'm telling you, Smalls, don't worry about Hagrielle. She's all talk."

I nodded, though I wasn't so sure.

"What class do you have next?"

"Chemistry," I answered, zipping up my bag then walking beside Morgan down the hall.

"I have shop." She made an evil face. "Power tools!"

I stopped short. "Power tools? Do you have access to a drill?"

"Uh, yeah." Morgan rolled her eyes. "Please don't tell me you're one of *those* girls, Smalls. You do know the difference between a flat head and a Phillips head, don't you?"

I didn't, so I ignored the question. "Could you do something for me?"

She pushed the head of her barbell between her lips. "Sure."

I dug into my pocket and withdrew the green stone Bastin gave me.

"What is *that*?" Morgan asked when I opened my palm.

I shrugged. "I found it on the beach. I was hoping you could maybe drill a hole in it so I could string it on a necklace or something. That seems a lot safer than carrying it around in my pocket."

Morgan took the stone from my hand and turned it over with her fingers. "Sure. But why are you carrying it around in your pocket in the first place?"

"Because I like it." But the truth was, I carried it with me because it reminded me that Bastin wasn't a dream I'd made up. He became real all over again every time I fingered the polished stone. I wasn't sure exactly why that should be important to me, but it was.

Morgan pocketed the stone and saluted me. "Okey-dokey."

With the stone out of my possession I felt a flash of panic. "Be careful with it, promise?"

"I promise." She narrowed her eyes. "Are you sure you found it on the beach?"

Before I could answer, the water fountain across the hall burst open spraying water straight in the air. Several underclassmen screamed and darted out of the way as the spigot clanked down the hallway.

"Hallway hurricane!" Morgan called out to the forming crowd of gawkers. She thrust her backpack over her head and yanked me forward by my wrist. "Stupid school is falling apart."

I nodded in agreement, but a nagging feeling told me there was something else going on.

I chewed on it during Chemistry. While Ms. Whitman prattled on about chemical compounds, I drew a table in my notebook and listed everything I could remember about the faucet leaks—from the type of soap in the bathroom to the weather conditions before the leaks happened. Then I circled common factors and drew lines to connect them.

When the end of class bell rang, I sat back and studied my work. Every instance had one thing in common: me.

A sour taste rose up the back of my throat as I stuffed my books into my bag and walked from class. So what did I have to do with the leaking faucets? The idea that my nearness could be causing them was ridiculous. Yet what other explanation was there? There had to be

~ ☾ ~

something I was missing . . .

"Hey! You look terrible." Morgan fell into step beside me. "Don't feel bad about it, though. Chem gives me hives. You think I could get a doctor's excuse?"

I gave her a half-smile.

"I have something that will make you feel better," she sang. "Ta Da!" She thrust her hand at me. The green stone sat on her open palm with hole drilled neatly through it.

"It's perfect!" I took the stone, feeling instantly better having it pressed against my skin. "Thanks so much."

She waved dismissively. "Don't mention it."

We walked to study hall together and, afterwards—after a quick change and makeup scrub in the girls' bathroom—out to the parking lot where I was pleasantly surprised to find my mom waiting for me. I said goodbye to Morgan before climbing into our tan minivan.

Mom smiled and motioned to Morgan. "Is that your new friend?"

After buckling my seatbelt, I stuck my hand into my jeans pocket and fingered the stone inside. "Yeah."

Mom shifted the van into gear and pulled away from the curb. "That's great. I told you all you needed was a little bit of time."

I didn't answer, only twisted the stone around and around with my fingers.

"So your father's very excited about being invited to the Base Commander's for dinner."

I nodded.

A Journey song came on the radio and Mom hummed along. When it was over, she turned the volume down with a sigh. "How are things going, Edi-girl?"

"Um, okay I guess." It wasn't like I could tell her about spending the night with Bastin or being accused of murder by Gabrielle in front of the whole school. That type of behavior wouldn't work for the daughter she'd believed I was—even though it was a lie.

She cleared her throat. "I received a call from your principal today."

My chest tightened. I should have known I'd get busted one way or another. "What did she want?"

Mom looked at me. "She said you didn't attend any of your classes yesterday."

I chewed on my lip as my heart pounded against my ribs. "Does Sir know?" My voice was barely a whisper.

She shook her head. "I don't think that's necessary."

The knot in my chest loosened. "You don't?"

"No," she continued. "But I want you to promise not to make this a habit. After everything you've gone through, I know how difficult it must be for you to return to class. As long as this was a single occurrence—*not* to be repeated," her voice took on a threatening tone, "I think we can keep the skipping between the two of us. Sound like a deal?"

I bobbed my head, realizing how close I'd come to disaster. "Deal."

Mom smiled at me before returning her attention to the road. "Great. I've got plenty to deal with at the moment without having to worry about you. Would you believe that when I got up this morning, all of the faucets were dripping? Even the toilets were running. I called a plumber to come look at it and when he showed up, everything was working fine and he couldn't find anything wrong. Can you believe that?"

I shook my head, hoping I didn't look as pale as I felt.

~ ☾ ~

Chapter 14

Shortly after I pulled my nightgown over my head, there was a knock at my door. "Just a sec!" I quickly rolled my jeans up my calves then smoothed my nightgown over them. "Okay. Come in."

Mom walked in, still wearing her tattered cooking apron, and shut the door. "Getting ready for bed a little early tonight, I see."

I tugged on the gown and prayed my jeans wouldn't unravel underneath. "Yeah. I'm . . . not feeling so well."

"Mm-hmm." Mom sat down on my bed and patted the area next to her. "I noticed you hardly touched your dinner."

That surprised me. I hardly *ever* touched my dinner—but tonight she'd *noticed*. Meat didn't agree with me. If I had a choice I wouldn't eat it at all. But in this house, being a vegetarian was as bad as being a baby killer or a Democrat. I shrugged and sat next to Mom on my bed. The smell of lemon dish soap overpowered her English rose perfume. "I guess I'm still recovering."

She nodded and patted my knee. I stiffened but relaxed when she seemed unaware of the denim underneath. "I won't keep you up if you need your rest. But how about a quick Dog of the Day before you go to bed?"

"Sure." I smiled.

Mom stood and walked to my desk, ripping yesterday's dog from the calendar. "Today's dog is the Havanese." She showed me a picture of a dog that looked like an overturned dust mop.

~ ☾ ~

I wrinkled my nose. “Uh-uh. You don’t even have to read the description.”

She studied the picture. “You can tell just by looking? What are you, *The Dog Whisperer?*”

I laughed and tugged on a lock of my hair. “No. I just don’t want a dog that has longer hair than me.”

She smiled and set down the calendar. “Maybe tomorrow’s dog, then.”

“Maybe.”

She walked over and kissed my forehead. “Hmm . . .” She straightened, her brow furrowed, and pressed a lemon-scented hand against my forehead. “It’s a good thing you’re going to bed. You feel flush.”

Understatement of the year. In anticipation of my escape, adrenaline coursed through my veins like an electric current, igniting my nerves and forcing my heart into a gallop.

“I’m fine,” I said, sliding out from under her fingers and wiggling under my covers, careful not to expose my pants. “Night, Mom.”

“Night.” She hesitated, twisting her ring around her finger several times, before finally backing out the door and shutting it behind her.

I counted to ten before exhaling loudly. She was gone.

Now all I had to do was wait for Bastin to appear.

My stomach twisted at the thought of seeing him again. Last night, when I’d sat beside him on the grass, I’d felt really and truly alive for the first time in my life. I was aware of every beat of my heart, every breath in my lungs, and I couldn’t wait to feel that way again.

Earlier in the night, I’d fashioned an anklet from hemp, weaving the two remaining pearls from my Aunt Margie’s necklace into it, along with the green stone Bastin gave me. I curled my knees into my chest so I could twist the green stone between my fingers. Its calming magic worked a little too well, because the next thing I knew, a sharp rap at the sliding door pulled me from the depths of sleep with a gasp.

A glance at my clock radio showed the time to be a little after one in the morning. From my bed, I could make out Bastin's orb-like eyes. But they paled in comparison to his smile, which sent happy tremors dancing along my skin.

Peeling back the covers, I slipped the nightgown over my head and straightened the T-shirt I wore underneath. Finally, I uncuffed my jeans and slid on a pair of flip flops before quietly letting myself into the backyard.

Bastin grinned. "I was worried you wouldn't come." He held out his hand.

I slipped my hand inside of his and his fingers wove into mine. My breath hitched in my throat and it took several attempts of clearing it before I could talk. "Why would you think that?"

He shrugged and led me down the same path we walked the night before. "Because of what I am. Because of what I let happen to you." His skin was strangely cool against the warm night.

With my free hand, I scratched at the bandage on my shoulder. "But it wasn't your fault. You didn't mean for Luna to hurt me."

"No. I didn't." His shoulders went rigid and his grip on my hand tightened. "I wish I had been there in time to stop her. You'd think that considering I'm a prince, I'd have more control over my father's guard." He shook his head. "But the reality is I have so little control over anything."

I nodded. "I know *exactly* how you feel. Sir, my stepdad, has been waiting for me to mess up so he can send me away."

Bastin stopped walking. "He'd banish you?"

I nodded. That was the perfect word for it: *banishment*.

Bastin looked angry, but he didn't say anything.

~ ☾ ~

Instead, he urged me forward with a gentle tug on my hand.

We reached the dock where we'd been the previous night, and this time I allowed him to lead me down the dried-out planks to the end where we sat, the wood smooth and worn under my legs. Bastin let go of my hand so I could take off my sandals. The water was too chilly to hang my feet in, so I drew circles on the water with my toes. Bastin, unfazed by the temperature, let his feet sink to his ankles. He leaned back on his elbows and stared at the stars.

My fingers itched, suddenly aware of the skin no longer pressed against my own.

"Do you think we'll ever be free?"

Bastin's question startled me, and I looked up to see my own wide-eyed stare reflected in the depths of his eyes. Free? Before Bastin, that word didn't exist in my vocabulary. But now, sitting next to him on the dock, a strange new sensation swirled inside of me, making me lightheaded. Hope. "I don't know. Sir controls everything in my life from the food I eat to the clothes I wear. Other than switching outfits at school, this is the first time I've broken orders."

Bastin grinned, warming the pit of my stomach. "Feels good, doesn't it?"

I grinned back. "You say that like you're familiar with the feeling."

"Probably a little *too* familiar." He chuckled, a sound that burned a path from my cheeks to my chest, then sobered. "But seriously, this stepdad of yours, why are you so afraid of him?"

I pulled my legs back onto the dock and hugged my knees against my chest. "Because he's scary. He's mean. Nothing I ever do is good enough, and he wants to send me away."

"He's only a man," Bastin said.

"And a pit-bull is only a dog."

~ ☾ ~

Bastin frowned. "Has he ever hurt you?" His eyes locked onto mine. "Physically?"

I shook my head. "No. It's not like that. He's never laid a hand on me." If fact, I couldn't remember the last time he touched me for any reason. "But I'm still scared of him."

"Okay, then." Bastin stood. "I'll be right back." Without waiting for me to respond, he turned and dove off the dock.

"But—" I looked around. The closest house was several hundred feet away. Where could he have gone? I crept to the edge of the dock and peered into the water. It was too dark to see anything in the night-soaked water. I watched for a ripple, an air bubble, anything to show me where Bastin had swam off to, but besides the gentle lapping of waves, the water remained still.

"Bastin?" I called. There was no answer. I paced the dock. His abrupt departure didn't make sense. We had been talking about Sir and he'd just . . . left. I wrapped my arms around my body to ward off a chill as a cool bayou breeze tickled my skin.

A minute passed. And then another. I stopped pacing and stood in the middle of the dock. Had I said or done something wrong? What if Bastin wasn't coming back? I took a tentative step back toward the shore. It wasn't like I could sit here all night. I waited another minute before deciding enough was enough. I turned to leave, and that's when I heard it—the splash of something breaking the surface of the water.

"Edith, where are you going?" Bastin called. "I have a surprise for you!"

I stopped, looked over my shoulder, and immediately wished I hadn't. Bastin stood knee-deep in the water, holding a three-foot-long thrashing alligator. He held the furious reptile, one hand clamping the alligator's snout shut and his other arm supporting the base of the alligator's tail.

~ ☾ ~

"Bastin, what the hell?" Instinct told me to get as far away from the reptile as I could.

He grinned broadly and held the alligator out to me like an offering. "Surprise!"

I shuddered and my skin pulled at my bones as if it wanted to break free from my body. I jerked back and nearly stumbled in my retreat off of the dock. I'd watched enough *Animal Planet* to know that even a small alligator, like the one Bastin held, would have no trouble ripping my face off. "I don't want that thing! Put it back!"

"Why would I do that?" he asked and walked out of the water toward me. For every step he took forward, I took a step back. "He wasn't easy to catch. Look! He's extra feisty!"

The gator glared at me with unblinking eyes and a look that, if he could talk, would call me every name in the book.

My leg muscles seized with the ache to sprint. "Bastin," I said, "the stone was enough. I don't want any more presents. Please put the alligator back in the water."

Bastin stopped moving. "Okay."

Relieved, I stopped, too. "Really?"

"Yes." He grinned. "I promise to put him back . . . *after* you hold him." He thrust his arms—and the reptile in them—at me.

"What?" I jerked back and tripped on a loose plank at the end of the dock. I landed on my butt on the sandy shore. "Are you crazy? There's no way I'm holding that thing."

"But you have to hold him. It will help you."

I stood on wobbly legs. Sand stuck to my ankles, making my skin itch, but I didn't dare pause to brush it off. "In what universe is getting my face bitten off considered helpful?"

Bastin snorted. "Please, Edith. Do you think I'd let

~ ☾ ~

that happen? Back home we keep these things as pets."

"Really?"

"No." He smiled. "Are you kidding? Alligators are mean as hell."

"Bastin!" I moved my arms as if to shove him but stopped when the gator whipped his tail. A squeak escaped my throat.

Bastin laughed and stepped forward. "I'm sorry, I couldn't resist. But seriously, I want you to take the alligator. You only have to hold him for a minute. I promise." He took another step, which put the gator within biting distance to me.

My pulse skipped as my heart played hopscotch inside my chest. "What's the big deal? What does it matter if I hold the stupid alligator or not?"

"It matters," he answered, "because you told me that you're afraid of your stepdad because he's scary, mean, and he wants to send you away. But I can guarantee you that this alligator is scarier, meaner, and—not only does he want to send you away—he'd like to eat you. Wouldn't you agree that makes him worse than your stepdad?"

"Yes. But I still don't see—"

"The point is that you're going to face this alligator. You're going to overcome your fear, and you're going to survive. After that, how bad can your stepdad really be?"

I licked my lips. His words made sense in a crazy sort of way. "But what if he bites me?"

"He won't." Bastin's eyes locked onto mine. "I'm here, and I won't anything happen to you. I promise."

I believed him. All I had to do was look into his eyes to know that he only wanted to help. And since he went through the trouble of catching the gator, the least I could do was try. "O-okay. I'll do it."

The grin he gave me made the threat of an alligator bite totally worth it. "Good." He held out his arms. "Now I want you to slide between the alligator and me."

~ ☾ ~

I swallowed hard and ducked beneath the thrashing reptile. When I stood I pressed myself against Bastin's chest in order to put as much space as possible between me and the jaws of death. Too many emotions rolled through me at once. The heart-squeezing anxiety of having an alligator invade my personal space coupled with the dizzying effects of Bastin's salty-sweet ocean scented skin swayed me on my feet.

"I want you to place your hands exactly where mine are," Bastin said. "One hand will grip his snout and the other will support his body."

I tried to concentrate on his words, but all I think about were the hard lines of muscles pressed against my back. *Focus, Edith!* With trembling fingers, I reached for the alligator's snout. The reptile's eyes narrowed and he jerked in Bastin's grip, his tail lashing dangerously close to my body.

I whimpered and shrank against Bastin's body.

"It's okay." Bastin tilted his chin down so that his breath warmed the skin below my ear and sent delicious shivers racing down my spine. "I've got you. Try again."

Slowly, I reached out and ran my fingers along the top of the alligator's snout. His scales were softer than I expected, leather-like. When I was convinced that I wouldn't drop dead from a heart attack, I gathered the rest of my courage and wrapped my hand around the gator's jaw.

"Good job," Bastin said. And while I couldn't see his face, I could hear the smile in his voice. "The muscles that alligators use to close their jaws and crush prey are very strong," he continued. "But the muscles they use to open their jaws are very weak. This is why we're able to keep their jaws closed with almost no effort at all. See?" He dropped his hand from the gator's snout so that my hand was the only thing keeping it shut.

"Oh my God," I whispered. I was holding an alligator's jaw shut. Me! And on top of that, I was still alive!

"You're doing great," Bastin said. With his free hand, he guided my arm under the alligator's body at the base of its tail. The alligator twitched once and went still. "Okay, are you ready for this?"

I swallowed. "I trust you."

"No." He leaned his head over my shoulder so that his cheek was next to mine. "Do you trust yourself?"

I couldn't answer right away. My head spun from Bastin's nearness. What exactly was I supposed to trust myself to do? Keep my grip on the alligator? Try not to die? Or something more? "I-I think so."

"Good. Because it's all you, now." He dropped his arms, stepped back, and left me alone, with a struggling alligator in my arms.

My heart leapt inside my throat, thick and hard. But, despite my inability to breath, I held on. "I'm doing it." I wasn't sure who I was talking to; me, Bastin, or even the alligator. I pivoted on my feet so I could face Bastin. The gator writhed and twisted, but I held on. "I can't believe this. I'm doing it!" I laughed out loud.

Bastin laughed, too, but held his hands up. "Careful where you point that thing. It's loaded."

"This is amazing!" In my hands, I held a creature that wanted me dead. And yet I was okay. For the first time in my entire life, I felt strong—almost invincible.

"Are you afraid?" he asked.

"No." My heart hopped inside my chest like a bunny with ADHD, but I wasn't afraid. In fact, I felt like I'd lived more in this moment than I had in my entire life.

"Why do you think that is?"

"Because . . ." But I wasn't sure why. The animal in my arms could easily kill me. That alone should have my knees quaking. But I felt elated. That, if it wasn't for the added weight from the reptile in my arms, I might just soar into the sky. "Because I can handle it."

He nodded and held out his hands. I placed the

alligator back into them. When I was sure Bastin had the reptile firmly in his grip, I let go. "That's not the only thing you can handle," he said. "Don't forget that." He turned, stepped onto the dock, and walked to the edge where he dropped the reptile back into the water. It swam away without a backward glance.

With the alligator safely back in the water, I couldn't help myself. I ran down the dock and threw my arms around Bastin's waist, pressing my cheek into the hollow of his neck. No one had ever forced me to examine who I really was on the inside. I was used to being torn down by Sir's snide comments and threats. I'd thought I was weak. But that wasn't true. Before this moment, before Bastin came into my world, I'd never realized the strength I had. "Thank you," I whispered against his chest.

He tensed, his arms rigid at his side. For a moment, I wondered if I'd made a mistake by hugging him. But, slowly, Bastin relaxed and returned my embrace by wrapping his arms around my shoulders. "You're welcome."

We stayed that way for a long time. Me, not wanting to let go, and Bastin not making me. I couldn't remember a time when I'd been held so close or felt as safe as I did in that moment. I never wanted it to end. It wasn't until exhaustion got the better of me that I felt myself being lifted and carried down the dock. As hard as I tried, I couldn't keep my eyes opened, and I worried that if I fell asleep, when I finally woke, I'd discover that Bastin had only been a dream.

But then I heard the words, "I really like you, Edith," whispered from a distance. I couldn't be sure that I'd heard them correctly, so I pried my eyes open just in time to see Bastin slip through the sliding glass door of my bedroom. Only then did I feel safe enough to let myself fall.

~ ☾ ~

Chapter 15

I spent most of the next day in an exhausted haze. I didn't remember getting dressed, or even my ride to school. And, despite guzzling an energy drink, I dozed during my classes and spent lunch nodding—but not really listening—while Morgan prattled on across the table from me.

It wasn't until that night, as I pulled my night gown over my jeans and T-shirt, that the fog of sleep deprivation clouding my mind finally lifted. In fact, I felt energized. My body hummed in anticipation of Bastin's arrival. My blood burned through my veins like a spark on a fuse of a firecracker. How much longer until I exploded?

The minutes passed like hours until, just after midnight, a familiar shadow appeared at the door. I was out of bed and outside before Bastin had the chance to knock. Once outside, he and I walked hand-in-hand to our dock, where I kicked off my flip-flops and sat down on the sun-bleached wood, my legs draped over the side.

Bastin sat next to me. He grinned and invisible needles crocheted intricate knots inside my stomach. "How's my alligator wrangler?" he asked.

"Retired," I answered, then laughed.

"That's okay. You've got bigger beasts to wrangle." He nudged me with his shoulder. "How did things go with your stepdad?"

His touch electrified my skin to the point that I was surprised I didn't see sparks. A blush burned from my cheeks to my throat and I ducked my head before Bastin could see it. "It didn't. I'm . . . working up to it."

"Ah." Bastin tilted his head to the sky. The moon reflected off of his silver hair making it look like it burned with a blue fire. "You mean you chickened out."

"Hey!" I nudged Bastin back which made him laugh. "Rome wasn't built in a day. And it certainly wasn't built by alligators."

Still laughing, Bastin shook his head. "I have no idea what that means. But I do know what it's like to have an overbearing father." He leaned back on his hands, stretched his legs out on the dock, and crossed them at the ankles. "If my father knew I was here, talking to a human, he would fillet me." His voice changed to a regal tone in what I guessed was an impersonation of his father. "Fraternization between the human and mer worlds is strictly forbidden. To do so would be at threat to all mer-kind."

I giggled. "That's crazy. I would never do anything to hurt you."

The humor drained from his eyes and was replaced with sadness. "Maybe not you specifically, but your species seems determined to kill us."

The smile died on my lips. That was news to me. I didn't realize other people knew about mermaids, much less tried to kill them. "What are you talking about?"

He turned his attention back to the sky, which spread before us like a velvet blanket littered with diamonds. "Humans care nothing for the ocean. They leak pollution and disease into our world, destroying our homes and making my people sick."

My eyes drifted to the soda bottles and beer cans that littered the shore. "Yeah, well, I'm not so sure that too many people care about the land, either."

Bastin nodded. "And that's why so many tribes want you dead."

"What?" I whipped my head around to see if he was

~ ☾ ~

joking. His face was impassive, as if murder were as casual a topic as baseball and the weather.

He settled back onto his elbows. "Well, not *you* specifically. Just humankind."

"Oh, *just* humankind." I waved my hand dismissively. "That makes me feel *so* much better."

Bastin cocked his head to the side, as if my reaction amused him. "Not all mers feel that way, Edith. My people don't. In our kingdom, we are forbidden from making contact with humans, but we don't wish them dead. There are other tribes, though, that would prefer to see your kind exterminated. Like the mers who attacked your friends."

"You mean like Luna?" I shivered, remembering her cruel smile and claw-like nails.

He shook his head. "No, Luna and I tried to stop them. The only reason she attacked you is because you saw her face when she took your purifiers."

The more Bastin talked, the more questions piled into my head until my temples throbbed under the pressure. "Purifiers?"

"That's right, you call them something else. What's the word I'm looking for?" He was quiet for a moment, and then snapped his fingers. "Pearls."

Reflexively, my fingers went to my throat and grasped for my missing necklace. "Why on earth would you be so concerned over a few pearls? The ocean is full of them."

"Not as many as you think." Bastin shifted his weight on the dock. "And our need is great. Pearls contain a chemical—calcium carbonate—that is vital to our survival. It helps us fight off the excessive levels of CO_2 that your kind has polluted into our waters. Without calcium carbonate, we would die."

My hand dropped to my side. When he put it that way, I doubted I'd be able to hold onto my broken necklace grudge. "Oh."

Bastin continued, "The other tribes, however, would

use calcium carbonate for another purpose. They would put excessive levels of CO_2 into your atmosphere—to melt the polar icecaps—and bury your land underwater."

It was hard to imagine a threat to human existence had been going on without anyone realizing it. I swallowed hard. "They could do that with pearls?"

He nodded. "Pearls are part of it, but there are other stones in the deepest part of the ocean—deeper than humans are able to explore—that contain concentrated levels of calcium carbonate. We call them nicite. These stones are very powerful and very rare. My kingdom has only one. We've been attacked numerous times by other tribes trying to steal it."

"What would happen if they got it?" I asked.

Bastin blinked one of his too-fast-to-be-human blinks. "They would destroy your land. You would die."

Acid climbed up my throat and burned my tongue. "Then why not destroy your nicite thing?"

He tilted his head away and stared at the ocean. "Because, then, my kind would be dead. It's capable of cleaning more of the ocean than all our pearls combined."

I opened my mouth, but the question died on my tongue. Something stirred in the distance. A barely audible swish as it pushed through the dry grass down shore.

Bastin leapt to his feet before I'd had a chance to move. "Humans!" he hissed in alarm.

I crouched behind him, my muscles tense with the urge to flee. "Who would be out here this time of night? Well, besides us." I peeked around his legs. Whoever they were, they were too far away to make out more than a silhouette. But even from this distance, I could see their stumbling legs and grasping arms.

Oh. Relieved that it wasn't Sir leading a search party, I sat down and smothered a giggle behind my hand.

Bastin looked at me and frowned. "What is it?"

~ ☾ ~

Down shore the couple dropped onto the sand in a tangled heap. "Um, I don't think they're going to bother us."

Bastin's look was disbelieving. "How can you be sure?" He turned his head back to the couple. "What are they doing, anyway?"

I couldn't help but laugh, drawing another narrow-eyed glance from Bastin. "You can't tell? They're kissing." The figures were now pressed so closely that they shared the same shadow. "Okay. Maybe that's not *all* they're doing." I held my hand in front of my eyes before the PG rating turned R. "Do you want to go somewhere else?"

"Are you kidding?" His voice held a hint of excitement and he craned his neck as if to get a better look. "We can't leave now. I've always wanted to see a kiss." He stared at the couple with unblinking eyes. "Fascinating."

I couldn't believe it. "You've never seen anyone kiss before?"

"No. Mers don't kiss." He sat back down next to me and leaned forward like an eager student. "Explain it to me."

Explain kissing? I might as well explain nuclear fission because I had the same amount of experience in the subject. "Um . . . when two people like each other . . . they just . . . press their lips together," *said the girl who'd never kissed a guy*. Sure, I'd simplified it. But how much more to it could there be? They were only lips. Everyone had them. They weren't special.

Or at least I hadn't thought so. But now that I studied the soft curve of Bastin's mouth, I wasn't so sure. I leaned in for a closer look. His lips were full, yet wide, complimenting the line of his jaw. I couldn't help but wonder what they would feel like against mine, if they would taste as salty-sweet as Bastin smelled.

A slow burn spread from my chest into my limbs until my entire body was consumed with uncomfortable warmth. I jerked back, stopping myself just before I could . . . well, I had no idea what I was about to do but I'm sure it would have been embarrassing. "Anyway," I pretended to study a star just above Bastin's shoulder—as if that had been my reason for moving closer. "That's pretty much all there is to kissing."

"It's a sign of affection, right?"

I nodded.

With superhuman speed, Bastin leaned over me, trapping me between his arms. Before I could so much as blink, his head lowered, so I could smell the ocean on his skin and feel the heat of his breath against my cheek.

Instinctively, I flattened myself against the dock which enabled him to swing his leg over mine and pin me down. "Um, Bastin, what are you doing?" I tried to sound casual but my voice came out a pitch higher than normal.

He tilted his head so that his hair slid over his shoulder, cutting me off from the rest of the world in a curtain of silver. "I'm going to kiss you."

My breath hitched in my throat as a shockwave of shivers tingled down my spine. "W-w-what?" I swallowed several times but still couldn't generate enough saliva to coat my suddenly dry throat. "Why?"

His lips stopped a breath away from mine and his eyes opened. Two shimmering black pools—deep enough to drown in. "Why not?" His voice was amused.

Why not? Why not? Why not? The question replayed over and over in my mind. "It's not that I don't want you to . . ." Because, boy did I want him to. I bit my lip and fought the urge to squirm. His hips hovered inches above my own. A strange ache ignited within me, low and forbidden. I wondered what would kill me first; drowning is his eyes or burning in our heat? "But we've only just met. Don't you think we should get to know each other better?" I knew it was a load of crap but it was the best my melted pudding-brain could come up with.

But the real reason I didn't want Bastin to kiss me was that I was scared—scared to let him get closer to me than he already had. What if I let him kiss me and whatever magic spell had been cast that brought him to my door each night unraveled? I knew that if I lost another person I cared about it would undo me—and there was so little holding me together to begin with.

Bastin settled his knees between mine, crossed his arms over my chest, and rested his chin on his clasped hands. He looked entirely too comfortable while I, on the other hand, felt like a fly twisted in a web. As if reading my mind, he said, "You warm-bloods and your complex feelings. How do you stand it?"

I could taste my own heartbeat, thick and frantic on the back of my tongue. The world shifted around me, spinning from the blood rushing through my head. What was happening? What did I *want* to happen? Both questions unraveled until they were nothing but a tangle of threads. "It's not easy," I said.

He shook his head, the movement spilling some of his silver hair across my cheek. Its weight surprised me—so much heavier than it looked. "I'm glad I'm a mer. We don't need to express ourselves the way you humans do."

"Obviously. You have no concept of personal space." I balled my hands at my sides. My fingers couldn't be trusted—so badly they itched to explore the muscles along his wide shoulders.

He smirked but made no attempt to let me up.

"And what do you mean, you don't need to express yourselves?" I tried squirming out from under him, but it was useless. The weight of his body kept me trapped. "You guys reproduce, right? How do you choose the person you want to do that with? Are you telling me there's no dating or romance involved?"

"Nope." He lifted a lock of my hair and wrapped it

around his finger. "We don't choose mates, Edith. That's what I've been trying to tell you. We're not people—we're fish." He let go of my hair, rolled off me, and swung his legs off the end of the dock. His eyes stared off into the blue-black horizon.

What just happened? I pulled myself up, careful to move slowly as I was still reeling from having Bastin pressed against me.

"Our procreation is purely for species survival," he continued. "Our females lay eggs and the males fertilize them. Simple as that."

"Wow. That sounds . . ." *Horrible* was my first thought. But then I thought about it. If humans behaved that way, then my mom wouldn't have been so devastated when my real dad took off. She wouldn't have felt the need to marry Sir. I might have had a normal life. That didn't sound horrible at all.

Bastin looked at me, waiting.

"That's sounds wonderfully uncomplicated," I finished.

"It was." He nodded. "*Life* was—until the pollution started. That's when our kind divided on how to handle the situation and formed different tribes. At first, my father wanted nothing to do with the other tribes' plan to flood the earth. But now, I'm not so sure."

A lump formed in my throat, jagged and hard. "But if your father changes his mind . . ." I tried to make sense of not only what Bastin had said but what he left hanging in the air. "Bastin, why are you here?"

His shoulders stiffened and he returned his gaze to the ocean.

"If what you've said is true," I prodded, "and your father decides he wants to kill off humans, then, that includes me. So what's the point of you being here?"

He was quiet a moment before answering, "I was curious."

Curious? Angry heat burned up my neck into my

cheeks as I tried and failed to keep my words even. "So, what? I'm like some sort of science experiment to you?"

He appeared to think about it before nodding. "Yes."

I pressed my lips together. Wasn't that nice? His every move had been a calculated effort to gauge my reaction, and, like the idiot I was, I'd fallen for it. I ran my fingers through my hair and smoothed the wrinkles in my shirt, trying as best I could to regain some dignity for allowing myself to be mounted like an animal *by* an animal. Stupid teenage hormones.

"You don't understand, Edith," Bastin continued. "Our kind do not touch. We live in tribes only for the sake of hunting and species survival. In fact, the males of our species raise the young because our females are vicious predators and can't be trusted not to kill their own offspring. We don't form attachments or bonds." He leaned toward me and I backed away until I had nowhere to go but in the water. "At least I didn't think so. But now . . . everything is so strange and confusing. When I am with you, Edith, my stomach twists—like I've eaten bad shrimp."

I glanced at the water and back at Bastin. Somehow he'd managed to trap me again. "So what are you telling me, exactly?"

He laughed. "I have no idea! Isn't that great? Everything I've been taught you're proving wrong."

I clung to the dock, the wood damp and sponge-like under my fingernails. "And . . . that's a good thing?"

"Not really." His smile was slow and sad. "But that doesn't matter. I'm next in line for the throne. Then it will be up to me to decide how to proceed against the human threat. I had to find out for myself if you were really as bad as I've been told."

"Are we?"

"Not you." He lowered his head to mine so that his nose was only inches from my own. His eyelashes glittered in the moonlight, like strands of a spider web.

~ ☾ ~

"I know humans talk about love—how would I know if I love you?"

It was as if the world itself had slipped out from under me. One minute I'd been holding on to the dock and the next I'd been so stunned by Bastin's words that I'd lost my grip on the edge and tumbled into the bayou. I couldn't see. Worse, I couldn't move. The water wasn't freezing but just cold enough to tighten my muscles. Just treading through the water, it felt like I was pushing myself through a vat of peanut butter.

Before I could panic, two arms wrapped around my waist and pulled me forward.

I broke the surface, then gasped. My feet found footing in the soft claylike marsh. Bastin held me against him. Standing this close I had to crane my neck to look up at him, his eyes the same color as the night sky that framed him. Water glittered on his face like stars. So brilliant, it was as if he swallowed the moon and it glowed through his skin. Leaving me breathless.

"Tell me, Edith," Bastin said, "What does love feel like?"

Using the last of the air in my lungs, I whispered, "I don't know."

He tightened his hold so there was nothing left between us but thin wet cotton. "Then how do you know that I'm not in love right now?"

It took me several tries before I could answer. "That would be impossible."

"Why?"

So much heat. It burned through my blood until I thought that my fingertips might sear the skin on Bastin's chest or bring the water around us to a boil. "Because we just met. You can't love someone you don't know."

He smiled, causing me to sway lightly in his arms. "I think I know you well enough."

He slid a finger under my chin and lowered his head.

~ ☾ ~

And then I knew—I was about to receive my first kiss.

Terror coursed through my body. I wasn't ready! I had no idea how to move my head, my lips, not to mention I had no clue what to do with my hands. Bastin would realize all this and be disappointed.

Scarier still were the words he'd spoken. Did he really love me? Or was this just another one of his *experiments*? Did I love him back? Was that even possible? If there really was a heart beating underneath my scars and Bastin uncovered it, what would stop him from destroying what little bit existed?

His lips were so close I could almost taste the salt on his skin.

"You're going to hurt me," I whispered.

He paused, his breath a cool breeze on my skin. "Kissing hurts?"

"No. Love does."

He brought his free hand up and wove his fingers into my hair. "I'll risk it." Before I could protest further, his lips were on mine. A soft brush of velvet. His tongue whisked against my bottom lip, tentative, then bolder until it slid further in my mouth where it was met with my own. His fingers curled against my scalp, entwining my hair in the same way that our tongues did in our mouths.

Something heavy and cold broke inside of me, and I pulled away from Bastin with a gasp.

He lifted his hand and brushed away the tears I hadn't known I cried. "Are you okay?" he asked.

No, I wanted to answer.

No. No. No. No. No.

Instead, I bit my trembling lip and wrapped my arms around his waist, digging my nails into his flesh, unable to get close enough, wanting only to sink inside of his skin. It'd only taken one kiss, but Bastin had not only found my heart, he'd stolen it.

We stayed that way, wrapped in each other's arms

and standing waist deep in the water, for what felt like hours. Only when the stars disappeared did I unwind from Bastin like a string pulled loose from a knot.

"I have to go," I said.

He frowned, tucking my now tussled hair behind my ears. "I know. I do, too. Before the others notice how long I've been gone."

I gazed at the bayou, still shimmering in the faint moonlight, and wondered what it would be like to live beneath its surface.

Bastin, as if reading my mind, said, "I wish I there was a way I could take you with me without—"

"Without?" I whipped my head back around so I could search his face. "Without what?"

His chin ruffled my hair as he shook it back and forth. "Forget I said anything. It is impossible."

I sighed, deflated. Of course it was. I could no more learn to breathe underwater than Bastin could grow permanent legs. Then a thought crossed my mind; if Bastin couldn't survive out of the water and I couldn't survive in it how could we ever really . . .

No! I shook my head, hoping to dislodge the notion that rolled my stomach in terror. *Stupid Edith.* Why did I always have to do that? Why did I always assume that every gift given to me was a moment away from crumbling in my hands? Well, not this time. I was going to cherish every moment I had with Bastin. I wouldn't, *couldn't,* consider the alternative.

When I shivered Bastin rubbed his long fingers down my arms. "We need to get you out of the water," he said.

I didn't answer, only fumbled my way through the sticky mud until I emerged on the shore. Even then, I kept moving forward—without looking back and without saying goodbye. I couldn't stop, too afraid that if I did I'd run back into his arms.

So I walked. And Bastin swam.

Each of us to a place the other could never go.

~ ☾ ~

Chapter 16

"Morgan saves the day again! Please, no need to thank me."

I stopped rummaging through my schoolbag to find a cardboard cup waving in front of my face.

I took the cup and sniffed the contents. "Marble latte?"

"Triple shot." She grinned. Today, Morgan had skipped her usual short skirt in favor of a pair of jeans that looked like they'd been run through a meat grinder. The pointed tips of snake-skin cowboy boots stuck out from under the frayed hems, dirty from dragging along the floor. "You looked a little run down first period, so I skipped calc and made a coffee run."

"You *are* my hero." I took the cup and greedily gulped it down, not caring that it was still hot enough to burn my tongue. I'd only managed to sleep three hours after returning home from my night with Bastin. Remembering our kiss, I shivered happily. I'd quit sleeping all together if I could manage it. Bastin was worth it.

Morgan arched an eyebrow as she leaned against the locker next to mine. "Everything okay?"

I nodded. "I'm having a little trouble sleeping is all." It was close enough to the truth. Sleep *was* nearly impossible when you were out in the bayou in the middle of the night making out with a merman.

"Well, you better rest up. We're going to having so much fun this weekend!"

~ ☾ ~

I gave her a look to show her I was less than convinced. “You forget that Sir is going to be at your house. A Pap smear would be more fun.”

“Bah!” She waved a hand dismissively. “Don’t you worry, Miss Negativity. I know how to deal with Sergeant Shithead.”

“If you say so.” I turned back to my locker. Once I twisted my combination into the dial, I pulled the door open only to have a piece of paper float out and land at my feet.

Morgan craned her neck over my shoulder. “What’s that?”

I picked up the paper with the caption, “Lady Death” scrawled on the top in permanent marker. On it, my head had been Photoshopped on the body of the Grim Reaper. The photo had obviously been taken in the school hallway with a cell phone. My face stared back at me from within the folds of a hooded cloak, my eyes worn and tired, my lips set into a thin line. One skeletal hand clutched a scythe.

“Ohmigawd!” Morgan ripped the picture from my hands. “This is hysterical! Don’t you think this is hysterical, Smalls?”

“Not so much,” I whispered. It was as if invisible hands had wrapped around my neck and squeezed. I struggled, just trying to remember how to breathe. So, this is what my classmates thought of me? That I was the harbinger of death? It was happening again. Just like before.

A tremor coursed through my body. First the accusations and then the blame. I pressed my palms into my eyes to keep tears from forming.

“Aw, Smalls!” Morgan slid her arm around my shoulder and gave me a squeeze. “Don’t let them get to you. It’s what they want. I think you should embrace being Lady Death. It’s a wicked cool nickname. Take this picture and make it your profile pic. That’ll show ‘em.”

~ ☾ ~

I looked at her, eyes brimming with tears that I refused to let fall. "But it's not my fault! I had nothing to do with it. I didn't kill them. I didn't kill Russell. It was an accident! Just like my brother!"

"Whoa, wait up." The reassuring smile fell from Morgan's face. "Your *brother*?"

I turned away, horrified by what I'd let slip, and started down the hall. What happened to William was nobody's business but my own. "Forget I said anything."

"Smalls, wait!" Morgan snatched my elbow, but I shrugged her off. She was my friend. I could take a lot of things, but I couldn't take the look of horror that always came when people learned I was responsible for my brother's accident. Like I really did belong locked up in some institution. I couldn't take that—not from her.

Morgan backed away with her hands up. "It's cool. Whatever."

I didn't say anything, just pushed past her and fled down the hallway to my next class. Running had always been my answer for difficult situations. Only now it was apparent that like the remnant of death that clung to me like a stain, some things followed no matter how long you ran.

***

"You're quiet tonight," Bastin said as we sat, perched on the end of our dock, later that night.

I pulled my knees against my chest. "Sorry. I had a rough day."

Bastin swept his hand in front of him, an indication for me to continue.

I sighed. "Everyone at school is blaming me for the boat accident. They're calling me 'Lady Death.' Like I personally murdered everyone who died."

Bastin snorted, which brought a smile to my lips. "That's ridiculous."

"Right? I wasn't the one doing a strip tease on the edge of a boat. If anything, the accident is Gabrielle's fault. She's the one with blood on her hands."

He frowned. "That's not what I meant."

I looked at him, searching his face. "Okay. What *did* you mean?"

"I meant to imply that it's ridiculous for the other humans to blame you for those kids' deaths when they're not even dead."

My dropped as I felt the wind knocked from my chest. It took several moments before I could breathe, let alone talk. I'd heard the words he'd said, turned them over inside my head, and still my mind refused to make sense of them. "*What* did you say?"

He inclined his head toward the water. "They're not dead."

My eyes fluttered and I had to tighten my hold on the dock to keep from toppling over like I did the night before. "Not dead? What do you mean *not dead*? They disappeared under the water and never resurfaced. How could anyone survive that?"

Bastin continued to study the bayou. I followed his line of sight but couldn't make out anything more than the ripple of waves of dark waves. "There are ways—" He snapped his mouth shut and flexed the tendons in his jaw. "You know what? I shouldn't have said anything."

"Bastin!" I pulled on his shoulder. "You have to tell me where they are. Their families are worried."

He shook his head. "Impossible."

"Bastin, look at me!"

He didn't.

"Bastin!" I crawled in front of him and placed my hands on his face, trying to get those onyx eyes to meet my own. "What happened to my classmates? If they aren't dead, you have to tell me where they are. Maybe I can find them and get them back."

He whirled his head in my direction so fast that I

~ ☾ ~

stumbled back, shocked at his speed. "No," he said. "That is the last thing you are going to do."

I shrank against the dock. "Why not?"

"Edith." His voice lost the harsh edge and he lifted a hand to my hair and pushed it back behind my ears. "You have to forget about the others. They're not coming back. Ever."

"But why?" My voice was a whisper.

"Because." His eyes found my own and I immediately became lost in their depths. "They belong to the ocean now."

"What?" My hand flew to my mouth, holding back the scream that sat just beyond the edge of my lips. I tried to process the information but it was like my mind had blue-screened, error messages flashing behind my eyelids. "How can they be underwater and not dead? That's impossible."

"It's not." Bastin pressed his lips into a thin line. "And it's not that I don't want to tell you because I want to keep a secret from you." He refused to meet my eyes as he sat down. "It's just that after I tell you, you'll think my kind are monsters."

I put my hand on his shoulder. "It's not fair of you to make assumptions about what I'll think. Give me a chance."

"Right." He took a deep breath. "Your classmates have been taken as slaves by the tribe that attacked them. They now live underwater in the deepest part of the ocean."

Shock paralyzed me. It was several seconds before I was able to blink, to breathe, to speak. And despite my best attempt, I was unable to hide the tremor in my voice. "Slaves?"

He nodded. "Please understand that my father's tribe doesn't believe in taking on human slaves. It's a common practice between many of the tribes we are at war with."

~ ☾ ~

"But . . ." So many questions swirled through my head that I had trouble grasping onto a single one. I wasn't sure how long I remained frozen before I was able to form the words on my tongue. "How do they survive underwater?"

"There are ways." Bastin took my hands within his. "Please don't ask me to explain them to you because there are consequences. Horrible consequences."

"Okay." A lump had formed in my throat, and I fought to breathe around it. "But is there a way to bring them back? Can we rescue them?"

He dropped my hands and turned his attention back to the water. "No."

"But why?"

Bastin may not have been human, but he had an Adam's apple that bobbed along his neck after a lengthy pause. "Once a human has been brought to the deepest part of the ocean, a place where sunlight does not reach, they can never return to the surface. To do so would kill them."

Everything inside of me—my blood, my bones, my muscles—all of it turned to ice. "Never return? You mean to tell me that my classmates are underwater right now, serving as slaves, and there is absolutely no chance that they'll ever return to their families?"

"Yes."

"Oh my God." I shivered despite the warm night breeze. "But why? I don't understand."

"You don't want to understand, Edith. It's horrible. Once a human descends to the bottom, they can never return to the surface. The decompression would either kill them or drive them mad."

"Wait, are you talking about the bends? Diver's disease?"

"Partly." He nodded. "We have ways of adjusting humans to adapt to the pressure of the ocean—just no way of adjusting them back."

~ ☾ ~

I chewed on my lip, trying to take in the horror of it all.

"Do you think I'm a monster, now?" he asked.

"What?" My head snapped up and I stared at him. "How could you think that? I have no more right to blame you for the actions of others than I can be blamed for the boat accident. It's subjective. You said it yourself that humans are polluting your home and making you sick. Doesn't that make us monsters, too?"

He appeared to consider this.

"Bastin, I could never think of you as a monster." I scooted closer and took hold of his hand. "The more time I spend with you the more I realize we're *not* that different."

He chuckled, a sound that broke apart the ice inside of me and sent my heart into happy flutters. "Edith, only *you* could think that. I'm a creature of the sea. You're human. My blood runs cold while yours runs hot. We think differently, live differently," he gestured to the water, "we *breathe* differently."

"That may be," I argued, "but you're *here*. And I'm *here*. On the dock, enjoying each other's company. Isn't that *something*?"

He wrapped his arms around me. "Yes, it's definitely something."

I sighed happily. "We may be different species, but we're the same, you and I. We're both renegades for starters."

"How's that?"

"It means that you're not supposed to be here and neither am I."

He laughed. "Again, true."

"See." I settled against him, laying my head against the soft curve of his neck. "We're not so different, after all."

~ ☾ ~

Chapter 17

The next night, my body fought me as pulled myself out of bed. *This is insane, Edith*. My muscles ached and my eyelids begged to remain closed. Each step outside the house drew me that much closer to getting caught, yet the threat of military school and my loss of freedom were no longer enough to hold me back. Not when Bastin waited.

I quickly slid on a pair of worn jeans and a T-shirt and slipped into the night. I found Bastin perched at the end of our dock. My exhaustion from a week without sleep was extinguished the second he smiled. The warmth that spread through my body as a result sent my pulse into a ripple of skips and hops. He stood and extended his hand, which I eagerly accepted. This time, instead of settling down to dip our feet in the water, he led me along the edge of the bayou. I hung slightly back, shielding my face from the scratching branches that Bastin didn't seem to notice as he pushed through to a clearing where a large boulder leaned over the water.

Bastin climbed to the top with the grace of someone who'd been born with legs. I, however, had more trouble, my still sore shoulder refusing to let me grasp the edges of the rock. It wasn't until Bastin offered me his hand, again, that I was able to leverage my way to the top, which was just flat and wide enough for the two of us to lie next to each other.

We stayed that way for I don't know how long—on our backs, our fingers woven together, wordlessly watching the night sky. I was getting used to Bastin's silence and no longer felt the urge to fill the space between us with useless words.

Finally, he sighed, a happy sound. "I like touching you."

I turned my head to find him staring at me. In that moment, I wished for nothing more than to be like him. If he wasn't completely happy in his own silence then he was letting me know exactly how he felt. No head games. No inhibitions.

"I like touching you," I answered. My cheeks burned as soon as the words left my mouth, though, I couldn't figure out why I should feel embarrassed. Sure, admitting how he made me feel . . . if it was anyone else I would have braced for laughter—but Bastin's honesty was teaching me to let go of my fear. Still, there was something inside me, a part so terrified of getting hurt, that I couldn't open myself completely. I only hoped Bastin was happy to fit inside the space I'd given him.

"It's strange," he continued. "My people don't touch often. The majority of our contact comes through battle. But your kind . . . your kind touches all the time. I like that."

He shifted closer so that our bodies touched from our shoulders to our hips. His skin, always several degrees cooler than mine, sent a ripple of shivers through my body.

Bastin stilled. "Are you cold?"

"No."

"But you shivered."

I wondered if Bastin could feel my blush as it burned its way from my cheeks to the rest of my body. "Because of your touch."

He smiled. "Is that a good thing?"

I laughed nervously and directed my attention to the sky. "You sure ask a lot of questions."

His grin widened. "And that bothers you?"

~ ☾ ~

I shook my head. “It’s just . . . awkward.”

“Why?”

I fidgeted on the rock. It was as if I could feel Bastin inside my mind, poking around, digging things out that I longed to keep buried. “I guess I’m just not that comfortable talking about my feelings.”

“Oh.” Bastin turned his head away from me and gazed at the moon. “My kind is the same. We don’t talk about our feelings, either.” He was quiet for a moment. “Sometimes I think most of them don’t have any.”

Sir’s image floated in my mind, and I grunted in agreement. “I know what you mean.”

In a flash, Bastin was above me, his hands on either side of my face. “But you feel, don’t you, Edith? You can feel this?”

He leaned over and pressed his lips against mine. Softly at first, but then followed by an urgency. The taste of him spread through me, sea salt mixing with my blood. His kisses became fevered, his arms twisting behind my back, pressing me into him, as if he could sink into my skin and underneath, to find the answers to all the questions he asked.

When he finally released me, I felt an immediate longing to close the space between us. “I definitely felt that,” I whispered.

“Good.” He grinned, a sight that ignited a flame deep within me. “The way you make me feel—” And the smile was gone.

My heart clenched tightly. “What’s wrong?”

He closed his eyes for what felt like an eternity before looking at me. “It’s like you’ve brought me to life. No one has ever made me feel this way before. Do you think . . .” He paused. “Do you think you’re the only one that will ever make me feel this way?”

Picturing Bastin with another girl, even a mermaid, was too unbearable to think about. It took me several moments before I was able to answer him. “I-I don’t know. I guess only you can answer that."

He cocked his head and appeared to think about it. "I think, Edith, you're the only one who can make me this happy. Make me feel this alive."

I stared at him. The way his eyes, endless in their depths, still seemed to get lost in the light of the moon that controlled him. I wanted to answer him back, to tell him how when I was with him, the rest of the world fell away, as if it'd never existed at all. That all there was and all there would ever be were the two of us. But even as the words burned on my tongue, something inside of me refused to let go.

"Why do you think, of all the creatures on this planet, it's you who is meant for me?"

The world around me swam out of focus as my breath caught in my throat. Like a computer struggling to download a complex file, my mind locked up, unable to make sense of what he'd said. Bastin thought I was meant for him? How was that even possible? He was a mythical creature and I was . . . the kind of girl who wore underwear that came in packs of six. Boring. The answer to his question seemed obvious. "You're totally cursed."

Bastin laughed, a sound that brought a smile to my lips. "No more than you, it would appear." He leaned over and kissed me again, only this time it lasted much longer. We kissed until his arms could hold him no longer and he lay on top of me. We twisted and twined like vines growing along a tree until you could no longer tell where Bastin ended and I began.

Bastin pulled away first. He always pulled away first. I had a harder time letting go. Good things didn't happen to me, and Bastin was the best thing in the world. There had to be a catch. A moment when it would all come undone. Until then, I couldn't help but treat each kiss as if it would be our last.

"Edith," Bastin's voice was husky, and it made me

smile to hear a mer out of breath. "I want to give you something."

I blinked.

He continued. "Tell me what you want most in the world. Anything. I will find a way to give it to you."

"That's silly." I sat up beside him. "I don't need or want anything. I have you."

He took my hand in his. "But I want to do this. I can only be with you at night. I want to give you something that reminds you that I am thinking of you even when you're walking in the sun and I'm swimming under it."

Absently, I tapped my jeans over the anklet underneath. I didn't know if Bastin would be upset that I had a hole drilled through the stone, so I didn't show him. "You already gave me that beautiful stone."

His eyes darted away. "That doesn't count. That was to replace something that Luna took from you." He cupped both my hands. "Please, Edith, let me do this for you. You've done so much for me. Tell me what you want."

I was quiet for a moment before I shook my head. "What I want most in the world I can't have."

Bastin squeezed my hands. "What's that?"

I leaned my head against his shoulder. "You. With me. Forever."

He sighed and wrapped me in his arms. "And there's nothing else?"

"Someday," I said, "when I can get away from Sir, I want to get a puppy. I've wanted a dog for as long as I can remember."

"This is your great wish? A dog?"

I laughed. "Pretty stupid, huh?"

I felt Bastin's head shake as his chin brushed the top of my head. "No. I like dogs. They're funny creatures. They always seem so happy."

"That's what I like best about them."

"There used to be a house up the coast," he gestured

across the bayou, "with a dog. Big and brown with ears that flapped in the wind. I believe I heard the owner call it a Chesa-" He frowned, searching for the words.

"Chesapeake Bay Retriever?" I offered.

He smiled. "Yes. That's it. Such a happy dog. Then the owner put some sort of a wire in the ground that kept the dog from running outside an invisible barrier—something to do with a collar. After that, they left him outside all the time. The dog was so sad, he used to howl pitifully. So every night I removed its collar and we played. We ran along the beach and swam in the ocean. I was quite impressed with the creature—he was almost as skilled as I at catching fish." Bastian chuckled. "If I were human, I would most definitely want a dog, too. One exactly like the Chesapeake Bay Retriever—a dog that loved water and loved to play."

"What happened to the dog?" I asked.

Bastin sighed. "The humans moved away, I guess. One night I came to visit the dog, only he wasn't there. I returned every night, in the hopes the dog would be waiting for me, until a month later, there was a dog. Only this one was small, white, and all it did was bark at me. It hated the water and didn't want to play."

I kissed the side of Bastin's cheek. "I'm so sorry you lost your friend. The Chesapeake Bay Retriever sounds like the perfect dog."

"Oh, he was." Bastin nodded his head emphatically. "The little white ones are not."

I laughed until tears sprang from my eyes. I couldn't remember the last time I'd been so happy. It was like life hadn't existed before Bastin, and in a way, it hadn't. The trouble with life, however, was it always ended. You start dying the moment you take your first breath. It was inevitable. And as soon as I had the thought, it was branded on my brain with a red hot poker. My time with Bastin was an hourglass full of razors, ripping through me as time ran out.

~ ☾ ~

Chapter 18

The following night, rain sprinkled from the few grey clouds streaked across the midnight sky. It wasn't enough to soak my clothes, but it did plaster my hair in annoying lines down my cheeks.

Bastin pushed a wet strand out of my eye and tucked it behind my ear. "I would like to show you something."

Another day of roaming the halls of my school in a half-awake stupor, leaky faucets, and dirty glances from Gabrielle and her friends, had led to this moment.

Totally worth it.

Slowly, as if Bastin were a creature to be swayed by fast movements, I uncurled my fingers and lifted my hand to his. In the moment before our skin connected, I could feel an electric current travel the air between his hand and mine. As if he was a magnet and I was metal, everything in me designed to follow the pull that was him.

When our fingers entwined I knew something dangerous was happening, but I couldn't see past the night's stars or, even brighter, the smile on Bastin's face. Blinded. The night fell away, followed by the world. And all that remained, all that *could* exist was the two of us.

I glanced at my hand, swallowed inside of his. Only it wasn't just my hand held captive. I wondered if there was anywhere he would lead that I wouldn't follow.

"Come with me," Bastin said. He led me to the water and I followed without a question. He waded deeper until the water reached his waist, and still, I followed.

~ ☾ ~

When the water reached his chest I inched forward on my tiptoes, straining to keep my chin above the small waves. If he took another step, I'd go under. Still, I couldn't find enough strength to let go.

My heart beat a frantic rhythm inside my head. Something intense was happening here. Something I'd failed to understand until just now, when it was too late. I'd thought Bastin to be safe but I'd been wrong. The danger had been just beneath the surface, waiting for me to open my backdoor that first night. And I was paying the price. Bastin was inside of me now, pulsing through my veins with each beat of my heart.

He dropped my hand long enough to fidget with something underwater. Moments later, he lifted his arm exposing the shorts dripping wet in his grasp. He tossed them on the beach.

My throat went dry and I couldn't help but move away from him. I'd never been around a naked guy before, and it felt far more dangerous than I'd ever imagined.

Bastin disappeared under the inky waves. Scared, but not sure why, I took another step back only to run into something solid. I turned to find Bastin standing in front of me, looking down at my face. He licked his lips, looking even more the predator. "I can hear your heartbeat under the water, Edith. Why are you scared?" His fingers found mine, and before I knew what was happening I was pressed against him, his skin so much different now that it was wet, slippery even.

Because I couldn't think past the curve of his hips pressed against my own, I stammered the first thing that came to me. "A-a-alligators. There are alligators in here."

Bastin laughed, a sound that twisted things deep inside my chest and below my navel. A pain so beautiful it ripped my heart and I was glad to bleed. "But you've already bested an alligator, remember? Besides, no alligators would dare bother us tonight, Edith. On that you have my word."

"How can you be so sure?"

His smile would have brought me to my knees if he hadn't been holding me inside his arms. In that moment, I wouldn't have cared if we were surrounded by a hundred gators. I still would have followed him—straight into their hungry mouths.

"Come on!" Bastin released me and took a couple of strokes away from the shore.

I didn't move. "Where are we going?"

Bastin, his head bobbing above the waves, only smiled.

"You know I can't swim the way you can," I said.

"You can with me."

"How?"

Instead of answering, Bastin disappeared into the water. Alone and nervous, I considered trudging back to the shore, but before I could even take a step back, something wrapped around my waist and forcibly pulled me under.

It was too dark, the water too murky to make out more than a few feet in front of my face. Still, there was no missing the enormous, glittering fishtail that made up Bastin's lower body. I'd believed him when he'd said he was a merman. I'd watched him disappear into the ocean every night. Yet I couldn't seem to make sense of the image before me. He floated in a sea of black silk. A rainbow of emerald, ruby, and sapphire-colored scales shimmered down the length of him until they disappeared into his pearl-colored skin. Behind him, his hair fanned behind him like a silver cloak. It was too much. Not only did his beauty hurt to take in, it also served to remind me how different we truly were.

I tried to look away and failed.

As if reading my mind, Bastin's lips moved and I heard him speak as plainly as he did above the water. "I thought you should see the real me."

I wanted to answer back, to thank him for opening himself up to me. But unlike him, I couldn't speak. And I couldn't stay underwater much longer. My lungs were beginning to ache for oxygen and my shoulder burned in the saltwater.

Bastin stopped smiling. It was as if he understood what I'd been thinking only a moment ago. He couldn't exist in my world and I would die in his. He swam toward me, and, while I would have liked to wait for him, my need for air was too great. I kicked for the surface but a hand ensnared my wrist before I could break free.

I whirled around and found myself staring into the depths of his eyes. What was he doing? Didn't he realize I needed air?

I struggled in his grip until he whispered in my ear, a trail of bubbles tickling along my cheek. "I'd never hurt you, Edith."

Despite the burning fire consuming my lungs, I relaxed in his arms.

Bastin brought his mouth to mine. I felt the faintest brush of his tongue tracing the outline of my lips before he breathed deeply inside my throat.

The barbed wire encasing my chest disappeared. Oxygen! With his lips still on mine I continued to breathe from him. I wrapped my arms around his chest and clung to him, drinking him in, as his tail moved beneath me, pushing us along. Bastin secured one arm around my waist and slid his other hand behind my head. I closed my eyes and tried to imagine what it would be like to be a mermaid, to be able to be with Bastin forever. There was nothing for me on shore. Everything I wanted was under the water where I could never stay.

I opened my eyes and watched the reflection of the stars dance above us. It was like we were no longer in the ocean but flying above it. Into the sky. Soaring. Leaving everything behind. Proving that there was a place for us, after all. If we couldn't be together on land and we couldn't be together in the ocean, we would always have the night sky.

Bastin pulled away and our gliding ceased. It was like I'd fallen from the moon back into the ocean. Without his arms around me, I was suddenly aware how cold the water was.

He said nothing, just stared at me, blinking his too-rapid blink. If I hadn't already been in the water, the weight of his eyes would have left me holding my breath.

"I wish I could keep you," he said.

I wanted to answer. I wanted so much more.

He shook his head, sadly. "It's time to take you home."

Before I could protest, his lips were on mine. Breathing into me. Drinking me down, like he was trying to suck a piece of my soul inside him. If I could I gladly would have given him a piece. Bastin belonged to the sea. I belonged to the land. But in a way, we belonged to each other. That had to count for something.

We broke the surface, both of us gasping, and neither from lack of oxygen.

"Every night," he said, brushing a strand of wet hair from my eyes. "Every night I say it will be the last that I visit you. And then I find myself at your door the very next day."

The impact of his words ensnared my heart like a thousand fish hooks, each one pulled from a different direction. "What do you mean? Is this the last night we'll be together?"

"I hope so."

When the hooks could pull no harder, they simply ripped through, leaving my heart tattered ribbons of meat.

Bastin continued, "Every time I visit you, I find I lose

more of myself."

I didn't know how far we'd swum or where we were. Definitely beyond the bayou as the shore stretched wide a good hundred yards from where we bobbed. I doubted I could swim the distance on my own but still, I pushed myself away from him. "Why, Bastin?" I choked back a sob. "Why did you do this to me? If you knew you were going to leave, why did you keep coming back? Did you *want* to hurt me?"

But hurt wasn't the right word. Because I'd let him in, because I'd opened up, I was bleeding from the inside out.

He shook his head and pulled me to him. I wanted to fight, to get away, but lacked the strength. "I didn't know, Edith. If I knew what this would feel like, how much I would need you, I would have stayed away. I'm addicted to you. No good can come from that." His voice softened. "Every time I leave you, I spend the entire day trying to figure out how we can survive together. There is no way."

"That's just great, Bastin. I'm glad you have it all figured out." As much as I hated to, I clung to him. Otherwise the weight of my grief would have pulled me under. "Maybe you can tell me something, then?"

He blinked at me.

"If there's no way for us to survive together, just tell me, how are we supposed to survive apart?"

His silence was my answer.

***

I ran the entire way home. My eyes burned with tears that refused to fall, blurring my vision, which made it even harder to stick to the animal trail cloaked in darkness. Sharp underbrush clawed at my flesh as I tumbled through. But the pain barely registered. Bastin's words had numbed me from the inside out.

~ ☾ ~

A tree root snagged my foot and sent me toppling to the ground. Without a word, I got up, wiped my dirt-streaked hands on my shorts, and continued on. When I finally burst through the trees into my backyard, the sun was beginning to drape banners of pink across the sky. Panting, I reached out toward my bedroom door.

And froze.

Tiny hairs rose along the back of my neck. Something was wrong. I surveyed the yard—nothing looked out of place. The window to my parents' room remained dark. All was quiet.

Swallowing past the copper taste of fear that rose in my throat, I grasped the door handle. As I did, it moved under my fingers. With a yelp, I jumped back. My legs tangled, sending me falling against the wooden deck.

Sir stepped out of my room and stood over me. Wearing only a pair of running shorts and a white tank-top, I could see that every muscle in his body was taut. It was as if God had run out of skin halfway through making him, stretching what he had to make it fit.

Sir didn't move. And like any small rodent under a viper's stare, neither did I. My mind raced to come up with an acceptable excuse to explain my absence—but I couldn't think under the weight of his gaze. I dared not breathe, dared not move, for fear that Sir would snap out of his trance and lash out. Not that it would help. The end was coming—I was only delaying it.

He cleared his throat, the break in silence causing me to flinch. I tried to think of the alligator I'd held my second night with Bastin. But instead of conjuring up the confidence I'd felt when I conquered my fear, all I could think about was how I'd never see Bastin again, which broke my heart all over.

When Sir spoke, his words were soft and low. A very bad sign. "Where have you been?"

I opened my mouth and closed it. Again, a thousand excuses ran through my mind. None of them ended with swimming in the ocean with a merman. Finally, I managed to squeak, "Outside."

"Do not play games with me!" Sir roared.

I shrank back against the wood, ignoring the needle-like splinters of the deck as they dug into my skin.

"I can't believe you'd leave your bed in the middle of the night and then have the nerve to be smart about it."

Oh, he couldn't be more wrong. There was nothing smart about me at this moment. "I haven't been gone all night." I hated the way the trembling of my voice betrayed my fear.

Sir crossed his arms. "Is that so?"

"Y-yes." Feeling a little better that Sir's hands were no longer in grabbing range, I climbed to my feet. As I did, a plan began to formulate in my head. "I was having trouble sleeping—you know, the pain in my shoulder and all."

Sir didn't look the least bit concerned over my sleeping habits.

"And I remembered your advice about exercise and how it promotes healthy sleep cycles," I said, quoting directly from a Sir lecture. "I decided to go for a run. I thought a little exercise and fresh air would help." This was a dangerous gamble. My only hope was that Sir hadn't noticed I was missing until recently. If he'd known I was gone half the night, I was sunk for sure.

He blinked for the first time and dropped his arms to his side. "You went for a run?"

My heart did a back-flip. Somehow, I'd said the right thing. "Yes, Sir."

He stepped away from the door so that only inches separated us. Despite my best attempt not to, I flinched, just like I always did. And it was funny, because Sir never hit me. He didn't have to. His presence was enough.

"If you're so interested in exercise, then by no means let me discourage you. I find physical fitness is lacking

~ ☾ ~

in the youth of today. Too many lard-asses playing their video games."

He walked a slow circle around me. I struggled to keep my eyes forward and my body straight despite every instinct screaming at me to run.

"So I have an idea. Since you're suddenly so interested in exercise, I propose I lead your morning PT. Every day. Effective immediately."

Physical training with the sergeant? My stomach fell into my knees. This was officially the worst morning of my life. First I'd lost Bastin and now this. It looked like karma had finally found a way to punish me for being happy.

He smiled and stroked his morning stubble. "Yes, I'd say that's a great idea. Don't you agree, Ed? Besides, you'll learn a lot more from me than you ever could from some marshmallow-fluff gym teacher."

"Yes, sir."

"Very good. I can't think of a better way for a father and daughter to spend time together, can you?"

There was that word again. *Father*. Waves of nausea rolled inside of me. "No, sir."

"Good." After looking me up and down he nodded his head. "You're dismissed."

I could only blink. Surely it wasn't going to be that easy? Before he could change his mind, I stepped around him and darted for my bedroom. I was halfway through the door before he stopped me.

"Ed."

My heart wedged itself in my throat. Choking me.

So here it was, the part I'd been waiting for.

I turned. "Sir?"

"If I find out you lied to me, there will be consequences."

I tightened my grip on the door handle. Unable to breathe, knowing if I could just shut the door between us the pressure building inside me would ease. "Yes, sir."

~ ☾ ~

His eyes narrowed. “Good. And to reinforce that fact, I’ve taken the liberty of packing a bag for you. You’ll find it on your bed. It’ll save us some time in case I find out that you haven’t been straight with me.”

I glanced at my bed where a suitcase lay opened. Even with my room’s dim lighting, I could see it was stuffed to the brim with clothes taken from my closet and folded too neatly to be Mom’s handiwork.

“Don’t bother unpacking,” Sir said. “You never know when we might need it.”

“Yes, sir.” Tears pricked my eyes, but I wouldn’t let them fall. If I could keep it together, I’d be okay. Fall apart and it’d be that much worse. Like a spreading infection, all Sir needed was an open wound. I wouldn’t give him one.

He waited for several heartbeats, as if anticipating the tears that he could use against me. When they didn’t come he pushed past me, through my room, and into the house beyond.

When I was sure he was out of earshot, I shut my bedroom door and collapsed on my bed. But the numbness that always followed Sir’s departures didn’t come. Bastin’s abrupt goodbye was still fresh on my mind and seared on my heart. Still, a small part of me was relieved. I knew Bastin was right. The longer we continued on, the more pain we would cause each other. Even now I’d felt as if a hole had been carved from my heart, a dull ache throbbing inside my chest with each beat.

I hoped for a miracle, despite knowing it wasn’t possible for girl and a merman to exist together. Bastin knew it, too. Hell, even the suitcase next to me knew the direction that my life was pointed, and it didn’t include the ocean.

Angry, I slapped the side of the suitcase. How much of a reminder did Sir think I needed? My whole life was proof of his control.

~ ☾ ~

I hated him.

The revelation startled me, and I sat up. It was the first time I realized that my relationship with Sir had no chance of getting better. What little hope I'd had of Sir's acceptance was gone. He would never love me. We would never come to some tearful understanding that happens in the movies. There was no happily-ever-after. This was it. The end. The actors had taken their bows.

Now we were just waiting for the credits to roll.

~ ☾ ~

Chapter 19

Whoever penned the word "heartache" sure knew what they were talking about. I didn't know why I allowed myself to get so wrapped up with Bastin over the last week, but knowing that I would never see him hurt unlike anything I could have imagined. It was as if my ribcage had collapsed inside my chest, the jagged bones grinding into my heart like a nutcracker grinding into the meat of a pecan.

Luckily, between classes, Morgan was more than eager to distract me from both my thoughts of heartbreak and Sir's threats with talk about her parents' dinner party—something I had dreaded but now looked forward to. A night away from Sir, my bedroom, and all reminders of Bastin, was exactly what I needed.

That evening, Sir turned into Morgan's subdivision at five before seven. He hadn't spoken the entire trip. Mom, however, prattled on about her Apple Brown Betty and whether she should have baked a Bundt cake instead.

"Mom," I assured her from the backseat, "your Apple Brown Betty is the best in the world. They'll love it."

She turned to smile at me. "Edith, you're such a sweet girl. Thank you." She glanced in Sir's direction, as if waiting for him to comment, too. He didn't. I had to give her credit, though, for thinking he would. She hadn't given up. I wasn't sure what to make of that. Hope was one thing, delusion another.

At the end of the road, Sir pulled into the circle drive of a house unlike any I'd seen outside of a reality show.

In fact, calling it a house was like calling the ocean a pond. Despite the modern windows and pillars supporting the two-story archway over the front door, because of its size and textured stonework, I half-expected Rapunzel to lean out a window and drop down her hair.

"Wow," Mom whispered. "It looks like a movie star's house."

I could only nod.

Sir shifted in his seat, drawing my attention. His knuckles paled as he tightened his grip on the steering wheel. I wondered what had him so upset. I thought he'd be jumping for joy at the chance to meet with the Base Commander.

"Have you ever seen anything like this?" Mom asked him.

His jaw flexed but he didn't answer. He was too caught up in staring at something. Following his gaze, I saw what had him so bent out of shape. Morgan skipped down the front walk wearing what could only be described as a black leather and pink tulle tutu, complete with matching leather corset, pink fishnet stockings, and a pair of Doc Martens that laced just below her knees.

"Oh, my." Mom held up a hand to smother her smile. "Isn't she . . . colorful?"

I bit my lip to keep from giggling. Morgan was exactly the kind of person Sir loathed, and since she was the Base Commander's daughter, he would have to play nice. Maybe Morgan was right after all—we'd only just arrived and already I was having fun.

Morgan pulled me into a hug when I got out of the 4x4, whispering in my ear, "What's with the getup?"

I assumed she was talking about my clothes, a plain khaki skirt and pink cardigan. Unlike Morgan, I had to pass inspection before I left the house. I wondered what it would be like to have parents who didn't care what I wore. Who actually cared what I thought and listened to what I had to say. It must be like having wings.

When she released me, I rolled my eyes in Sir's direction to let her know the reason for my clothes.

She gave me a knowing glance then turned my Mom. "Hi. I'm Morgan."

Mom gave her a warm smile and held out her hand, which Morgan shook. "It's so nice to meet one of Edith's friends."

Morgan turned to Sir, who was at the front of the 4x4 scowling, and curtsied. I knew she had to feel the waves of heat radiating from his eyes. Instead of shrinking back like I would have done, her smile widened. "Come on. You don't want to keep Daddy waiting."

Sir said nothing but followed as she flounced down the driveway.

That was the moment I realized why Morgan and I were friends. What she wore and how she dressed didn't matter to me. What made Morgan special was the fact that she was free in a way I could never be. Alive. Every movement she made, every twirl of her skirt and twitch of her lips radiated with energy. I only wanted to stand next to her and soak some of her color into my grey interior.

"Come on. Come on." She waved impatiently. If I didn't know better, I would have sworn she was getting a kick out of ordering my father around. I know I was. She was fearless. Laughing at the threat while I allowed it to devour me whole.

Sir grunted, causing Mom to automatically reach for her wedding ring and begin her nervous twisting, which wobbled the dessert dish in her arms.

"Carol," Sir hissed. "Watch what you're doing."

Mom released her wedding band and laughed nervously. "Sorry. You're right. I am so clumsy."

He didn't comment, only followed Morgan into the house.

~ ☾ ~

Once inside, I felt like I'd walked into a museum. Oil paintings taller than me in their carved wooden frames decorated every wall. Even the windows looked like works of art. Silk tassels pulled back the embroidered tapestries.

"Welcome!" A woman appeared around a corner, the heels of her shoes clicking sharply on the granite tiles. She wore a pair of silk drawstring pants, a silk blouse, and a matching yellow sweater draped over her shoulders. Her blond hair, cut in layers that framed her face, accented her plump—and I was willing to bet surgically-enhanced—lips.

A sculpted man with black hair and skin the color of freshly tilled dirt followed her. "So, where's the girl who saved my baby's life?"

"This is her, Daddy." Morgan motioned to me with a dip of her chin, snapping her heels together and lacing her fingers behind her back. The picture of an adoring, obedient daughter. She winked at me. Everything was a game to her. As if life was something to be enjoyed, not dealt with.

Sir puffed his chest and snapped his head into attention.

Morgan's father laughed, a deep and pleasant sound that echoed off the marble archways. "At ease, soldier. You are a guest in my house." He held his arms wide. "You are *all* guests. Especially *you*, young lady." His amber-colored eyes met mine. "I don't know how I can ever thank you for what you've done. My daughter means the world to me." He smiled at Morgan, who beamed back at him. "I'd invite you into the parlor for refreshments, but it appears the cook has finished early. Please allow me to escort you to the dining hall."

We followed Colonel Pratt and his wife down a long hallway until we reached a room with a table long enough to serve a small army. Pictures depicting fights from the Civil War were mounted on cream-colored walls. Mrs. Pratt took Mom's dessert and disappeared

~ ☾ ~

into the kitchen. Colonel Pratt positioned himself at the head of the table and motioned for us to take a seat.

Moments later, Mrs. Pratt came out of the kitchen with a pitcher of iced tea. "Sorry it took me so long to get the sweet tea. It's the strangest thing, but it appears our kitchen sink has sprung a leak."

Morgan glanced at me from across the table, and I quickly dropped my eyes to my plate.

"That is strange," my mom agreed. "We've had some plumbing issues ourselves this week. What's really weird is that it's not consistent. One minute the faucets are dripping and the toilets are running, and the next, everything is fine.

"That *is* really weird," Morgan said. I could feel her eyes burning holes in my forehead, but still I refused to look at her. "We've had plumbing issues at school, too. Don't you think that's weird, Edith?"

"Weird," I said. As long as I kept my eyes on my plate, maybe no one would be able to see the fear in them. This only confirmed my suspicion that I was somehow the cause of all the faulty plumbing. Then I had another thought—it wasn't until after my first encounter with the mermaids that the leaky faucets started.

The clinking of glass and ice pulled me from my thoughts as Mrs. Pratt filled my glass with sweet tea. I smiled my thanks before taking a drink.

"So, Edith," Mrs. Pratt said before sitting down, "why don't you tell us how you and Morgan met? It isn't often we are so lucky to be able to entertain Morgan's friends."

"Sure," I answered, thankful to have the topic steered away from faulty plumbing. I set my tea on the table but held onto the glass to keep my fingers from trembling.

Sir leaned forward, as if this too, was a subject that interested him.

Mom, however, looked at her lap, inspecting the napkin's lace trim with a smile. So happy, and yet so clueless. She really thought we were here for a dinner party, but I knew exactly what was at stake.

My mouth went dry and I cleared my throat in hopes of removing the paste that seemed to have locked my tongue to the roof of my mouth.

"We met at a strip club," Morgan chimed in. "Edith was tossing back shots of tequila while I was working the pole. Geez, Mom, we met at school. What did you think?"

Morgan's parents laughed. "Kids," her dad said, rolling his eyes. "You never know *what's* going to come out of their mouths next."

Sir and Mom only sat in stunned silence.

I attempted to grin and failed miserably.

"Well, regardless." Colonel Pratt smiled. "Janie is right when she says we rarely get to meet Morgan's friends. I'm so very glad to meet you, Edith. And I'm glad your family was able to come tonight."

He looked at Sir, who managed to pull the corners of his lips into an almost smile. He looked constipated. "We're honored to be here, sir."

"No, no." Colonel Pratt wagged a finger at him. "We're all friends at this table, right girls? Please call me Cliff."

Morgan rolled her eyes. "Daaaad," she moaned. "Can you please stop making such a big deal about it, already? Did you maybe think that I don't invite friends over because I know you guys are going to embarrass me? You know, like you're doing right now?"

Cliff laughed. "Oh, teenagers. You know what I'm talking about, don't you, Michael?"

Sir stiffened under the use of his first name. I don't remember anyone ever using it before besides Mom. "Right," he answered with another tight-lipped smile. But then he shot me a glance—a warning—that had me sinking into my seat.

Morgan smiled at Sir. "You must be pretty proud of Edith for saving my life."

~ ☾ ~

If I could have reached under the massive table I would have kicked her. I knew how to deal with the man sitting to my left. Just play dead around the growling bear and he would eventually leave. Under no circumstances should you poke the bear. Unfortunately, Morgan was oblivious to my psychic plea for her to shut up.

Sir shifted in his sit so he could lock eyes with her across the table. “I would love to hear more about that.”

“As would I!” Cliff smiled.

Janie and Mom, nodding, set down their drinks.

It was as if I were in two different places, half of me in an interrogation office while the other half was at a dinner party. I didn’t know who to look at or how to respond. I looked from Morgan’s parents to Sir. What was the correct answer? What was the question? The walls shifted, pressing into me until there wasn’t enough air to breathe.

“I’ll tell the story,” Morgan said. “After all, we know how modest Edith is. She wouldn’t want to brag.”

I gave her a weak smile.

Mom looked up from the napkin ring she’d been twirling around in her hand. “Oh, yes. Edith is very modest.”

Morgan leaned forward and splayed her hands across the table. “Well, there I was, all alone in the bathroom, in between classes, with my throat closing up on me. It had started with a little wheezing. I thought I had time, but in a matter of seconds, I realized I was in big trouble. And by then, it was too late. I was totally screwed, all because I was careless enough to leave my inhaler in my car.”

“Morgan.” Her dad tsked. “You know better than to forget your inhaler. How many times do your mother and I have to remind you?”

She dropped her eyes to the table and stuck out her bottom lip. “I know, Daddy. I’m sorry.”

~ ☾ ~

Cliff waved his hand in the air. "That's all right, baby. It's neither here nor there, now. I just worry about you. Go on with the story."

"Okay, Daddy." She looked up and addressed the table. "At this point I was collapsed on the bathroom floor."

Janie gasped.

Morgan continued, "I thought I was done for. But then Edith appeared! She yanked me off the ground—never minding the fact that she had her own injured shoulder to deal with—and half-dragged me to my car, where she was able to get my inhaler. She saved me!"

"Well done, Edith," Clifford said.

Janie clapped her hands while beaming at me.

Sir, however, folded his arms and leaned back against his chair. "You say this occurred between classes?"

Morgan nodded.

And just like that we had fallen into Sir's trap. Only Morgan didn't realize it yet. I wanted to scream at her to stop talking but, with Sir's eyes searching my face for the lie that was written there, I could only stare at my hands clasped in my lap.

"It happened right before last period." A smug smile appeared on Morgan's face. She thought she had him.

"But I found you two in the parking lot at the end of the day."

There it was. Morgan paled slightly as panic flashed through her eyes. Next to me, Mom began her incessant ring twisting.

"So what you're telling me," Sir continued, "is that you two missed a whole period of class."

Janie and Cliff seemed oblivious to the warning in Sir's voice. They cocked their heads, waiting for their daughter's explanation. I only hoped she had one.

Morgan crossed her arms. "It was a bad asthma attack. And I'm not a little girl, Mr. Small. It took Edith awhile to drag me outside."

~ ☾ ~

Sir leaned forward, a cobra ready to strike. "What I find appalling, is that no one—no faculty, students, or janitorial staff—witnessed what took place."

I dared a glance at Morgan, who stared at me with a helpless expression.

Cliff frowned. "You know, Michael, you raise an excellent point. I find it disturbing that my daughter had a medical emergency and it went undetected. First thing Monday morning, I'm going to contact the administration."

Morgan's eyes widened. "Daddy, don't you think that's going a little overboard? I'm fine. No harm, no foul, right?"

Cliff shook his head. "No, angel, I don't think so. You could have died. The fact that another student had to come to your aid is unacceptable. The school board will hear about this."

Sir leaned back with a satisfied smile. "I think that is an excellent idea. In fact, I'll place a few calls of my own." He said the last part while staring straight at me.

I had to take a quick swallow of tea to stop the acid climbing my throat. We were sunk. And apparently, with Morgan pressed against the back of her chair like a deflated balloon, she knew it too. All it would take was a phone call to the school for Cliff and Sir to discover that we had skipped every class that day. There would be no explaining that. Especially after the asthma story Morgan had crafted.

I didn't know what kind of trouble Morgan would be in, but a packed suitcase was definitely in my future.

Janie stood as a woman in uniform entered the room carrying a silver tray loaded with plates of steaming food. Attention diverted. Despite the mouth-watering smells of poached chicken and garlic potatoes, I only picked and played with the food on my plate. It was definitely one of the nicest dinners I've ever had, and that too made it feel entirely too much like my last meal.

~ ☾ ~

Chapter 20

I'd been sitting on Morgan's black bedspread for almost an hour, waiting for her to wear a tread in the carpet with her nonstop pacing.

"Your dad is a complete douche bag!" She threw her hands in the air. "Seriously. He needs a colonoscopy to get out whatever the hell is stuck up his ass."

I didn't say anything, only picked imaginary lint from her pillowcase. Ranting wouldn't help. I had a bag packed for me and it was would be used very soon. No amount of name calling and shouting could change that.

Morgan groaned and leaned against a picture of a band I'd never heard of. In fact, I didn't recognize a single name on the posters plastered against her wall, but they all had one thing in common: I wouldn't want to meet any of them in a dark alley. I liked my bands to sing about pain—not look like they inflicted it. Everything about them looked sharp, from their spiked jewelry to their pointed nails. Even their hair was cut at jagged angles.

"You're not saying much, Smalls."

I shrugged. "There's no point. I'm as good as good as at military school."

She frowned. "The man's a dick, but would he really send you away?"

I drew my knees to my chest and tucked them under my chin. "He already packed my bag."

"Shit." Morgan sat next to me and leaned her head on my shoulder. "Don't worry about it, Smalls. I won't let him send you away. I'll think of something."

I shook my head. "Thanks, Morgan. It means a lot to me that you care, but my fate is sealed. Sir isn't one to be persuaded, and he's had his mind set on this for awhile. He's just been waiting for a reason. Now he has one."

"But what if I told my dad—"

I cut her off. "No. It won't do any good." Before she could argue, I stood. "Can we change the subject? I mean, isn't this supposed to be a slumber party? Aren't we supposed to be doing facials or having a pillow fight?"

She laughed. "You want a facial?"

"No. I'm just trying to get my mind off Sir and military school."

Morgan chewed on her bottom lip. "The truth is, Smalls, when I came out of the closet, my friend stock took a nose-dive. When you don't have friends, you don't have slumber parties. I'm kinda new to the whole thing."

I put my hand on her shoulder. "Well, you're in luck because I've never been to one. Since we both don't know what we're doing, I guess it's safe if we make up our own rules."

Morgan grinned. "My vote is for popcorn and horror movies, that is, unless you're too scared."

"I can handle it. I'm pretty tough." I flexed my muscles, which made us both giggle.

"Yeah," Morgan said. "I guess you wouldn't be afraid of flesh-eating zombies—not when you *live* with a monster."

She had a point.

***

"Smalls!" The girl's voice, barely a whisper, was laced with the unmistakable tremor of terror. Before I could open my eyes, sharp pricks stabbed into my arm. I sat up and peered at where Morgan held me. Even in the dark bedroom I could make out the tiny, red, half-moons left on my skin from fingernails.

The unfamiliarity of my surroundings disorientated me. It took me a moment to remember where I was—in a sleeping bag on the floor of Morgan's room. I rubbed my stinging arm before Morgan gripped the oversized T-shirt I wore.

"Smalls, you have to wake up," she hissed. "We need to move. Now." Her eyes darted wildly around the room.

"Wha—?" I stifled a yawn. This was the first good night's sleep I'd had in a week. I wasn't about to let Morgan ruin it because she'd watched one zombie movie too many. "What's going on?"

"Someone's knocking." Her voice was frantic. "Outside my window. I saw a shadow. Someone's lurking out there." She pulled me to my feet. "Come on! We need to get my dad and call the police."

I was instantly wide awake and fighting to keep her from dragging me out the door. "Are you sure you heard knocking?"

"Yes!" She bobbed her head up and down and managed to get me through the door, but I latched onto the doorknob before she could drag me down the hall. "What are you waiting for?"

A knocking in the middle of the night? A mysterious shadow? My breath caught in my throat. It wasn't possible. How did he find me? And, more importantly, why had he come? After last night's swim, Bastin had made it pretty clear he had no intention to visit me again.

Morgan snapped her fingers in front of my eyes and I reflexively jerked back. "Seriously, Smalls, this is not the time for another one of your emo trances. I need you to stay with me and focus." She tugged my arm but I wouldn't let go of the door. "What are you *doing*?"

I shook my arm loose from her grip. "It's okay,

Morgan. I know who's out there."

"You do?"

"Yes. It's a . . . friend. I better go see what he wants before he gets us into any trouble." I started down the hall and stopped when I heard the sound of bare feet padding after me. I glanced over my shoulder. "You better wait here."

"No way!" She darted in front of me. "I totally see what's going on here."

Somehow I doubted that.

"You have a boyfriend." She smirked.

I almost laughed. If only it were something that simple. "I don't have a boyfriend. He's just . . . a friend . . . a secret friend."

"*Secret friend?*" Morgan snorted. "I'm hurt that you don't trust me. I thought *we* were friends."

"We *are* friends!"

"Who're friends? You and me? Or you and your boyfriend?"

I rubbed two fingers against my now throbbing temple. "Now you're just messing with me."

She flashed an innocent smile.

"Look," I dropped my hand, "I'm sorry he scared you. Just give me five minutes and I'll make sure he leaves."

"Okey-dokey." She held up her hands to let me move past her, but when I did, she fell back in step behind me.

I stopped and sighed. "What are you doing?"

She leaned her head against my shoulder and batted her lashes. "I never said I was going to let you talk to him all by your lonesome, now did I?"

I mentally counted to ten before I answered. "If you're with me it might freak him out. He's not exactly, um, *social.* I'll just let him know that I'm okay and I'm sure he'll leave."

Morgan didn't look convinced. "Smalls, my parents' house is pretty big. The odds are more in favor of a burglar sneaking around than your boy-boy. I can't let you take that risk alone. If you're gonna get murdered, then I'm gonna get murdered with you." She shrugged. "It's what any good friend would do."

The soft throbbing under my temples became a steady pulse. What was I going to do? I knew that Bastin was persistent and wouldn't stop knocking on the window until I came out. I also knew that Morgan was stubborn enough to not let me go outside without her. Part of me thought that if Bastin was foolish enough to come looking for me at strangers' houses, then whatever happened wasn't my fault. Still, I cared for him and I didn't want to risk exposing him for what he was. Even in his human form—with his black eyes and silver hair—it was pretty obvious he wasn't *normal*. "Morgan, it's not what you think. My friend Bastin . . . he's really shy. He wouldn't like it if you were with me."

"Ohhhhhh. I get it." She nodded. "He's a real dog, huh?"

If I wasn't worried about making too much noise and waking Morgan's parents, I would have been tempted to beat my head against the wall. "It's not like that. He's just not that comfortable around strangers. It's why he only meets me at night."

Morgan squealed and clasped her hands together. "What? You guys are having midnight trysts? Really, Smalls, this is so scandalous. I didn't think you had it in you, and for that I apologize."

I rolled my eyes before continuing down the hall.

"But despite my awe," she was back at my side, "I cannot let you go outside alone. What kind of person would I be if I let you get attacked outside my home? That would be the end of my sleepovers, wouldn't it?"

I stopped and looked at her. "Why are you being so difficult?"

"Why are you?"

Touché.

I could see that I no longer had an option—Morgan

was coming with me. Maybe Bastin would learn that if he wanted to keep himself a secret from humans, he should stop tapping on their windows in the middle of the night.

"All right," I huffed. "You can come with me. But don't say that I didn't warn you. If you could do me one favor, though? Just try not to freak out. At least, not too badly."

"Smalls." Morgan rolled her eyes. "I see ugly people all the time. We go to school with Hagrielle, remember?"

"Gabrielle is a bitch, but she's not ugly."

"On the outside, no. But they don't come uglier than her insides. I'd rather befriend a hundred dog-faced mutants than have to sit next to her for an hour."

I nodded. "I get that. But Bastin's not ugly, either."

Morgan folded her arms across her chest. "Relax, Smalls. I'm not going to make fun of your boyfriend. I don't care what he looks like. All that matters is that he's not a creep to you."

I wondered if sneaking around outside my bedroom and taking me for a swim in the ocean only to dump me would fall under her definition of a creep. "I just want you to be ready. Bastin doesn't look like anyone else. So, please, just try not to freak."

She frowned. "You know this is really weird, don't you, Smalls? All this talk about not freaking out is starting to freak me out. He honestly can't look *that* bad."

I said nothing as we tip-toed past her parents' bedroom, through the dining hall, and into the kitchen.

"This is it." Morgan gestured to the French doors like she was modeling a prize on a game show. "Here we have door number one. Will it lead our contestant to the dog-faced man of her dreams? Or will she find an axe-wielding psychopath? Stay tuned."

I swallowed hard as I grasped the handle. Some of the hurt from last night resurfaced and I struggled to keep my breathing even. Bastin was out there. I didn't know what he wanted, but I knew I wouldn't be able to rest until I found out.

"Smalls?" Morgan touched my shoulder, her brows knit together with worry. "You okay?"

There was no way for me to answer that question because I wasn't sure. "Just, whatever you do, don't freak out."

She made a face. "I'm a big girl, Smalls. Don't worry."

"Okay." I took a deep breath and opened the doors. Instantly, the smell of surf and sand enveloped me. Bastin. But I couldn't see him. Morgan's yard was dark except for the illuminated blue water of the lighted in-ground swimming pool several feet away.

"Edith." As much as I wanted to be angry at him for what he'd said to me, the moment I heard him say my name I was lost. He stepped halfway out of the shadow cast by Morgan's house and stopped to sniff the air. "You are not alone."

As if on cue, Morgan jumped forward with an exaggerated wave of her arm. "Hi there!"

I wasn't sure if it was Morgan's forward greeting or her appearance, but something about her startled Bastin. He took a step backward only to step on a foam pool noodle. The noodle rolled under his foot which made him stumble backward.

"Bastin!" I ran forward, but I was too late.

He teetered on the edge of the pool for just a second, his arms pin-wheeling and grasping for something to hold onto before he fell in.

I dropped to my knees next to the pool and watched, helpless, as the pale flesh of his legs twisted and shifted until all that remained was a glittering fish tail.

"Holy shit," Morgan whispered, just before crumpling to the ground.

~ ☾ ~

Chapter 21

I didn't know who to address first: the merman or my new best friend. But before I could move, Bastin broke the surface of the water next to me. He threw his sopping wet shorts onto the concrete beside me.

"Sorry," he said, frowning at Morgan's unmoving body. "I can't always control the change when I'm underwater."

"It's okay," I said. "Just get out of the pool so you can help me."

He nodded and pushed up on his arms.

"Stop!" I quickly grabbed his shorts and handed them back to him. "Before you get out."

Bastin smiled a devilish grin as he pulled his shorts back on. Apparently he'd managed to get rid of his tail and now had two legs again. After he'd secured the zipper, he climbed out of the pool and crouched beside Morgan. "Shall we?"

I nodded. Together, we hoisted Morgan to her feet, dragged her across the patio, and set her down in a lounge chair. She immediately sagged forward, her head rolling like a flower with a snapped stem.

Bastin lifted Morgan's arm and then dropped it, letting it fall across her stomach. "She's pretty out of it."

"Seriously?" I gaped at him. "For most people, seeing someone like you is a bit of a shock. You should try being a little more discrete."

He frowned at my scolding. I don't know if he expected me to jump into his arms upon seeing him, but

I was still hurt and angry over the way he left things between us . . . even if he was right.

I huffed. “What did you come here for, anyway?”

His eyes narrowed. “I was worried. I didn’t feel good about the way things were left between us. So I went to your house, but you weren’t there.”

I took a step forward despite my best attempts to stand my ground. Even angry, I couldn’t fight the impulse I had to be close to him. “That doesn’t explain how you found me here.”

“I followed your scent.”

I shook my head. There was no way I heard that right. “Wait, you what?”

“I followed your scent,” he repeated, motioning to the bandage on my shoulder. “Your blood—it’s a skill we share with the sharks—I can smell it from miles away.”

“But my shoulder is almost completely scabbed over.”

He nodded. “I know. It’s getting harder to scent you out—but I can still do it. Barely.”

I made a face. “I can’t decide if that’s romantic or disgusting.”

He threw his hands in the air. “I don’t get you. You talked about how your stepdad wants to send you away. When I couldn’t find you, I thought he might have done just that. So I decided to rescue you, but instead I’ve repulsed you.”

And just like that, the anger simmering my blood cooled. I smiled. “You really came here to rescue me?”

“Apparently not.” His frown unfolded into a smile.

“Okay. Then what? Where would you take me?”

His smile withered. “I hadn’t thought that far ahead.”

Right. I sighed. “It doesn’t matter. I wasn’t in any danger, anyway.”

“I’m sorry,” Bastin said. “I didn’t realize my presence would be so upsetting.”

A laugh escaped my mouth before I could smother it with my hands. “What did you expect? Humans aren’t used to seeing mers swimming in their pools. I don't think you have to worry about Morgan. She's cool, but other humans wouldn't be so understanding. I bet some would even want to study you." I shivered at the thought of Bastin on some scientist's table.

He lifted his chin. "Don't worry about me. I'm careful."

I folded my arms. "Even so, I couldn't bear it if you were taken to a lab and cut up into little pieces."

"That won't happen."

I really hoped so. But if Bastin was going to keep taking risks by showing up unannounced, he had to know the consequences.

Morgan groaned and I kneeled by her side. "Are you okay?"

She stared at Bastin, rubbed her eyes furiously, and then stared some more. "Holy shit." With my help, she climbed to her feet and scrambled behind me, peering at Bastin from over my shoulder. "He's really real." She removed an inhaler from the pockets of her sweatpants and breathed in the mist.

Bastin didn't move.

"It's okay." I took her hand and patted it in what I hoped was a reassuring way. "This is Bastin. He's my . . ." The sentence hung in the air, growing heavier the longer it sat. What was Bastin? I knew I'd told Morgan earlier that he was my friend, but now that he was next to me I was reminded how much more he really was.

"Merman," Bastin finished for me. He stepped forward and offered his hand. I wondered where he'd learned that particular human custom. Especially when he told me that his kind didn't touch.

"Um, okay." Morgan squeezed his hand and dropped it like it burned. She turned to me and whispered, "He's your *merman*?"

I gave her a weak smile.

Morgan looked from me to Bastin to back at me.

~ ☾ ~

"This is insane. I must still be dreaming."

"I know it's a lot to take in." I clasped both of her hands and squeezed. "But you can't say anything about Bastin to anyone. Please. Promise me."

Morgan opened her mouth to answer, but before she could, a new voice spoke out from the shadows at the back of the property. "She doesn't have to. Because I promise that if either of you says anything, I will kill you both."

~ ☾ ~

Chapter 22

It was as if ice water had been dumped inside my veins. I'd recognize that voice anywhere.

"Luna." Bastin didn't sound happy.

She stepped out of the shadows and regarded us with a sneer, then shook her head, causing waves of midnight-blue curls to spill over her shoulders. "My prince, you are in a world of trouble."

His shoulders tightened. "Am I?"

She walked up to us, clothed in an oversized dirty shirt. The fabric, tattered around the hem, was barely long enough to cover the important bits. "I've searched the entire ocean over for you. I never dreamed you were exposing our kind to the parasites on this dung heap they call land. The king is not going to be happy when he hears about this."

Bastin clenched his fists at his side. "Then I have nothing to worry about, because the king won't find out about my visits to the surface."

Luna closed the distance between us and crossed her arms. "And why's that?"

His hands swung up, reaching, but I stepped between the two mers before they could collide. "Are you two crazy?"

Luna jerked her head toward me and hissed.

Bastin tried to reach for Luna over my outstretched arms. "If you so much as touch her, Luna, I swear—"

"Stop it!" I took his hand in my own and he relaxed his stance. "If you keep this up, you're going to wake

Morgan's parents. I can't risk any more people finding out about you."

The two mers regarded each other silently, as if unsure how to proceed.

"Come on, you guys," I pleaded. "Can't you save the fight for the water?"

Luna's eyes didn't leave Bastin. "I'll make a deal with you. I won't say a word to the king about your land excursions, providing you return to the water with me right now. And never come back."

I swayed on my feet, as her words stabbed my heart. He was going to leave me. Again.

As if reading my mind, Bastin tightened his hold on my hand. "I can't do that."

Luna's eyes grew impossibly wide and I knew mine looked much the same. "What are you talking about?"

"I've tried, Luna." Bastin turned away from her so that he stared down at me. "What have you done to me, Edith?" He took both of my hands in his, pleading. "Why can't I leave you?"

"Are you ill?" Luna grabbed him by the shoulder and wrenched him around before I could respond. "Or perhaps just crazy? Don't you know the dangers of venturing into the surface world? You could pick up a disease, or worse, get caught."

"I know the risks and I don't care."

Luna hissed, only this time it was more frustrated than angry. "Bastin, I will take you under by force if I have to. As a member of the King's Guard, it's my duty to maintain your safety and the safety of our people. You endanger us all with this . . ." she waved her hand in the air as she searched for a word, then said, "liaison."

Bastin straightened himself to every inch of his six-foot-plus frame. "I'd like to see you try."

Luna appeared to weigh her options.

"Besides," Bastin said, "if you're so worried about my safety, stay with me. Then you can see what really happens on the surface—you can meet some humans instead of condemn them from a distance."

Luna scoffed and threw her hands in the air. "I don't need to meet them. They're all murdering parasites. Their trash and their oil infect our home. Their military sonar inhibits our ability to find food and is a never-ending source of my migraines." She dropped her hands and lowered her voice, as if suddenly afraid someone might overhear. "Have you even considered what would happen if the other tribes found out the heir to the Aridonian throne has gone insane? Your fondness of humans doesn't just make you weak, Bastin; it makes *all* of us weak. We'll be under attack as soon as the word spreads."

He shook his head. "Stop being dramatic, Luna. I'm not insane, in fact, the opposite. I'm figuring things out myself for the first time in my life."

"This is all *your* fault." Luna locked eyes with me and closed the distance between us in a matter of seconds. She smelled nothing like Bastin. Gone was the scent of salt and surf, overpowered by the stench of fish and blood. Her eyes narrowed into black slits. "I'd sooner kill you than allow you to manipulate our future king."

She reached for me. But before her claw-like nails could graze my neck, Bastin moved like a blur, shoving her to the ground. "You will not harm her!" He stood over Luna, his chest heaving, clenching and unclenching his fists. Anger spilled from him in hot waves and, at that moment, I had my first glimpse of the prince he claimed to be. "I swear to you, Luna, if you so much as touch Edith, I will see to it that you do not make it back to the water before sunrise. You can shrivel and die on the land that you hate so much."

She blinked several times. "You wouldn't."

"I would."

Luna brought her hands to her throat as if the burning in her lungs had already begun.

~ ☾ ~

"Edith." There was a tug on my sleeve and I turned to find Morgan had moved beside me. With everything that had happened, I completely forgot about her. She stared at the mers with unblinking eyes. "I have a question."

I nodded, even though I knew there wouldn't be an answer—at least not one that I understood.

"Just tell me," Morgan began, "am I really seeing what I think I'm seeing? Are there two mermaids about to throw-down in my backyard?"

Actually, that seemed to sum it up nicely. I nodded.

"This is the best day ever!" she squealed, clapping her hands together.

Bastin and Luna seemed to forget about their staring contest, as they turned their attention to Morgan.

"Seriously," Morgan continued. "This is the most awesome thing that's ever happened to me. Look at you guys with your shiny hair and wicked eyes. You're real!"

The mers blinked.

"Wow." Morgan shuddered. "That über-fast-blink thing you do with your eyes is a little disturbing."

Bastin looked at me but I could only shrug.

"Anyway, here's the deal." Morgan pointed to a window at the edge of the house. "That's my dad's room. If you guys keep it up, you're going to wake him and that would be a bad thing. So, if you want to hang out for a bit, you can come inside. My room is on the opposite end of the house and my parents won't be able to hear a thing."

"Luna?" It may have been a question, but the tone of Bastin's voice didn't leave room for argument.

Luna dropped her arms to her side but her hands remained fists. "Absolutely, my prince. Let's go inside the human's filthy den. Whatever you want." As she brushed past me she mumbled, "Consorting with humans. This can only end badly."

Yeah, I thought, holding Bastin's hand as we followed Morgan inside. *Tell me something I don't know.*

~ ☾ ~

Chapter 23

The four of us marched, single-file, down the hall to Morgan's room. The soft pad of our bare feet on the marble tile was another sign that this wasn't a dream. Even though I'd been reluctant to share Bastin with anyone else, now that Morgan was involved it was almost a relief. The fact that another person could see the mers proved I wasn't hallucinating—that Bastin *was* real, something I couldn't help but question every time we parted.

He slid his arm around my waist, dissolving the tension that had built to muscle-aching levels inside me. I wanted nothing more that to fold myself against his body, to fall into the world that was just the two of us.

Morgan ushered us inside her room and shut the door. She pulled a cigarette lighter out of a desk drawer and began to light the dozens of votive candles strategically placed around her room. Afterward, she turned her stereo on low and flopped down on the floor, motioning for us to do the same.

Luna dropped to the ground, grunting. Bastin ignored her, pulling me onto his lap and wrapping his arms around me.

Morgan, who'd been watching, wriggled her eyebrows. "*Just friends,* eh Smalls?"

My cheeks burned.

"What do you mean?" Bastin asked. "Is there something better than friends?"

"Oh, sure." Morgan flashed a sly grin. "FWB. Friends with benefits." She giggled.

~ ☾ ~

The burning in my cheeks spread from to my neck and the tips of my ears as I silently pleaded with her to stop.

"I've never heard that expression. What does it mean?" Bastin asked.

Morgan looked at me and must have seen the desperation in my eyes because she waved her hand in the air. "Nothing. Never mind." She winked at me before turning her attention to Luna, still sulking in the corner. "I absolutely adore your hair."

"Why?" Luna pulled a strand of her blue hair in front to her face and examined it. "It's a common color."

"Not here." Morgan ducked her head, allowing several black and pink dreads to spill across her face. "I have to dye mine to get it this color."

"It is more desirable to have hair like Bastin," Luna said, pointing at him. "Only those with royal blood have silver hair. That's how we know he's the heir to the throne." She said the last part like it left a bad taste in her mouth.

"That's cool," Morgan said. "I'd love to hear all about your culture and stuff."

Luna glared at her.

"Right." Morgan jumped to her feet. "Where are my manners? I'm being a terrible hostess. Do you guys want something to eat?" She walked to her desk, opened another drawer and examined the contents. "I have Doritos, gum, or—" she withdrew her hand and inspected the package in her hand. "Sour straws!"

Both Bastin and Luna held out their hands and Morgan placed several pieces of the sugary-sour candy into their palms before sitting next to Luna.

Luna eyed Morgan as she shoved all the candy into her mouth, smacking her lips as she chewed. "Why are you sitting so close to me?"

"It's what humans do," Bastin said. "They like to touch and be close. It's wonderful."

~ ☾ ~

"That's a matter of opinion," Luna said after swallowing. "This food is disgusting, by the way." Still, she held her hand out for more.

Unfazed, Morgan scooted closer and handed her the bag. "I was wondering . . ."

Luna shoved more candy in her mouth. "Yes?"

"How are you able to transform your tails into legs?"

"Because of the moon," Bastin answered. "We're ruled by it. When the moon is out, we can trade our tails for legs if we want. But we need to be back in the water before sunrise, otherwise we'd suffocate as would any fish trapped on land."

"It doesn't happen often," Luna said. "*Most of us*," she glared at Bastin, "hate taking human form." She wiggled her toes and shivered. "Disgusting."

"Oh, I don't know." Morgan inched closer to her. "I think they're kinda cute."

Luna's face remained blank, oblivious. But I couldn't help but feel a sense of dread come over me. Of all of the people in the world to flirt with, why had Morgan picked Luna? An actual shark would have been friendlier.

"It's so sad that you can't be out during the day," Morgan said. "There are so many things I'd love to show you."

"We can," Bastin said. "Once a month."

"What?" I looked up at him. This was news to me. "How?"

"The three days of the full moon," he answered. "That's the only time the moon is strong enough to allow us to walk under the sun."

Morgan stood and grabbed her school planner off her desk. "The full moon is next weekend!" She hopped up and down. "What do you guys want to do?"

"Stay in the water," Luna said.

"No way!" Morgan tossed the calendar on her desk and flopped next to Luna. "You'll have legs for three days straight. We have to use that time to do something epic!" She clicked her tongue ring against her teeth as she thought.

"Morgan," I said. "I don't think that's such a good idea." I couldn't imagine Bastin, even with legs, being able to go unnoticed among humans. Even fully clothed, there was no way of altering his silver hair or black eyes.

"Don't you start, Negative Nancy." She silenced me with a wave of her hand. Then, "I got it! This is the best idea ever. Are you guys ready?"

We stared at her.

She rolled her eyes. "Whatever. Here it is . . . the greatest idea ever . . . you guys are gonna freak."

I sighed. "Well?"

"Disney World."

She was right. I did freak—but not in a good way. "No, Morgan. There's no way that would work."

"What's Disney World?" Bastin asked.

Morgan ignored me. "It's an amusement park with rides and roller coasters. You guys have to go. You'll love it!"

"Morgan," I said. "We can't go to Disney World. It's six hours away. There's no way we could take them that far from the ocean. Besides, they don't exactly blend in."

"I could drive us. My mom and dad have a timeshare. We could stay for the weekend." She continued to click her tongue ring, then snapped her fingers. "They could wear disguises! All we'd need are some wigs and dark sunglasses."

"But could you survive out of the ocean for that long?" I asked Bastin.

He nodded. "Yes. As long as we had enough water to drink."

Luna's mouth dropped. "You can't possibly be considering this, Bastin. You've done some stupid things—"

Bastin cut her off. "We're going."

Morgan squealed and clapped her hands.

~ ☾ ~

"You sound like a porpoise," Luna grumbled.

Morgan only smiled and nudged her. "I was wondering something else, too."

Luna stared at the spot on her arm where Morgan had bumped her, as if waiting for hives to break out. "What now?"

"When you get your legs . . ."

Luna blinked at her. "Yesssss?" she hissed.

"Do you get all the human parts or just the legs?"

"Morgan!" I covered my eyes with my hand. "I can't believe you just asked that."

"What?" She asked. "I'm curious. Just pretend I'm a scientist. Besides, you can't tell me that you haven't wondered yourself."

"Me? That's . . . I . . ." I refused to look up at her, to expose my burning cheeks. "Of course not."

"Liar liar, pants on fire," Morgan sang. "Unless . . ."

Oh God. I glanced at her, silently begging her with my eyes to stop the direction of this conversation.

"You've never seen one." She folded her arms and smirked at me, as if daring me to disagree. When I didn't, her eyes widened and she brought her hands to her face to cover her gaping mouth. "Oh. My. God. It's true. You've never seen one."

I crossed my arms, trying to copy her defiant pose, but I only managed to look defensive. "And you have? I thought you were into girls."

She laughed. "Honey, did you ever think that maybe I'm into girls because I *have* seen one? And wasn't impressed."

My mouth flapped open and closed like a screen door banging in the wind as my mind scrambled to come up with a good comeback.

"What are you talking about?" Bastin asked.

"Your boy parts," Morgan answered with a wink. "Edith's never seen what's under a guy's zipper."

"Oh." Bastin slid out from under me and undid the

top button on his shorts. "Why didn't you say so? I'll show you."

I gasped. "No!" My hands flew back to my eyes.

Across the room, Morgan fell onto the ground in a fit of laughter.

I still hadn't removed my hands from my eyes. "I don't want to see!" My face seemed to sear my fingertips, my skin was so hot. Before I could stop myself, I felt the first teardrop trail down my palm, followed by a stream. I dropped my hands and glared at Morgan. "Thanks a lot for embarrassing me." Before she could answer, I ran from her room, back outside, where I hoped the cool night air would melt the heat washing over me.

It wasn't long before a door open and shut behind me. Without looking I said, "Morgan, I really don't want to talk to you right now."

But it was Bastin who answered. "I'm sorry for upsetting you."

I quickly wiped away the remaining tears before I turned to face him. "It's not your fault. You didn't know."

He nodded. "Yes, but I still don't understand. I was just trying to help."

The burning returned to my cheeks. "People don't usually show their stuff to other people, Bastin."

"Why not? Our kind has no problem with nudity. We only cover when we're on land so we don't draw attention to ourselves. We're ashamed of nothing."

"I don't . . . I don't know." I sighed. "While your way sounds liberating, here, on the surface, we keep our clothes on."

"You're *never* naked?"

The blush spread from my face, creeping down my neck, until there wasn't a place on my body that wasn't warm. "I . . . well . . . there are times when people get naked, I guess. When we bathe and . . . other things . . ."

He moved in front of me, tilting his head so that we

~ ☾ ~

were removed from the world, under the curtain of his hair. "What kind of things?"

His breath brushed my cheek like a velvet glove, sending delicious tremors coursing down my body. I had to lock my knees to keep from toppling over. "Um, sex."

"Sex," he repeated, settling a hand against my hip and drawing me closer so not even the night air stood between us. "What the sailors wanted."

I was suddenly aware how alone we were and just how dangerous that was. "What sailors?" My voice was a whisper.

"Years ago, several tribes would have their younger maids lure sailors into the water by displaying their nakedness. I never understood why the sailors would plunge to their deaths before now. The pull I feel to you is"—he shuddered—"almost painful. If I were a sailor, and you the maid, I would already be dead."

My mouth went dry and I felt myself wanting to pull away from him. What was wrong with me? This was Bastin. My Bastin. Why was I suddenly so afraid?

Bastin lifted his hand to my face, but stopped before his skin touched mine. Tilting his head to the side he sniffed the air and frowned. "I can smell your fear, Edith. Why are you scared of me?"

I tried to speak, swallowed, and tried again. "Not you." My voice trembled. "I'm scaring myself."

He blinked.

"Because," I continued, "you're looking at me as if you'd like to devour me. And all I want to do is let you."

"Good." And then he had both arms around me, moving so fast that it brought a startled cry to my lips—a cry that was quickly swallowed by his mouth. And then, it was as if he really was devouring me—melting together in a tangle of limbs and hungry mouths. So much so, that when the morning finally came, and Bastin would return to the ocean, I wondered just how much of me would be left.

~ ☾ ~

Chapter 24

I spent the rest of the weekend holed up in my bedroom, trying to stay under Sir's radar. Aside from my midnight visits with Bastin, I did my best to blend into the background, hoping Sir would forget about his threat and the suitcase propped next to my bed.

I really should have known better.

Monday morning, I awoke to a banging outside my bedroom door. Unlike Bastin's soft taps against the glass, this knock wasn't asking permission.

After rubbing the grit from my eyes, I glanced at my clock radio; four-thirty AM. My heart sank, as it did every day, when the confusion of morning cleared and my dreams dissolved, leaving behind the very real nightmare.

"Get up!" A voice growled from outside. "You have approximately ten minutes to get yourself dressed and on the deck."

Oh God. My stomach clenched painfully. I grabbed four antacid tablets out of my nightstand. With everything that happened at Morgan's house, I'd nearly forgotten my punishment for being caught outside. The physical training had begun.

I dressed as fast as my protesting shoulder would allow by throwing on a T-shirt and running shorts before meeting Sir outside.

He narrowed his eyes at me—I'd almost forgotten. Quickly, I dropped my arms to my side, stuck out my chest, and snapped my head up in attention. "Sir."

~ ☾ ~

He nodded. "On the ground. Push-ups."

Good morning to you, too. Why yes, I slept very well. Thanks for asking. I lowered myself to the ground, my shoulder screaming under the weight of my body.

Sir dropped to the ground beside me and did three pushups for every one of mine. He turned his head, shouting in my face, things like, "You call that a pushup? I've seen five-year-olds who could do better. You wouldn't last a second on a battlefield. You're soft. They're going to eat you up and spit you out!"

I didn't know which was going to make me pass out first—that my shoulder felt like it was on fire, or the fact that Sir had yet to brush his teeth and every time he shouted at me little flecks of spit landed on my cheek.

"Pathetic," Sir said, standing up. "It's making me sick to watch you. Get up."

After saying a quick prayer to the Lord of Mercy, I did.

He placed his hands on his hips. "Now, we run. Originally, I'd planned a nice five mile course with hills and obstacles, but I realize you're still recovering from an injury. So a three mile jog around the neighborhood will have to do."

Apparently, the Lord of Mercy was out of the office today. Maybe I could appeal to the Lord of semi-trucks to send a big-rig to mow me down and put me out of my misery. Tears pricked the corner of my eyes and my face flushed with pre-crying heat. To keep the crying at bay, I bit down on my tongue and fluttered my eyelids, trying to blink back the tears. It worked, which was nothing short of a miracle. The man in front of me was trying to kill me and crying would have made it that much worse.

Sir took off down the street and I had to sprint to keep up with him. After a mile, his breathing and pace were the same as when we'd started. The only sign that he was working out was a thin sheen of sweat that glittered on his bald head. I, however, was gasping for every breath with an aching cramp that ripped into my side. Still, I managed to keep up.

The last mile, it was all I could do to remain upright.

When our house came into view, my knees gave out and I stumbled onto the gravel.

Sir glared at me but kept running. “Don’t sit down. Do you want your muscles to knot up?”

It was too late for that. My entire body was a guitar strung too tight.

“Walk it off!” he yelled.

“Yes, sir,” I stood on shaky legs and brushed the rocks off my knees, at least the bits that weren’t embedded in my skin. After limping home, I was relieved to find that Sir wasn’t waiting for me in the yard. I used that opportunity to dart into my room and jump in the shower. Afterward, I’d twisted the handles off but water still drizzled from the showerhead. I had enough on my plate without worrying about leaky plumbing.

I pulled on a Sir-approved blouse and crammed a black T-shirt and my makeup case into my backpack. After walking into the kitchen, I found Mom standing before the sink with her hands on her hips. Water trickled from the faucet.

“Stupid thing,” she muttered. “It was working fine a minute ago.”

Sir walked in a moment later and positioned himself at the table. “What’s going on?”

I sat next to him without making eye contact and carefully unfolded a napkin, smoothing it around my legs.

“Oh, nothing.” Mom turned and gave him a smile, though her eyes were a little too wide to make it look natural.

Sir didn’t answer, only grunted as he opened the newspaper that waited for him on his plate.

A pop from the stove startled Mom. She picked up a wooden spoon and gave the steaming pot several turns.

Next, she grabbed a jar of cinnamon and gave it a few shakes before turning the stove off. "Finished," she announced with a smile. "My grandma's famous oatmeal."

Sir peered at her from over his paper but didn't return the smile. "About time. We're going to have to rush to not be late."

Mom's smile twitched. "Sorry about that. I guess I fell a little behind this morning."

Sir took the bowl she offered and dug in. "If that's the case, Carol, you might want to consider getting up earlier. I can't have you making me late because you can't make a pot of oatmeal in under thirty minutes. I think you can microwave the stuff for less than five."

She stared at her hands, as if straining to keep from reaching for her ring. "Yes, you're absolutely right."

Anger flooded my veins like acid. Sir was a jackass. I was used to his constant belittling of myself and my mom. But something I'd never grown used to was the way she accepted it—like a beaten dog ready to roll on its back at the first sign of tension.

She handed me a bowl before sitting down with her own. "I just want to say how wonderful it is the way you two got up early this morning to exercise. It's great to see you spending time together."

I almost choked on my oatmeal and had to take a swig of milk to swallow it down. Sir eyed me dangerously until I'd composed myself enough to resume eating. Leave it to Mom to put a twisted spin on his abuse.

I couldn't stand to be around them for another minute, so I inhaled my breakfast. When I stood to put my dishes in the sink, a car horn blared from outside.

"What the—" Sir was on his feet in an instant and at the window even faster.

I dared to peek around his shoulder. Outside, parked in our drive, was a red convertible, the top down.

~ ☾ ~

Morgan sat behind the wheel, a scarf tied around her head Thelma and Louis style.

Mom came up behind us both and clapped her hands. "Well, look at that. It's your new friend, Edith. I bet she's here to give you a ride to school. Isn't that wonderful, Michael? Now you won't be late for work."

He didn't answer but kept his gaze fixated on Morgan. If a look could turn one to stone, Morgan would have been lovely sitting in a garden somewhere with a bunch of pigeons on her head.

I snatched my backpack off the floor and dashed for the door before Sir could stop me. "I'm off to school!" I turned back to sketch a quick wave. Mom smiled. Sir opened his mouth to say something, but I'd shut the door before he had the chance.

Morgan didn't look at me as I climbed in next to her. Wordlessly, she handed me a scarf—black with white skulls wearing pink bows—and peeled out of the driveway. The scent of burnt rubber following us for several miles.

"You're really trying to get me into trouble, aren't you?" I asked above the rushing wind. Quickly, I tied the scarf around my head to keep my whipping hair from stinging my eyes.

She lifted one shoulder in a half-shrug. "We're already in trouble, don't ya think?"

She had a point.

When I didn't answer, Morgan turned to me with a smirk. "The way I see it, if we're already in trouble, then it doesn't matter what the hell we do."

Another good point.

Her grin turned sinister. "Besides, your stepdad's an ass. I can't help but screw with him. I can tell he's not used to it."

"He's not," I said. "Because most people know better. It's not that I don't appreciate you pissing him off, but he's really good at revenge. And, like you witnessed at dinner, you're not untouchable."

"Maybe not." She remained quiet for several minutes, staring at the road.

Soon, the silence became uncomfortable and I attempted to distract myself by fidgeting with the seatbelt. Morgan hadn't mentioned the mers once since they left her room early Saturday morning. I wondered what she really thought about the whole thing but was too chicken to bring it up. *So, what did you think about my merman boyfriend* just didn't feel like a good conversation starter.

Morgan eased her foot off the gas pedal and turned into the strip mall where we'd played hooky only a week ago.

"Morgan." I bit my lip. "I'm up to my ears in trouble. I can't skip school again."

She rolled her eyes. "Relax, Smalls. We're not skipping. School doesn't start for an hour and I can't go without my java fix. Want something?"

"Sure." I followed her into the coffee shop, where she ordered two marble lattes.

Morgan settled into a corner booth, then tore the lid off of her cup and blew on her drink, splattering the table with dots of whipped cream. After another couple minutes of awkward silence, she looked up at me. "Okay, I've been thinking . . ."

I paused mid-sip and set my cup down. So this was it—when she told me that what happened over the weekend was too insane for her and she could no longer be my friend. I mentally braced myself for impact.

"This weekend," she continued, "we didn't do any drugs or drinking that I'm aware of, did we?"

I sucked in a gulp of air before answering. "No."

"No," she repeated as if saying the word out loud made it more real. "Good. I gave that shit up a long time ago. I hate feeling out of control, you know?"

I nodded even though I didn't agree. While I'd never

done drugs or drank even a sip of alcohol, I loved the out of control, loosing myself feeling that came over me whenever Bastin was near.

"But . . . it was crazy, wasn't it? Surreal." She lowered her voice beyond the level of a whisper, so much so, that we had to duck our heads together so I could hear. "I just want to make sure that I'm not losing it. That it really happened. That there were mer people in my bedroom."

I nodded, bumping our foreheads together. It probably looked to the passersby like we were sharing an intimate moment—not that it bothered me. Nothing about Morgan bothered me. That's why I was so afraid to lose her.

She surprised me by leaning against the seat with a grin. "Wicked." A dreamy look glazed her eyes. "So very wicked. I've been waiting my whole life for something like this."

I couldn't hide the shock in my voice. "Really?"

"Oh, yeah. I always knew there was more out there. That this," she gestured to the room around us, "couldn't be all there is."

Unsure how to respond, I took a sip of my latte.

"That's why I knew we were gonna be good friends, Smalls. You get it. I could tell from the moment I saw you sprawled on the bathroom floor that there was something different about you."

Different. The word echoed around my brain like a gong. I couldn't help but think about the leaky faucets and wonder if my being *different* had something to do with that.

"Do they visit you all the time?"

I took another sip before answering. "Bastin does."

"Wow." Morgan scooped her finger into her latte before licking the whipped cream from the tip. "You two are pretty tight then?"

I didn't answer, I didn't have to. The telltale blush

burned on my cheeks. "It's not as simple as that. Bastin and I . . . we both know that we can't be together."

"Why not?"

"Mers can't survive on the surface." I stared at the liquid in my cup, wondering what it would feel like to be able to suck water in through my nose like air. "And Bastin says that if he takes me under with him, I'll be in constant pain. So he won't do it."

Morgan sputtered on the coffee she'd gulped. After her coughing spell passed she splayed her fingers on the table. "Hold the phone! Mermaids can take people underwater?"

I nodded. "I don't know how it works, but they can do something to a human so they survive. But Bastin says the people down there are miserable. He says you'd feel like you were drowning and the weight of the ocean curves your spine. He also says that once you've been taken under, you can never return to the surface."

"Interesting," she murmured. A strange look came over her face, causing a chill to run down my spine.

"Morgan . . ."

She blinked a couple of times before she was able to focus on me.

"What are you thinking?"

She waved the question away. "Nothing. I just find the whole thing fascinating, don't you? I mean, who'd have thought it would be possible for people to live underwater?"

I took another sip. "But I don't know that I'd call it living. Bastin says it's a miserable existence."

Her eyes narrowed, all of the excitement they'd held replaced by something dark. "And this isn't?"

She had me there.

Morgan lowered her eyes to the table. "There are other ways to cause agony than physical pain."

It was as if invisible hands were clawing their way into my stomach. I'd wanted Morgan's life to be perfect—needed it, even. I'd long ago accepted the fact that my life was a joke and Sir was the punch-line. I'd surrendered to my fate but carried the hope that happy families did exist. That mothers, fathers, and their kids spent weekends curled up on the couch watching movies. They took vacations to Mount Rushmore and returned home with bobble-headed presidents. That was not only my hope, but my dream for the future. If a happy family was nothing more than a myth . . . what was the point of living?

Morgan scooped more whipped cream from her drink and shrugged. "It doesn't matter, anyway. I'm just curious how they do it. Maybe if they didn't take you to the deepest part of the ocean, there could be a way around all that bone-crushing pain."

She held so much hope in her voice that I didn't want to voice my disagreement. Because, if there was a way for Bastin and I to be together, he would have said something . . . wouldn't he have? But doubt burrowed into my brain like a botfly. What if he didn't want to be with me the way I wanted to be with him? What if I was just something fun and different and when the novelty wore off, he'd return to the ocean using the excuse he'd given as a way to leave me behind?

My stomach cramped in nauseous waves and I pushed my drink away. On one level, I realized that I was letting my insecurity eat me alive. On another, I found myself sliding out of the booth pulling my backpack with me.

"Smalls?" Morgan was next to me, though I hadn't noticed her get up. "Where are you going? Did I piss you off?"

"No." But I didn't stop walking. I had to get outside. It was suddenly hard to breath. "I'm fine—just not feeling well all of a sudden. Sir had me run three miles this morning. Probably a side-effect from that."

"Jesus," she said. "Don't worry about it. I'll drive you

~ ☾ ~

to school."

I shook my head. "If it's all right with you, I'd rather walk. School's not that far and I could use the air."

She frowned. "In case you didn't notice, I have a convertible."

"I-I-just . . ."

Morgan's eyes softened. "You know what? Don't worry about it. I get like this, too. Take a Midol and I'll see you at lunch."

I smiled, relieved. "See you at lunch."

Morgan climbed into her car as I started down the sidewalk. The air really did feel good on my skin, not as thick as it had been in the coffee house. It blew through me and loosened the knots of tension inside, allowing me to think clearly.

Bastin had told me that there was no way for a human to live underwater without being in pain—and I believed him. If there was a way for the two of us to be together he would have said something. I believed that. I had to. Because if Bastin lied to me . . . I didn't think my heart could survive. Once again, I was reminded that there was no good way for this to end. Either I could convince Bastin to take me underwater with him, or we'd be torn apart when Sir sent me to military school. It didn't matter if I was underwater or above it—there was no escaping from pain.

~ ☾ ~

Chapter 25

When I'd told Morgan that I'd meet her for lunch, I had no way of knowing that I wouldn't make it past first period. Ten minutes into homeroom, the intercom announced my presence was requested in the principal's office.

I'd expected this—just not this fast. I took my time shoving my books back into my bag, ignoring the whispers and stares of the students around me. It didn't matter—nothing mattered now.

The hallways were quiet as I walked through them. The heels of my sneakers squeaked on the fresh wax, as if trying to warn me to turn back. When I arrived at the office, I reached for the handle only to have the door burst open. Gabrielle stood before me, her face swollen and blotchy—a sure sign she'd been crying. When she saw me, a cruel smile curled the edges of her lips, signaling an end to whatever act she'd been performing. She closed the door behind her and leaned against it.

My skin tingled as the blood underneath boiled. "Move, Gabi."

She tilted her head. "I wouldn't be so eager to go in there if I was you. I told them everything."

My hands tightened in fists. Normally, I avoided confrontations and would have backed away and found myself a nice, dark corner to hide in. But now, with nothing to lose, I no longer cared. "By *everything* I assume you mean your *lies*."

She pushed away from the door and strode toward

me so that only inches separated us. "I told them you were responsible for the boat accident because your lesbian lover put you up to it. Oh, I also told them you'd been skipping school and doing drugs with that freak." She adjusted the brace around her neck. "Your dad looked really pissed."

"You lying bitch!" Before I could stop myself I thrust my arms out and shoved, sending Gabrielle staggering backward.

She regained her footing before hitting the door and lunged for me. She grabbed my shoulders and rammed me into a locker. My head snapped back and connected with metal, sending jolts of pain down my spine. I blinked several times to clear the blurriness from my vision.

Gabrielle still held me, her fingernails digging into my skin like claws. "Better a bitch," she whispered next to my ear, "than a murderer."

Murderer. There was that word again. The accusation that'd followed me every day since the death of my brother.

A red haze blurred my vision and I no longer cared about Sir, military school, or anything else. In that moment, my sole purpose of living was to kick Gabrielle's ass.

I clenched my hand into a fist and reared back, but just before I plunged my fist into her three-thousand dollar nose, a faint rumbling sounded overhead.

"What the—" She released my arms. We both looked up at the florescent lights shaking overhead. Seconds later, the fire sprinkler directly above burst open, showering us with water.

Gabrielle shrieked and darted away, only to land in the path of the next sprinkler that turned on. She shuffled back, fell on her butt, and scrambled up again as she tried in vain to shield her hair from the pouring water. Her screams alerted the office staff, who came to the window to stare but didn't dare come out in the downpour.

Gabrielle spared me one last withering look before she fled down the hallway, screaming after each sprinkler she ran under burst open.

I smiled when she disappeared behind a corner. A smile that quickly disappeared the moment a hand clamped down on the curve of my neck.

"Clear out your locker," Sir's voice rumbled from behind me. "You're officially enrolled at the Saratoga Military Academy."

~ ☾ ~

Chapter 26

Sir drove me home, where I immediately ran to my room and collapsed on the bed. My worst nightmare had come true. In the car, Sir said that because the boat accident was caused by my drinking (as told by Gabi), that I'd skipped school and lied about it, and I was apparently worshipping Satan (as evidenced by my clothing and hidden stash of makeup), he felt it necessary to send me to Saratoga, California, where I could be molded into the kind of person society deemed "useful." I'd toured a military academy before and knew the term "useful" was just another word for compliant.

It wasn't like I hadn't known this was coming; Sir had been threatening to send me away for years. But after Sir had packed my bag, I'd hoped I would have more time to be with Bastin. The only good news was that my bus to California didn't leave until Friday afternoon. That gave me three days . . . hopefully enough time to convince Bastin to take me into the ocean.

Mom checked on me a couple of hours later. Her eyes were glassy and her face flushed, like she'd been crying. Still, she said nothing as she placed today's assigned dinner—beef stroganoff—on my desk. No reassuring words. No Dog of the Day. Just a few sniffles and she was gone.

When the door clicked shut, I threw my pillow against it. My hands shook and I hugged my chest to keep from throwing anything else. I wanted to scream but knew better than to attract any more of Sir's attention. Mom could do something if she wanted. She was my mother for crying out loud, and this man, this monster, was going to send me away. If she'd just speak up for once . . .

But the thought brought fresh tears to my eyes. She hadn't challenged Sir the entire time they'd been married—there was no chance she'd start now.

For the rest of the night I laid on my bed watching the shadows climb the walls. As the hours went by the shadows grew larger until the pressing darkness threatened to swallow me whole. I had to get out.

When the footsteps overhead quieted, signaling Mom and Sir were settled in bed, I was out the door and running down the paths to the bayou. It felt strange to navigate them alone—even stranger to arrive on the dock without Bastin. But I couldn't wait for him. Half of my heart was in the ocean, a part that I would cling to until I left.

I didn't know how long I sat on the sun-bleached wood, hypnotized by the gentle lapping of waves and glittering reflection of stars dancing on the surface. Eventually, one of the stars peeled itself from the water, growing larger as it moved, until it stood before me with arms stretched wide.

"Edith." A faint smile played on his lips. "I—" but he stopped short after catching sight of my face, his brow folding into lines of concern. In an instant he was out of the water. Even faster, and I was in his arms. Soft and warm. A place where I felt invincible when the rest of the world threatened to pull me apart.

Bastin tightened his hold, molding me against his side. The wind blew through the gaps of his arms and I shivered, reminding me again how different we were—how impossible our love.

As if sensing my thoughts, Bastin released me. I stood before the prince of the mers, nothing more than a silly girl. If only I could breathe underwater or fly us into the

~ ☾ ~

stars. But instead, I was no more special than a reed lost to the ocean, unable to choose my own direction, helpless to go where the currents pushed me.

"Something's happened." Bastin ran smooth fingers along my bare arms, and I was unable to surpass the shiver that followed. "What is it?"

I opened my mouth, but the words wouldn't come. I was afraid that if I said them they would cut up my tongue they way they'd cut my heart.

"Edith, please." His voice cracked.

Seeing him upset tore the words from my throat. "They're sending me away. And I don't know . . ." I chocked down a sob and buried my head against his shoulder. "I don't know how to let you go."

Bastin sucked in a breath but said nothing.

After several minutes of deafening silence, I begged, "Please, Bastin. Say something."

More agonizing seconds, and still he stayed quiet.

All of my attempts to keep from crying failed as the first tear spilled from my eye, trailing down my cheek where it clung to my chin for just a moment before letting go.

Bastin reached out—faster than humanly possible—and snatched my tear out of the air. He stared unblinkingly at the shimmering drop balanced in the middle of his palm. Finally, he clenched his fist and dropped it to his side, groaning. "If I could, I would breathe you in." He pulled me against him and buried his head on top of mine, his hair falling around us like a curtain of stars. Sealing us inside of our own world—a world I would give anything to stay inside of forever.

"Please," I whispered. My tears streamed down his chest. "Take me with you. Under."

He shook his head. "You are asking me to kill you."

"No." More tears. A sob escaped my throat before I was ready. "I'm asking you to save me."

He pulled away and held me at arm's length. "By

~ ☾ ~

crushing your spine? Condemning you to a life without sunlight and air? Never would I do that to you."

"Don't you think I'd rather have my spine crushed than my heart?"

Bastin closed his eyes pulled me against him. "We were such fools."

I clung to him with every ounce of my strength. "So what do we do?"

Bastin dipped his chin and I lifted my face. His lips met mine, but gone was the tentative brush of velvet. This time his kiss was hard and desperate, like a suicide note without the words. His mouth whispered of hope lost and love never ending.

I locked my arms around Bastin's neck and he wove his fingers into my hair. We pulled each other tighter, almost to the brink of pain. Bastin went to his knees and I followed him to the ground, never taking my lips from his, too scared to lose a second for fear that it would be our last. Carefully, Bastin leaned over me and laid me against the soft earth. Settling his weight between my legs, he propped himself up on his arms, shielding us behind a curtain of silver.

"You are so beautiful," he said, tracing his thumb along the line from my ear to my chin. My eyelids fluttered under the wave of tremors that coursed along my skin. "I was told all my life that humans are ugly vicious creatures. But you have proved otherwise. You've changed everything . . . you've changed me."

If it wasn't for the lingering taste of salt on my lips, I would have been sure I was dreaming. "You've changed me, too," I whispered. "You brought me to life."

He bent down, wrapping his arms around me, and kissed me. I drank him in, the sea, the night sky, and the moon, everything that made Bastin who he was. If only I could breathe him in entirely—hold on to him forever. Because if this moment was my last, it would be enough.

Bastin ran his hands down my sides and I shivered in

response. He ventured under the edge of my T-shirt and brought a small gasp from my throat when his hands moved up, tracing small circles along my skin.

The wind across the bayou picked up, tangling our hair together as we kissed. From a far away place, I realized I should have been cold—but the warmth of him, the warmth of us, was a fire that consumed me.

In each other's arms, we burned. Flames so hot that it'd felt like I'd died, only to be brought back to life by a backlash of white-hot flames that seared the blood in my veins. His pulse beat through his chest into my own until I couldn't tell where the beating of my heart ended and his began. Or, maybe, we'd shared one heartbeat all along.

When he finally pulled his lips from mine, I breathed in and drank the scent of him.

"Edith," he whispered as he settled himself next to me, "I—"

"Shhh." I shook my head against the sandy ground. "You'll break it."

"What?"

"The magic in the air." I sighed. So fragile. Every moment hung in webs of crystal—destined to be broken under the weight of what lay ahead. "I just wish—"

"I do, too," Bastin said, placing a kiss on my temple. "But it would never work."

I knew that, of course. I just kept hoping there was some obvious answer that we hadn't thought of, yet. I rolled on my side so I could stare into his eyes. "So what was the point?"

"The point?" His eyes widened. "How can you ask that? Look what you've done to me, Edith. If it weren't for you, I would have lived the same numb, miserable human-hating existence as the rest of my kind. I understand what it means to feel now—because of you. *That's* the point."

Tears pooled in my eyes and I blinked over and over

again until I was sure they wouldn't fall. "I just wish we had more time. After I leave . . . do you think we'll ever see each other again?"

He looked at the sky. "I don't know."

I laid my head against his chest, still slick from sweat. "I'm afraid of what life will be like without you."

"It will be full of sun. Something I could never give you in the water." He placed a finger under my chin and tilted my face to his, a sad smile on his lips. "You'll live, Edith. That's all that matters."

But he was wrong about the sun—I didn't need it. All the sun in the world wouldn't stop a flower from dying—if it had no one to care for it.

***

When the sky turned the color of smoke, I trudged back to my room more aware than ever how truly alone I was. But, at least I *was*. Finally, in a state of being. Before I'd met Bastin, I'd been numb inside. Now pain ripped through me like talons. And despite it all, it was better this way. The hurting inside of me reminded me that I could finally *feel*. I was painfully aware of every ragged breath, every tear trailing down my face, and the deepening rip in my heart.

I pulled the covers tight against me—a poor substitute for the arms that held me only an hour ago.

Bastin was gone.

And it was my fault. I'd wanted it too much. If I hadn't been so selfish—if I could have just been happy with the way things were. But with only two years left until graduation, I had to screw it up by skipping school with Morgan. Now I'd lost everything.

I twisted my fingers into the blanket and buried my face in my pillow, hoping to silence the sobs shuddering through my body. I cried until my tears ran dry and my chest ached from the tremors. So much pain. How was it that only a couple of hours ago I'd felt happier than I had in my entire life and now I was the most miserable?

As the morning sunlight crept into my room, I pulled the covers over my head, hating the reminder of everything I couldn't have. In three days, I would be on a bus bound for military school. If only I could convince Bastin to take me under. To make him understand that a life buried beneath the ocean had to be better than no life at all.

~ ☾ ~

Chapter 27

When I opened my eyes, there was a peanut butter sandwich and a bag of chips on the nightstand. Now that I was about to be sent away, I guess it no longer mattered when I woke up. Still, it bothered me that Mom hadn't said a word to me since Sir pulled me out of school.

But whatever. It wasn't like she'd actually stand up to him. I ripped the covers off and walked to my desk, where I grabbed the Dog of the Day calendar and threw it into the trashcan. It didn't matter anymore. Nothing did.

Next, I took the peanut butter sandwich and opened the sliding glass door so I could eat outside. What I hadn't expected, however, was to find Morgan wandering around in the backyard, peering into the windows.

"What are you doing?"

Morgan jumped back and then sighed when she saw it was me. "Oh, thank God, Smalls. I had no idea which room they had in lockdown." She looked around. "Is it safe?"

I nodded. "Sir's at work and Mom's avoiding me." I sat on the wooden deck and took a bite of my sandwich. "He's sending me away, you know. My bus leaves Friday."

She smiled. "That's great!"

I stopped chewing. "How can you say that? I thought you were my friend." I threw the sandwich in the yard, no longer hungry. "What are you doing here, anyway?"

~ ☾ ~

Morgan's mouth dropped. "I'm insulted. I *am* your friend. That's *why* I'm here. *Duh*. You know how prisoners are given a last meal before their execution?"

I nodded.

She grinned. "Well, I'm giving you a last hurrah! We're going to Orlando and we're leaving Friday."

"But my *bus* leaves Friday."

She waved her hand. "Military school will still be here when we get back."

"Yeah, and so will a very pissed off Sir."

Morgan rolled her eyes. "Seriously? You're worried about getting in trouble? They're sending you away—what *more* can they do?"

She had a point. Still, I wasn't so sure skipping town was a good idea.

As if reading my mind, Morgan said, "The mers are down with it."

That got my attention. "How do you know?"

A sly smile spread across her face. "Luna. She promised they would go last night."

A knot of worry tugged at my insides. "You've been hanging out with her?"

"Yeah." She leaned her head back and smiled at the sky.

I pulled at a piece of grass that had poked it way through the deck and began shredding it in my lap. I didn't like the fact that Morgan was involved with Luna. If something happened to her . . . "Morgan, you know Luna is dangerous, right?"

She looked at me, her smile widening. "*Oh, yeah.*"

Uh-oh. I went back to shredding. "Just be careful, okay? Hanging out with them, well, just look how messed up my life got."

The smile fell from her face. "I'm glad you brought that up. You'll never believe what I read in study hall yesterday."

I brushed my hands together, scattering my grass

confetti across the deck. "What?"

She shifted her weight so she could pull something out of her back pocket. "I Googled mermaids."

"Okay." I shrugged. "And you found a bunch of sites devoted to cartoons?"

"Yes. But there was something else." She handed me a folded piece of paper. "It's a Japanese folktale."

I made a face as I unfolded the paper. "I don't see what a folktale has to do with me."

"Oh, nothing . . . except everything!" She sighed loudly. "Just read it, already."

I smoothed the paper on my lap, my pulse throbbing in my fingertips. I was so desperate for hope I was willing to latch on to anything even if it was just splotches of ink under my skin.

Morgan snatched the paper from my hands. "For crying out loud. I should have known you'd go into another emo trance. Why don't I save us a couple of hours and tell you what it says?"

I folded my arms across my chest. "I was going to read it."

"When? A week from now? 'Cuz I'll tell you, Smalls, we don't have that kind of time."

I rolled my eyes. "Fine. What does it say?"

She cleared her throat dramatically. "Like I said, it's a Japanese folktale. It's about this fisherman who catches a mermaid in his net."

I cringed. "Does he let her go?"

"Not exactly. You see, he takes her home and decides to cook her. Apparently he's having a dinner party and didn't have time to catch any other fish."

"Oh, my God." I pressed my fingers against my lips as if that action alone could keep down the bite of peanut butter sandwich now churning in my stomach. "That's disgusting."

"I know, right? And that's what the dinner guests thought, too. Because one of them walked into the kitchen and found the mermaid laid out on the table. Afterwards, he hightailed it back to the dinner party, waited for the fisherman to go into the kitchen, and told everyone what was in the other room. So they're totally grossed out, and instead of eating the mermaid, they hide the meat inside of their napkins."

The sickly taste of bile burned the back of my tongue. "Seriously, I really don't like this story."

Morgan held up her finger, motioning for me to hold on. "I swear there's a point to this—I wouldn't gross you out for nothing. Anyway, everyone parties and gets wasted. On their way home, they throw out the napkins with the hidden meat in them—except for one guy. By the time he left the party he was stupid drunk and had forgotten to take the napkin out of his pocket. So he stumbles his drunk ass home, but when he gets there his daughter is up waiting for him. He no sooner walks through the front door when she's up on him, demanding a present."

I raised an eyebrow at her. Where the heck was this going?

"This guy is totally shit-faced," Morgan continued. "He wants nothing more than to shut the brat up, so he reaches into his pocket and pulls out the first thing he finds."

I gasped. "The napkin!"

She nodded. "And the girl just gobbles it up."

I hugged my stomach only to feel it gurgle angrily under my arms. "I thought you said this story had a point."

"I'd get to it if you'd quit interrupting."

I made a show of pretending to zip my lips shut.

"That's better," Morgan said. She looked at the paper in her lap. "The point is, after the girl eats the mermaid, she goes on to live a long healthy life."

"Wait, that's it?"

"Oh," Morgan tapped her finger against her chin.

~ ☾ ~

"Did I forget to mention that when she finally dies she's over five hundred years old?"

My cheeks tingled as the blood drained from my face. "What did you say?"

Her grin turned wicked. "I thought you might like that. One more bit of info; throughout this girl's five hundred years of life, her appearance stayed the same—like she never aged a day." Without waiting for me to respond she stood, folded the piece of paper, and tucked it into her back pocket. "Well, I'm out. I'll pick you up Friday morning. How's four AM work for you?"

The backyard seemed to tumble in on itself in a kaleidoscope of colors and I struggled to digest the information given to me. "Wait—where are you going?"

Morgan glanced at her watch. "Back to school, unfortunately. I figure I can't skip more than one class a week until this whole thing your stepdad started blows over." She bent over and gave me a quick hug.

"But, Morgan—" I gripped the edge of the deck to keep from toppling over. "What am I supposed to do with this information?"

She hesitated. "Whatever you want, Smalls."

"But . . . it's just a folktale, right? It can't be true."

"Well, Smalls, I imagine it can't be truer than the existence of mermaids." With that, she winked at me and disappeared around the house.

***

I spent the next hour in my room going over Morgan's story in my head. If it was true, that ingesting mermaid meat extended your life, then I was willing to bet that was how the mers kept people alive under water. But if the price for that life was a several-hundred-year extension . . . I shuddered at the thought. One lifetime was grueling enough.

An hour or so before Sir was expected home, I heard

the front door open and shut and a car start outside. *Probably Mom going to the grocery store*. I didn't think anything of it until after I used the bathroom. When I finished washing my hands, I twisted the knob off only to have water continue to trickle from the faucet. That gave me an idea.

Alone in the house, I could finally experiment with the dripping water. I knew that I was the cause—even more so after my almost-fight with Gabrielle. I just didn't know how or why. So I pulled up the stopper on the sink and waited.

The water didn't speed up or slow down. It remained a steady drizzle as it filled up the ceramic bowl. Okay, so doing nothing did nothing. Big surprise there.

Next, feeling a little like an idiot, I held my hands in front of me—like a witch casting a spell—and concentrated on making the water run faster.

Nothing.

I shouted, "I command you to move, water!"

Nothing.

"Now, dammit!"

Still nothing.

I hopped around like a Native American performing a rain dance I saw once on TV. I tried jazz fingers. I lit candles and made up magical incantations.

Nothing. Nothing. And more nothing.

With a sigh, I leaned pressed my palms against the cool porcelain and stared into the almost-full sink bowel. Maybe the leaky faucets and exploding sprinklers had only been a coincidence. Still, lowering my face to the water, I couldn't deny the pull I felt to move closer. The water rippled as it devoured each falling drop—as if whispering my name, calling me forward.

Before I realized what I was doing, I dipped my face into the bowl. Maybe whatever the mers did to humans to enable them to breathe underwater was something

Bastin had accidentally done to me? Working up the courage for the next part of my experiment, I mentally counted to three—and then braced for what I was about to do.

I sucked in a breath.

And then I knew.

I could *not* breathe underwater.

My disappointment was almost as painful as the water that burned through my nostrils, chocking me with fire. Suffering through a coughing fit, I stumbled back from the sink, grasping blindly for a towel.

To my surprise, it was placed in my hands.

Still sputtering, I wiped my face, then looked up, only to find Sir standing in my doorway, staring at me as if I'd declared myself a member of the Communist party.

"What in the hell were you doing?" he asked, his eyes wide.

"Um . . ." My mind raced to come up with a plausible explanation as I dabbed the remaining water from my neck. My safest bet was to go with something Sir wouldn't question—something girly. "I was giving myself a facial."

He snorted but relaxed his stance. "Yeah, well, I think you're doing it wrong."

I shrugged. "I read about it in one of Mom's magazines. Not only is the warm water good for the complexion, but when you breathe it in, it opens up the nasal cavities."

"Uh-huh." He turned on heels but shot me one last warning glance over his shoulder. "If I were you, I wouldn't be too concerned with your *complexion*. Your skin is going to be the least of your worries where you're going."

With that, he was out the door.

~ ☾ ~

Chapter 28

Apparently, now that I was going to military school, Sir's threat of daily physical training expired. This made sneaking out of the house so much easier. Also making it easier was the fact that, with nothing left to lose, I no longer cared if I got caught. For the next two nights, I met Bastin on the dock where we knitted ourselves together like yarn, only to unravel when the sun peeked over the horizon.

And each morning I found it harder to let go as I left for home and Bastin for the ocean. Making it harder was that all my attempts to convince him to take me under had failed.

The third night Bastin didn't come for me. But that was all part of the plan. For the first time since I'd met him, I counted the seconds until the first morning light. I glanced at the alarm clock, realizing it was almost time. I sat up in bed and patted a nervous rhythm against my thighs. *Pat-a-tat-tat.* We had to time this just right. If they were late, then Sir would be up and I'd be caught. I was excited for my weekend trip away with Bastin but at the same time, dreading it. It signaled the end and reminded me that each minute passed was one less that we'd have together. My hands kept up their anxious pattern. *Pat-a-tat-a-tat.*

Another glance at the alarm clock told me they were late. What if something had gone wrong? What if they weren't coming? Fear pressed into my chest, digging my ribs into my heart like pins in a voodoo doll. What if I never saw Bastin again? *Pat-a-tat-tat.* My thighs were starting to burn.

A quiet knock on the sliding glass door eased the pinching inside of me, and I let my breath out in a whoosh. I peeled the covers back and emerged fully clothed, like a corpse leaving a coffin. And in a way, that's exactly how I felt—like I was coming to life. I grabbed the small duffel bag that I'd packed the night before, ignoring the suitcase next to it—the suitcase that would be waiting for me when I returned. I couldn't think about that right now. All that mattered was Bastin and spending time with him before I was sent away.

I opened the door, then couldn't help the gasp that escaped my throat. In front of me stood a stranger. Only not. Bastin smiled, the corners of his mouth curled into the mischievous grin I loved so much. He wore dark wraparound sunglasses and a baseball hat pulled down on top of a wig, shoulder-length and blond, tied back into a ponytail. It might have been a woman's wig, but that didn't matter. Whatever Bastin wore—or didn't—he always looked good.

"This is great, isn't it?" His voice, though a whisper, came out a few decibels too loud.

"Shhh!" I placed my finger against my lips, shut the door behind me, and pulled him away from my house. Traveling through the neighbors' yards, I didn't risk speaking until we were four houses away. There, I stopped and smiled at him. "You *do* look great."

His grin widened. "I've never been able to blend in with humans during the day. Especially not in crowds. This is so amazing—it's almost like being a human."

My smile slipped a little. Being a human wasn't exactly amazing, but Bastin was so excited I wasn't going to tell him any different. "Where's Morgan?"

Bastin wove his fingers into mine and guided me along. "Just ahead. That's another thing: I still can't believe I get to ride in a car!" He was so happy it was impossible not to share his excitement. His smile dissolved whatever thoughts of suitcases, buses, and uniforms lingered inside my head. It was just another part of Bastin's magic—his ability to make me forget about everything and just be . . . happy.

"Look!" Bastin squeezed my fingers almost to the side of pain. He nodded in the direction of Morgan's red convertible, its engine already growling. "We get to travel in that. Isn't that great?"

I laughed. "It's pretty great."

He pulled me with him as he broke into a jog, muttering under his breath about the slowness of human legs.

When we reached the car, two heads turned to look at us. Morgan sat in the driver's seat, her grin as wide as Bastin's. Luna, wearing her own pair of dark sunglasses, sat in the passenger seat, looking bored. She wasn't wearing a wig, but considering Morgan's pink dreads, blue hair wasn't that unusual for a teenage girl.

Morgan got out of the car so Bastin and I could climb into the back seat. When we were settled, she climbed back in, squealed, and clapped her hands. "I'm so excited. Are you guys up for a fun-filled weekend?"

"Yeah!" Bastin answered.

Luna shrugged. "It's not like I have much of a choice."

"Oh, you!" Morgan made a face at her.

Luna turned to stare out the window.

Morgan shifted the gear into first and pulled away from the curb. "I called the resort pretending to be my mother and told them to expect my daughter and her friends all weekend. Then I used my credit cart to buy park tickets—we're all set."

I looked at Bastin. "Are you guys really going to be okay out of the ocean for three days straight?"

He waved my worry away. "We'll be fine. As long as we're back before the end of the full moon cycle, we'll have no trouble."

~ ☾ ~

I nodded, despite the unease that rippled through my stomach. It seemed dangerous to me to take the mers so far from the ocean. I wished I could wave the worry away as easily as Bastin had. Luna, on the other hand, silent and solemn in the front seat, seemed to share my concern.

Bastin leaned forward and spoke to Morgan. “I was wondering if you might put the top down?”

She shrugged. “Sure. Why not?” When we came to a stop sign, Morgan pressed a button and the electric top whirred down and disappeared into the back of the car leaving the four of us exposed to the cloudless sun-filled sky.

Bastin laughed out loud and tightened the ball cap on his head as the wig whipped wildly around his face.

I yelled to be heard over the rushing wind. “Do you guys think this is such a good idea? What if the wind blows your wig off? People will freak if they see your hair.”

Either Bastin didn’t hear me or he pretended not to as he undid his seatbelt and stood up. Opening his arms like wings, he screamed, “Whoo-hoo!”

Luna twisted around to scowl at him. “What are you doing? You are making a scene.”

Morgan laughed. “Bastin’s got the right idea. He’s the only one beside me who seems to be enjoying himself. You know, the whole point of this trip is to let loose and have fun.” Lifting one hand in the air, she joined Bastin in screaming.

Luna settled back into her seat with her arms folded. “Fine. But when it all goes wrong, don’t say I didn’t warn you.”

Morgan dropped her hand from the sky and pressed a finger against the tip of Luna’s nose. “You’re so cute when you’re grumpy.”

To my surprise, Luna’s face softened and she dropped her arms.

“Edith.” Bastin extended his hand. “Come up here with me.”

~ ☾ ~

I looked around. Even though the early hour kept the interstate fairly deserted, I wasn't sure that was such a good idea.

"Edith!" He thrust his hand in my face. "You're missing it."

He had me. Of course I would take his hand. How could I not? He could stand on the edge of a canyon, ready to leap, and if he smiled at me like he did now, I would go with him. My frown faded away as I unfastened my seatbelt and placed my hand inside his. He pulled me next to him. Without the windshield for protection, the wind was more forceful than I expected and I stumbled back.

Quicker than humanly possible, Bastin pulled me against him, wrapping his arms around my waist. He laughed. "And you're the one with legs."

I jabbed him lightly in the ribs with my elbow, which made him laugh harder.

"Watch, Edith." He let go of me and spread his arms wide. "I can fly."

Cautiously, I peeled myself off of his body and twisted against him so that my back was against his chest.

He dipped his chin, his mouth next to my ear, and whispered, "Fly with me."

Slowly, like a butterfly uncurling new wings, I opened my arms, Titanic style. The wind ripped through my hair and fingers, pulling against me, as if it really wanted to lift me into the sky. I laughed and Bastin laughed with me.

"See? We can be birds and fly away."

My heart ached. If only it were so simple, as if by simply extending our arms we could soar into the sky—a place we could share instead of borrowing from the other.

I threw my head back and screamed so loudly it rattled my heart in my chest like the gong inside a wind chime.

~ ☾ ~

Morgan's eyes, reflected in the rearview mirror, lifted in surprise. Luna shook her head. But as the wind ripped the scream from my throat, the more I wanted it out of my body. It was as if the anguish I'd carried over a love that could never be, a lifetime of hate, and a brother lost, had all poisoned my heart. And now, I could finally rid myself of all of it. I screamed until throat hurt, my arms fell, and my body struggled to remain upright.

Exhausted, I sagged back into Bastin's waiting arms. Together we slid down into our seats. I thought I should feel empty after screaming the pain from my body. Instead, I felt fulfilled, near bursting with warmth and love.

After we fastened our seatbelts, Bastin reached over and took my hand. "I wish I could stay with you always. If there was a way . . ." He sighed.

"Take me with you," I whispered.

He stiffened.

"I don't care if I can't come back to the surface. I don't want to come back."

Luna twisted around in her seat, smirking at us. "Yes, Bastin," she said, her voice sugary sweet. "Why don't you take your human under?"

His jaw flexed. "You know what happens to humans underwater, Luna. Edith doesn't know what she's asking." He looked at me. "The life of a human underwater is unbearable. The ocean would curve your spine and pale your skin. Your eyes turn milky and you would lose your sight. Not to mention that you would be unable to talk." He squeezed my hand. "I would never do that to you. I'd die first."

~ ☾ ~

Chapter 29

We arrived at the resort midday. After Morgan checked us in, we took a shuttle to Disney. We bought ice cream, which both the mers liked so much we had to go back for more. After coming across a girl dressed like a mermaid, I explained the movie and both Bastin and Luna had a good laugh over it.

"As if such thing as a sea witch could exist." Luna snorted. But after spotting a tiara for sale in a gift shop, she persuaded Morgan to buy it for her and spent the next hour skipping around the park, announcing to anyone who would listen that she was a mermaid princess. Luckily, no one seemed to think that we were anything more than a group of teens goofing off.

When we reached Future Land, Morgan insisted we all ride Space Mountain. Despite my warnings, the mers agreed. Bastin sat in front of me and didn't make a sound or take his hands off the lap bar the entire ride. After exiting the coaster, his legs wobbled and he didn't respond to his name, which I called several times. He took a step forward and staggered. Immediately, I darted under his arm and let him lean against me.

Worried, I asked, "Are you all right?" It wasn't like we could take him to the first aid station. And who knew what the effects of a rollercoaster would be on a mer?

He shook his head but remained silent.

Morgan appeared a moment later, bracing Luna the same way I held Bastin. We shot each other worried glances as we led them through the exit. Outside, Bastin straightened himself and held a hand in front of me, stopping me in my tracks. He looked at Luna and they exchanged nods.

"We've decided to do that again," Bastin said.

"What?" I asked. "I don't think that's such a good idea—you can barely walk."

He shook his head. "Again."

"Again," Luna repeated.

I sighed and Morgan shrugged. We led them back through the line and back on the coaster. This time, instead of their previous white-knuckled silence, both Bastin and Luna waved their arms in the air, whooping the entire ride. The four of us were a mess of giggles by the time we stumbled from the coaster.

"Again!" Bastin and Luna shouted in unison.

So we rode again . . . and again. Five times, in fact, before I could feel the ground moving under my feet even when I was standing still. "Guys, I think I'm going to sit this next one out," I said. My knees jiggled beneath me, and this time it was Bastin who held out his arms to support me.

Luna frowned. "You're weak. Bastin's right not to take you underwater. You'd never make it."

Was that the reason why? Because I was weak?

Before I could react, Morgan tugged on Luna's arm. "Come on. I'll ride some more with you."

Luna nodded. "This one," she told me, "I like. She's stronger. She's got what it takes."

Morgan beamed.

Bastin waved her away. "Go on then." He looked at me. "I'll sit with you, Edith."

I leaned into him. The night was beginning to creep into the edges of the sky, like ink soaking into a sheet of blue paper. The air was sweet, filled with the smells of sugar cones and lemonade. Together, we weaved through the clusters of people that had formed along the walkways in anticipation of a parade. I wished I could be one of them—here to relax and have fun with their families. Not like me, on a stolen vacation with someone I could never have.

I slipped my hand from his arm and wound my fingers through his—so deceptively human. He had arms to hold me, fingers to touch, and yet . . .

I blew out a breath.

Bastin led me to a park bench and we sat. "You're upset," he said.

I took my time before answering, biting on my lip until I had the trembling under control. "I just wish I could have fun like everyone around me. I've been trying . . . so hard, but . . . every time I see a couple, smiling at each other, happy, I can't help but be reminded that we'll never have that."

Bastin said nothing, only ran his thumbs across my knuckles, an action I could barely feel through the aching of my heart. Finally, as if he'd digested what I'd said, he nodded. "We both knew this was going to end at some point. It just happened sooner than we thought." He kissed the top of my head and leaned his cheek against it. The muscles in his jaw flexed against my scalp as he ground his teeth.

"I guess," I said, "it's better this way. Each time I see you it makes it that much harder to leave. If we spent any more time together, it just might kill me."

"If there was a way, Edith . . ."

Just then, a brilliant spider-web of blue and red streaked across the sky in a thundering boom.

Bastin jumped on top of me, pushing me into the bench's wooden planks.

"Bastin!" My cry was muffled by his shoulder which pressed against my face. "It's okay."

"What do you mean it's okay?" He didn't move and I became aware of more than a few people craning their necks to look at the spectacle we made.

"It's only fireworks."

~ ☾ ~

Slowly, he climbed off me and I could breathe again. "Fireworks? This isn't another one of your wars?"

I tried not to laugh as I rubbed my aching jaw. "No one is fighting. This is . . . just a show."

"Just a show," he repeated. I felt his muscles loosen beside me. "There's no danger?"

I shrugged. "I wouldn't say that. Apparently, there's a crazy merman on the loose, flattening unsuspecting girls onto benches."

He laughed and then threw his arms around me. We stayed that way, watching the fire burn across the sky in pops and sizzles. With the castle in the background, the night felt like a fairytale—only this story would have no happy-ever-after. But we could have a happily-for-the-moment. I made a silent promise to myself that for the rest of the weekend I'd stop counting each second lost and focus on the ones I still held.

Bastin brushed his lips against my neck. "Remember when I asked you how I would know if I loved you?"

I nodded, my tongue suddenly thick in my throat.

"I figured it out—I do."

Time stopped. The world stopped. My lungs stopped. My heart stopped.

All because Bastin loved me. And I said nothing in return. Bastin didn't seem to notice as he went back to gazing at the sky. It wasn't that I didn't love him—I just didn't have the ability to speak. He'd left me breathless.

"You've shown me so much," he whispered to the night sky. "I understand things now, why humans pair up the way they do. Why they touch. Why they mate. It all makes sense now. My kind are taught to hate humans because of their pollution. I understand that. But we aren't taught about all the good things your species is capable of. I originally came to you to understand more about humans. The other tribes are putting pressure on us to join them in their quest to destroy the land. But I won't let that happen. Even if every other human were a parasite, if only for you, Edith, I will fight to keep your home safe."

I felt the first of many tears slide down my cheek. What could I say to someone who'd pledged to save the world for no other reason than I existed? I looked around at the crowd. The milling people were too focused on the sky to notice a pair of seemingly-normal teenagers perched on a bench. With shaking fingers, I reached toward his face and removed the sunglasses. The endless eyes stared back at me. The eyes that I'd wanted so badly to fall into and drown. It wasn't until that moment that I realized that I already had.

"What are you doing?" Bastin asked.

I put my hands to either side of his face. "I'm drinking this moment in so I can carry it inside of me forever. They may tear us apart but they can never take you out of my heart."

His arms were around me in an instant. Staring into his eyes, I ran my fingers over his face, memorizing each inch of his skin and the way it felt to have his chest rise and fall against my own. I was desperate to take it all in, so later, when I was alone, I could remember and be sure it wasn't all a beautiful dream.

Bastin kissed me under the rain of fireworks. We kissed and clung to each other as if the world really was under attack and we wanted to die in each others' arms. We kissed until the climatic boom of the grand finale ended and, in the silence, someone cleared their throat.

We pulled apart and Bastin scrambled for his sunglasses.

"That's disgusting." Luna stood in front of us with her teeth bared. "Why must you suck on each other like that? Especially when I might stumble upon the scene with a full stomach?"

Morgan laughed. "I think it's adorable."

Luna made a gagging noise.

Bastin stood and held out his hand to help me up.

~ ☾ ~

"Someday, Luna, you will understand. All of our kind will."

She folded her arms across her chest. "What's that supposed to mean?"

"It means that Edith has taught me how to love. "

"Love sounds like another human disease. I told you they were contagious. If you spread it to our people—"

"I hope I do. We've been wrong about them."

Luna opened her mouth to respond but Bastin silenced her with a wave of his hand. "Why do you think these humans invited us here? Why are they sharing all of this with us?"

She looked confused. "I don't know . . ."

"Has Morgan asked you for anything?" he asked.

"No."

"Has Edith?"

"No"

"And haven't they given us disguises? Made sure we ate? Given us shelter?"

She took a step back as if preparing herself for a dark truth. "What are they after?"

"Nothing," Bastin said. "It's just what they do. Humans share, they love, they *feel*. Don't you feel *anything*, Luna?"

Luna opened her mouth—but no words came out. Instead, she turned around and walked in the direction of the rollercoaster, grumbling about human diseases the entire way.

~ ☾ ~

Chapter 30

Bastin stood behind me munching on a handful of fries as I balanced the cardboard tray of sodas in one hand and rooted through my pocket for the room key with my other. We'd left Morgan and Luna at the condo while we walked the two blocks to McDonald's. I was nervous leaving Morgan alone with Luna while Bastin and I retrieved dinner. Having been attacked by Luna myself, I didn't trust her not to fillet my best friend while I was gone. What I hadn't expected when I inserted the key and turned the doorknob, however, was Morgan and the mermaid standing on the balcony with their arms around each other.

I froze as wave after wave of shock rippled through me. Bastin, still focused on the fries, bumped into my back which rocked me on my heels and sloshed the soda noisily inside of the cups.

Morgan and Luna glanced in our direction. Morgan quickly dropped her arms from Luna's waist and her cheeks burned several shades of crimson. Luna merely looked bored.

This wasn't good. Luna was vicious, bloodthirsty, and dangerous. Not exactly the qualities you'd want to see in the person your best friend is caught . . . um, kissing? Was that what they'd been doing?

"Finally," Luna said with the same amount of emotion in her voice as if we'd caught her brushing her hair. She walked inside the room, stepped around me without so much as a glance in my direction, and took the bag of food from Bastin. "I'm famished." She perched herself on the foot of a bed and began rummaging through the fries and nuggets as if nothing had happened. Morgan, meanwhile, made a point of avoiding my gaze.

I turned to Bastin. "Give us a second, will you?" Before he could answer, I thrust the drink carrier into his arms, marched out onto the balcony, and closed the door behind me. This was a tricky situation and I was conscious of keeping the panic I felt about Luna and Morgan's evolving relationship from showing on my face. I folded my arms across my chest in what I'd hoped was a casual stance and attempted a weak smile. "Sooo . . . What's going on with you and Luna?"

Morgan grinned lazily and balanced on her toes so she could bend over the rail of our two story condo. "I don't really know." She stared at me, her face upside-down and growing redder by the minute as more blood rushed into her head. "But I like her . . . a lot."

That's what I was afraid of. I gripped the rail beside her and immediately let go when rusty flakes of paint chipped under my palms. "You know she almost ripped my throat out, right? With only her fingernails." After wiping my hands on my jeans, I pointed to my injured shoulder.

"I know." Morgan stood with a sigh. "But she feels bad about that."

I arched an eyebrow.

"I think."

"Uh-huh."

Morgan flopped down on plastic lawn chair. "Is there a point to this interrogation, Smalls?"

I sat in the chair next to her and scooted it close enough that our knees touched. "I just . . ." But my throat tightened and I had to swallow before I could continue. "I've never had a best friend before." I looked down at my hands, clasped tightly on my lap. "And I don't want to see you get hurt." The way I was hurting. Bastin's declaration of love still clung to me, making me

~ ☾ ~

ache with longing.

"Aw, Smalls!" Morgan moved from her chair and into mine, making room by bumping me over with her hip. She threw an arm around me and squeezed. "You're my best friend, too, you know." Her voice hitched in her throat, and her eyes brimmed with unshed tears. "But you don't have to worry about me. I'm tough."

I made a face. "Luna's tougher."

Morgan's smile melted away leaving her expression serious. "She told me she was fond of me today."

I blinked, too shocked to respond. If it were any other person, I would have said that was no big deal. But from what I had gathered from Bastin and Luna herself, for Luna to tell someone she was fond of them would have been like anyone else pledging their undying love.

"Whoah," I finally said.

Morgan nodded. "I know." The tone of her voice matched the somber look on her face. "And that's what I really like about her. Luna doesn't play head games. She'll tell you exactly how she feels. It's a nice change." Morgan leaned her head back on the chair and looked at me. "But I get why you're worried. I know Luna's dangerous. And I know she's selfish, but . . ." She shrugged helplessly. "It's not like you get to choose who you fall in love with, right?"

She had me there. Because if it were up to me, I sure wouldn't have picked a mermaid prince to fall in love with. I'd bet a member of the chess team would be a much less complicated boyfriend. Heck, any boy as long as he was human would be a less complicated boyfriend. I sighed and leaned my head on Morgan's shoulder. "We're so screwed up," I said.

"Yup," she agreed and rested her cheek on my head.

Just then, the sliding glass door opened and Bastin leaned against the doorframe. "I'm sorry to interrupt, but if you girls don't come back inside, I can't guarantee the safety of your French fries. Luna's been circling me like a shark for the last ten minutes, and I don't think I can fend her off any longer."

Morgan and I looked at each other and laughed. "We better go in," I said.

"Yeah." Morgan shoved me to my feet. "Besides, what are you doing outside with me anyway? This is the last night you get to spend with your boy-boy."

Bastin held out his hand and I slipped mine inside his. I started to follow him inside the condo, but hesitated at the door. "It's my last night to spend with you, too. And you *are* my best friend."

Morgan smiled. "Then let's do it right." She jumped to her feet and rubbed her hands together. "First one to the remote gets to pick the movie."

"Oh God." I turned and shoved Bastin inside. "Move! Or we'll be stuck watching a zombie movie."

Bastin frowned. "Zombie?"

Before I could respond, Morgan barreled past me, laughing maniacally. She reached for the remote on the nightstand between the two beds but I jumped on her back before she could grasp it. We collapsed on the floor in a giggling heap only to have Bastin snatch the remote, flip through the channels, and settle on a car show.

Morgan looked at me and groaned. "That's what you get, Smalls, for teaching him how to use the remote." She sat next to Luna, who was exactly where we'd left her, perched on the end of the bed and devouring the last of the French fries.

"Oh well." I smiled and shrugged. While shows about cars certainly didn't interest me, I didn't care what was on TV. I climbed onto the other bed and snuggled close to Bastin, resting my head on his chest. His arm wrapped around me as his thumb traced slow lines down my arm.

I sighed. It was the closest to pure happiness I'd ever been, and yet I couldn't enjoy it. As much as I tried not to, my eyes were drawn to the alarm clock on the nightstand. Because Bastin had told me he loved me, and each minute that passed brought me closer to the moment I'd have to say goodbye.

~ ☾ ~

Chapter 31

Morgan cut the engine and we coasted the rest of the way down the block until she parked in front of my house. Three sets of eyes turned to me.

"I'll be all right," I told them. I just hoped they didn't notice the way my fingers trembled as I unfastened my seatbelt. It was early Sunday morning, two days after I was supposed to be on a bus bound for California. I swallowed but had difficulty pushing past the tightness of my throat.

"Edith." Bastin stared at his hands clasped in his lap. "I wish—"

"I know." I couldn't bear to hear the words, like knives, that would cut me to bits. "It doesn't change anything. I'm glad we had our time together." I sucked in a deep breath. "And now I have to deal with the consequences."

He licked his lips and nodded. "Maybe . . . maybe everything will work out."

"Luna." Morgan reached across the seat and snatched Luna's wrist. "The sun is rising. Don't you think it would be a good time to take a walk?"

Luna wrinkled her nose. "Are you kidding me? I've been walking on these cursed feet for two days. All I want to do is get back into the ocean."

Morgan sighed. "Just come with me, okay? They need a moment."

Luna cursed under her breath as she undid her seatbelt and slid out of the car. "Just because he's the prince I'm expected to keep enduring this torture?"

~ ☾ ~

Morgan grabbed her hand and pulled her down the street.

Alone with Bastin, I reached across the seat, removing his sunglasses and pulling off the wig. I wanted see him for who he was one last time.

He exhaled loudly and blinked his impossibly fast blink. "So this is it."

I nodded, unable to speak for fear of losing hold of the scream just on the edge of my tongue.

"I knew it would hurt," he continued. "I've *always* known it would hurt. I just never imagined how bad the pain would be . . . I feel like I can't breathe."

A tear trailed down my cheek and I quickly crushed it with the back of my hand.

Bastin reached out and traced his thumb along the length of my jaw. "I can't believe this is the last time I get to talk to you—to touch you." His voice broke and he looked away.

"It doesn't have to be," I offered.

His head whirled around so fast that the flashing silver left me dizzy. "Yes it does. I would never take you under. Don't you understand? You would be in hell. You would be in constant pain. You would . . . hate me."

I shook my head. "No, Bastin. I would never hate you."

A sad smile twisted his lips. "Words are easy, Edith. But they can't predict the future."

I didn't say anything for a moment. My last attempt to convince him to take me under had failed. But like I'd said only seconds ago, I could never hate him. "Bastin?"

He waited.

"Will you hold me? Just for a moment?"

No sooner had the words left my lips than his arms were around me. I pressed my face against his chest, making a damp mess of his T-shirt with the tears that bled from my eyes. This was it. Inside Sir would be waiting for me—probably with that damned suitcase in

~ ☾ ~

hand—ready to rip me away from the only person who'd ever made me happy.

Bastin leaned back and held my face between his hands. "Look at me. I want to memorize every detail."

I stared into the black pools of his eyes. "I won't forget you, Bastin. Ever."

His lips brushed mine, much softer than I would have preferred. As if the time we had was so fragile that even something as delicate as a kiss could shatter it.

And then, as I pulled away, it did. I could feel the end deep inside my bones, cracking through the marrow. It was time to face Sir. For too long I'd feared this moment. After years of watching my every move, I was too exhausted to continue on. So, whatever the ending, I was ready. "I have to go."

Bastin knotted a hand in my hair, as if he would hold me in place, then, slowly, his fingers released their hold and slipped away. "I know."

There was nothing left to say. The pressure building in my chest threatened to burst through. When my brother died, I'd lost all feeling inside. And when I met Bastin, he'd brought it all back. And now I couldn't remember the last time I'd felt such pain—not when Luna's fingernails ripped through my shoulder, not Sir's constant threats, not even my mom's vacant stares—nothing had ever hurt so much as climbing out of Morgan's car.

"Edith."

I stopped on the sidewalk but couldn't bring myself to turn around. If I saw his face, even a glance, it might be the thread that unraveled me. "Yes?"

"You'll keep the stone I gave you, right? Something to remember me by?"

"Of course." I thought it funny that the entire time I'd wore my anklet around Bastin, he hadn't realized how close I really kept it. "I promise."

"Good." His voice fell further behind me like the

fragments of a dream upon waking.

Miraculously, my feet marched forward. Despite the fact that I knew I would never see Bastin again, despite the fact I knew I was walking toward my doom, they kept moving me forward. One step at a time—each one bringing me closer to the end—until it was right in front of me in the form of a dew-covered doorknob under my fingers.

It was unlocked.

I'd forgotten my key in my room during my escape, so at least this way I would be saved from the humiliation of having to knock. It felt better to embrace the end by walking into it. Not so much if I'd have to wait at the door for it to come and get me.

Sir sat in his recliner, exactly where I thought he'd be. He'd probably been sitting there the entire time I'd been gone, poised and ready. Posture was everything to the sergeant. He appeared to be sleeping, but when the door clicked shut behind me, his eyes snapped open.

"Ed." His voice was gruff from sleep.

Outside, the sports car growled to life and tore down the street, taking my heart with it. Which, in a way, was a good thing. Now that I was cold from the inside out I could do this—I could face him. Having just lost everything, there was nothing Sir could take. Just the way I wanted it.

The sergeant rose from the recliner. We stared at each other. His eyes narrowed, and his gaze intensified as we engaged in a silent staring contest. After a minute of non-blinking silence, he spoke, "Get your bag. Since you can't be trusted to ride a bus, I'm taking you myself."

So that was it. I knew it would come to this, but still, I couldn't help but be surprised how easy it was for him. He could announce his intent to send me away with the same emotionless voice he used to order coffee.

Even so, I didn't flinch. If he'd expected tears or cries

of protest then he was going to be disappointed. Instead, I marched past him to my room and grabbed the suitcase that'd been waiting for my return. Before I left, I took a moment to glance around my bedroom. There would be no pink walls where I was going, no Dog of the Day, or homemade chicken noodle soup.

While my life crumbled around me, I couldn't help but wonder what Bastin was doing. He was probably back in the ocean, already a world away.

I grabbed the suitcase handle but hesitated, surprised by the weight. Unzipping a corner, I peeked inside to find that it had been repacked to fit every piece of clothing I owned, all folded into impossibly small squares and vacuum-sealed in plastic bags. It was as if I was going away and never coming back. The realization punched a hole through what tattered bits remained of my heart. *I wasn't coming back.* That was what he'd intended all along.

Angrily, I zipped the suitcase shut and hoisted it off the bed. I was almost out the door when I heard it—a faint tapping against the sliding glass door.

My heart jumped, pumping blood at a rate so fast that my fingers tingled. Hope bloomed like a field of dandelions in my chest. Bastin had come for me after all! He must have changed his mind and decided to take me with him.

In a second, everything had changed. Now, instead of suffering through years of torturous hell, it looked like I was going to get my happily-ever-after. I dropped the suitcase, then raced to the sliding glass door. I could barely contain my squeal of joy as I flung the door open where a merman waited for me on the deck.

Only it wasn't Bastin.

Sea shells of various sizes were woven into his braided green hair. His grin was no more reassuring than the hundreds of shark teeth dangling from his necklace. With the same super-human speed Bastin possessed, the mer yanked me from my room and placed a clammy hand over my mouth.

I never had a chance to scream.

~ ☾ ~

Chapter 32

The strange mer smelled like Luna—only the blood on his breath was stronger. "Hello, little sandpiper." His voice was like a jagged rock scratched along a mirror.

Every instinct I had screamed at me to run, and fast. I tried digging my heels into the ground, but my efforts did little to slow him as he pulled me into the trees behind my house and onto the same path Bastin and I traveled so many times.

He was taking me to the bayou.

And, with his claw-like grip on my mouth and stomach, I was willing to bet his intentions were less than friendly.

My pulse thundered in my head as my heart hammered against my rib. If this mer wanted to kill me, I wasn't going to let him do it without a fight. I twisted inside his arms, thrashing and kicking, but he only tightened his grip. I even bit his hand but instead of letting go, he laughed. "The little bird thinks it can peck a shark, eh?"

I kicked harder, making contact with his shin, only he didn't seem to notice.

Up ahead, I could see the water sparkling through the trees. My mind reeled. What could the mer possibly want with me? Bastin said the other tribes didn't bother with humans unless they wanted slaves—even then they only hunted at sea. It didn't make sense. This mer was obviously looking for me. The only question was, why?

It wasn't until he pushed me onto the dock that he finally released his hand from my mouth. Even then, the taste of fish remained ripe on my lips. I stared at the water, unable to see what lay beneath. "W-what do you want from me?"

"From *you*?" He laughed, a cackling sound, nothing like the melody of Bastin's. "Trust me, little sandpiper, there is nothing you have that I would ever want." He sneered, showing his repulsion as the idea. "Look at you."

I could feel the revulsion in his gaze as his eyed followed the lines of my body.

"You're scrawny, even for a human. Weak. Your spine would snap the second you reached the bottom of the ocean, and then what good would you be? I have no idea what that plankton-brained Aridonian prince sees in you."

So there it was. The mer wanted nothing with me. He wanted Bastin.

"You belong to a warring tribe, don't you?"

He jerked me against him so hard that my check landed against his chest. From there, I could feel his heart beat erratically beneath his slimy skin.

"Don't pretend that you know anything about what goes on beyond the waves, human."

The unexpected closeness was exactly what I needed to make my move. Because of my time with Bastin, I knew that when mers walked on legs, they inherited the parts that came between them. Using every ounce of strength I had, I brought my knee crashing into his groin.

The mer made a soft squeak-like sound before he crumpled against the dock. I jumped over him, not really sure where to go, just knowing that I had to make it to land. I scrambled down the rotting planks until my foot sunk into soft earth. I hadn't even a second to celebrate my success when something jumped out of the water and darted in front of me, trapping me.

Even with her purple hair, she looked like an average

girl my age—an average *naked* girl—but I knew better. Hissing, she closed in on me, her fingers curled into claws that—I knew from experience—were sharp enough to cut bone.

I took a step back, my pulse hammering its way up my throat so that I could taste the sourness of fear on my tongue. I wondered if Sir had discovered me missing yet. If so, maybe I could scream loud enough for him to hear.

But, even as the thought crossed my mind, two arms fastened themselves around my waist. I had a moment, when my feet left the ground, when I thought I might actually be flying, like that horrific moment when Russell's boat had shattered into pieces.

That was, however, until I hit the water.

~ ☾ ~

Chapter 33

My wrists were locked inside of two hands on either side of my body—hands that were pulling me deeper. During my struggle and fall into the water, I hadn't had a chance to suck in a decent breath. It wasn't long before the familiar burning of suffocation ignited my lungs. I fought, twisting and pulling against their grip, until tired and defeated, I fell limp in their hands. I didn't even have the energy to worry about my soon-to-be drowning.

Despite the curtain of black creeping along the edges of my vision, I could tell we were moving fast—speed boat fast. If the mers cared about drowning me they didn't show it. Seconds were all I had left. The pressure building inside my head let me know we were deep enough that I'd never make it to the surface in time. The blackness in my sight grew until it I felt a floating sensation that had nothing to do with being in the water.

And then a hand wrenched into my hair, yanking my head back. A pair of scaly lips pressed against mine, so forcefully that my teeth bit into the flesh inside my cheeks, and a blast of air was shoved down my throat.

I swallowed it greedily, despite the foul fish taste. I wondered if this was how the mers kept the humans alive—they waited until you were half-unconscious from oxygen deprivation before allowing you a breath of air. If so, then Bastin had been right all along—it was hell.

As the mers pulled me deeper, the light became less until it disappeared entirely, leaving me in floating darkness. A new wave of panic set in, itching along my bones like crawling centipedes. Deep in the pitch-black water, with no gravity, and no light, I could no longer tell which direction was up. If the mers were to let go of me—there would be no way to be sure I could find the surface. My fear brought to life things in the water that couldn't be real—like fingers pulling through my hair and scratching along my legs.

A scream bubbled in the back of my throat—a scream that would kill me if it made its way out. It rose higher and higher, until it sat on the tip of my tongue, trying to pry its way through my teeth.

But, before it could, I was thrust upward where my head broke through water. Unsure of how long I'd be there, I sucked in all the air I could in hungry gasps. Still, I was surrounded by darkness. It didn't make sense. How could I be above the water and still not see anything?

And then I was pushed on top of what felt like a jagged rock, and I knew. From my new position I was put under a sliver of light shining through a crack in the rock above. My eyes adjusted to my surroundings, which was really nothing more than rock. I was in a cave no bigger than my bedroom, with only a thin lip of rock to sit on, a crack too small and high to climb through, and an exit too deep to swim out of.

I was trapped, with literally no way out.

There was a splash and the green-haired merman and purple-haired mermaid were suddenly on either side of me. The merman brought his head dangerously close to mine, filling my nostrils with his fish stink. "Don't even think about escaping," he growled. "Not that you could."

I tried to scoot away but my back was met with stone. "So what happens next?"

"You wait."

"For what?"

He smiled, his teeth gleaming as brightly as the sharks teeth around his neck. "For Bastin, little

~ ☾ ~

sandpiper. That is, unless he decides you're not worth the trouble."

The mermaid giggled, a sound that raised the hairs on the back of my arm.

"For your sake"—the merman jabbed a sharp claw-like nail into my chest—"you better hope he comes. Your only value to me is as a bargaining tool. If Bastin doesn't make the trade, then you have no use." He grin widened, implying everything that he left unsaid.

"What do you want from him?" I asked, unable to hide the tremor in my voice.

He groaned and leaned forward to look at the mermaid. "I told you they were stupid creatures. The earth will only benefit from their extermination."

She giggled harder.

He turned his attention back to me. "Bastin has a rock, and I want it."

"A rock?" As soon as the words left my tongue, I knew. They wanted the nicite—the stone that purified the water for Bastin's people and could also bury the land underwater. It felt as if thousands of ice shards flooded my veins, ripping through me as they froze my blood. "There's no way he's going to give it to you," I whispered, hoping I was right.

His hand was around my neck in an instant, his fingers choking the gasp that would have escaped my throat. "You better hope, human, that you are wrong. Because without that stone you are worthless. Another disease-carrying parasite infecting the earth. A disease I intend to cure."

I pulled on his fingers with my hands, loosening his grip enough to say, "You want to drown the earth."

He cocked his head. "So maybe the sandpiper does know a thing or two."

He released me by shoving me back against the cave wall. The back of my head smacked the rock hard enough that spots of white flashed before my eyes. He spoke to the mermaid, "Come. We'll deliver the message to the prince's guard."

"How will they know we have her and aren't lying?" she asked.

The merman hesitated, considering. Slowly, the edges of his lips curled into a grin that twisted my stomach. "I guess we'll have to bring them proof."

~ ☾ ~

Chapter 34

I waited on the thin ledge of rock; tired, bruised, and a hunk of hair shorter.

It could have been worse, though. I hadn't been sure what to think when the merman removed a rusted knife from a braided-rope belt he wore at his waist. Despite the fact it had hurt like hell, when he began hacking into my hair I'd made it a point not to move or make a sound. I hadn't wanted him to change his mind about what to cut.

It was cold in the cave and the fact that I was wet didn't help. No matter where I scooted to, I couldn't find an inch of dry ground to sit on. So I sat, shivering, wondering what the chances were that I'd make it out of this cave alive. My only regret was not being able to see Mom one last time—not getting the chance to tell her that I loved her.

When my brother died, a piece of Mom died too. Ever since that day she'd retreated inside of her head, living in her imaginary world while she navigated the real world on autopilot. That was also when the ring twisting started. If she lost another child . . . No. I wouldn't think about that. Bastin would come for me.

After an hour, I stood and tried to walk around to bring some warmth to my muscles, but my tennis shoes had been lost during the swim to the cave and the rocks were jagged and cut into my feet. Defeated, I sat down again, and hugged my knees to my chest in the hopes of conserving body heat.

~ ☾ ~

Maybe a half-hour later—it was getting harder to keep track of time—the water gurgled and a pair of onyx eyes appeared under a tangle of purple hair. They blinked once and disappeared back under the water. The mermaid, checking to make sure I was . . . what? They knew there was no way I could escape. So the only other reason to check on me would be to make sure I wasn't . . . dead? The thought wedged a lump inside of my throat and my shivering turned violent. I had to find a way out of this.

I stood back up and carefully felt my way along the jagged wall until I stood directly under the crack. It was true what the merman said, its opening was small, but then again, so was I. Maybe if I could find a way up there I could squeeze my way through. It was a gamble—but if Bastin didn't come for me, then the mers were going to kill me—I had nothing to lose.

I ran my hands along the cave wall, inch by inch. Occasionally, my fingers ran across something squirmy and slimy, but I tried not to think about it. Finally, I discovered a small ledge. It cut into my fingers when I pulled myself up, but I grit my teeth and grunted through the pain. Balancing on my knees, I searched the wall all over again. This time, I found a purchase large enough to grip with my hand and a recess just below where I was able to wedge my foot. I was closer to the crack now, maybe eight feet away? I lifted my foot and felt along the wall, my toes finding another ledge, narrower than the others, but it was my only option. I raised myself again, fingers scrambling for something to grasp when I came across a small rock formation protruding from the wall.

Only three feet to go. And from this close, I could almost convince myself that I could fit through the crack. If I raised my arms and shimmied like a snake . . . Sure, the rock looked sharp and I'd get sliced pretty good, but that didn't matter in the long run. Only living.

~ ☾ ~

That was the only thing that mattered.

I pulled myself up another foot and searched for another ledge, rock, shelf, *anything* I could put my foot into. Stretching, almost to the point of losing my balance, I found a small recess big enough for the front half of my foot but far enough away I'd practically be doing the splits. If I could maneuver it, I would be close enough to the crack to pull my way out.

I tightened my grip on the wall and reached my foot across the gap until my toe brushed the ledge. I strained to close the distance but couldn't reach. The only way to give myself the extra inch would be to loosen my grip on my hand hold—which is what I did.

My foot reached the rock, but my lack of balance kept me moving forward. I scrambled to reclaim my grip on the ledge I could no longer reach, and two of my fingernails were bent backwards as I clawed my hands into the rock, desperate to find something to cling to. But there was nothing.

I was air born. My flight of two seconds ended in an explosion of hurt. Landing on my already injured shoulder, pain shot like an electric jolt down the length of my body. At the same time my ankle throbbed a burning ache. I tried to rotate it but a breath-stealing twinge shot from it like a bottle-rocket on July Fourth. Not broken—but definitely sprained. The last of my aches came from my elbow. I touched it only to come away with warm, sticky fingers smelling faintly of copper.

Blood.

The cave was dark but my vision swam in a rainbow of color. I wondered if I hit my head on the way down. The fact that the cave was spinning around me like a Tilt-A-Whirl suggested I had.

Great. As if I didn't have enough on my plate.

Slowly, I pulled myself into a sitting position, fighting the waves of nausea that squeezed my stomach. "You're okay, Edith," I whispered. "Everything is going to be okay." I had to stay calm and not panic.

And then, quite suddenly, the pounding of my pulse inside my head began to soften into the gentle hum of a lullaby. I was calm—tired, even. So extremely tired. I leaned my head against the rock wall and fought to keep the weariness threatening to pull me inside of myself. From far away, I heard a noise, and it wasn't until after I shook my head a couple of times that the static noise buzzing between my ears softened enough to let me know I was hearing my own moans.

It was more than likely I had a concussion. I remembered from my last trip to the hospital, only two weeks ago, that the worst thing you can do is fall asleep.

So what was I going to do? I couldn't just sit here and wait to die—and yet, I had no other options.

And then the water gurgled again. The same black eyes and nest of purple hair appeared. She lifted her head above the water and sniffed. "Ugh." She made a face. "You stink. What have you been doing?"

I stank? My fuzzy brain tried to make sense of her words. It must because of my blood . . . my blood! Without realizing it, she'd given me an idea.

"If you don't stay put, human, I'll have to subdue you. Do you understand me?"

I dared not speak or risk having her detect the excitement in my voice. Instead, I nodded, praying she couldn't read the plan formulating in my head.

That seemed to satisfy her, because a moment later she'd disappeared again. I waited five minutes, counting three hundred Mississippis under my breath until I was sure she was a good distance away. I only hoped it was enough.

Carefully, I inched my way on all fours to the edge of the rocky ledge. I knew from the swim up that the drop was severe, and in my condition, I doubted I had the strength left to tread water. The room tilted back and forth around me, as if the entire cave had been placed on a teeter-totter. Bile burned the back of my throat as I fought the urge to throw up. Inch by inch I crawled along the rock, chipping the fingernails that hadn't been broken during my fall.

Almost there. One more inch.

And then my searching fingers grazed the surface of the water. I heaved myself to the edge of the rock, tearing my shirt and scraping my stomach in the process. But really, at this point, what was a little more blood?

The edge of the rock was covered in thick moss, like a slippery shag carpet. I leaned over the ledge and lowered my elbow to the water a foot below. Unable to reach, I shimmied closer to the edge, but with my vision still wavering, I overcompensated. The balance of my weight shifted against the slick surface and I slid off the ledge, headfirst into the water.

The ocean water felt like an attack of bumblebees on my head, stomach, ankle, and the hundreds of other cuts and scrapes along my body. I screamed, flooding my mouth with saltwater. I kicked forward and broke the surface, coughing and spitting. My eyes burned, blurring my vision. Blindly, I held my arms in front of me to prevent any more head and rock collisions, feeling along the wall for an exit.

But there was a problem.

The lip of the rock I'd been perched on was a foot overhead at an angle too steep to climb. I held on with my hands, my legs pin-wheeling for traction but only managing to look like a cartoon character running in place.

"Shit!" My scream bounced off the cave walls, echoing around me.

So where was Sir's voice *now*? Was our connection so severed that even the imaginary version of him inside my head abandoned me? Or was it something else?

~ ☾ ~

Maybe, instead of Sir trying to push me away all these years—I'd succeeded in shutting him out?

Despite the frigid water I shivered in, a warmth spread through me. Earlier, when he'd challenged me to a stare down, I hadn't looked away. And I hadn't cried when he'd sent me for my bag.

Bastin had been right in having me wrestle that alligator. I was no longer afraid.

I almost laughed out loud. A decorated war veteran had spent the last fifteen years trying to destroy me . . . and had failed. He was nothing more but an angry, pathetic old man. I'd held shut the snapping jaws of a gator who'd wanted to eat me. Sir had nothing on that gator. And he had nothing on me anymore. The thought brought a smile to my lips, despite my current situation. Edith Small could not be so easily crushed.

There was a tiny splash behind me, but before I could turn around, a fist wound into what was left of hair and yanked me underwater. Edith Small may not be easily crushed—but she could be drowned. The scream I'd started became nothing but a stream of bubbles until I was released and resurfaced with a gasp.

The purple-haired mermaid was inches from my face. She hissed. "What do you think you're doing?" Rather than let me answer, she pulled me back underwater. Luckily, my scalp was too numb to feel the handfuls of hair being yanked about.

My instinct was to fight, which I did, briefly. But I was too dizzy to keep it up for long. Too tired. Too numb. On land, I couldn't fight someone with the strength of a shark, let alone in the water. Battling the gator had been more than using brute strength. Bastin had also shown me how to use my brain by clamping its jaw shut—using its weakness against it. Time for brains, not brawn. Signaling defeat, I went limp in her hands and was rewarded with a yank to the surface.

"I know what you were trying to do," she growled.

~ ☾ ~

Several large blue scales were stuck between her teeth. “But it won’t work. He’s too far away. The only things you’ll successfully call are the sharks.” She released her grip from my head and shoved me hard against the side wall. “And they can have you.” She paused, tilting her head. “On second thought . . .”

A crude ivory colored knife appeared from the water. It looked to have been made carved from a bone of some sort.

“You might actually have a good idea. Only, if Bastin is going to smell you, we’re going to need more blood. Possibly all of it.”

She was beside me in a heartbeat, a clammy hand pressed against my throat. “If you don’t struggle, this will be fast.” Her lips twisted into a sneer. “But if you fight me, I can promise the pain that will follow will have you begging for death.”

What did I do? What *could* I do? Struggling was pointless. I was trapped and, considering my beaten state, in no condition to fight back.

The blade bit into my neck, pulling a whimper from my throat. Despite the cool water, I could feel the first trickles of warm blood as it trailed down my neck.

~ ☾ ~

Chapter 35

"I hope you do attract a shark," the mermaid said. "That would be one less filthy human body stinking up our ocean."

The knife was jagged, tearing as it cut. It was funny. Before, I'd been so ready to embrace death. Eager to move on from this world of pain.

Desperate to see my brother again . . . to find out if he forgave me.

But now, with the end only moments away, I couldn't help but feel the loss of it all. There were things I'd never get to do—places I'd never get to travel.

"Goodbye, human," she whispered. She forced the knife deeper, and despite my best effort, I screamed. It hurt too badly not to. Like a thousand needles digging into my skin at once.

I heard a splash followed by a sharp intake of breath. "Desmar, stop!" a voice ordered—a voice I never thought I'd hear again. My lip trembled; it was too much to hope for. I wanted to look but instead squeezed my eyes shut, too afraid that the voice I imagined had been a hallucination from my head injury.

The knife stopped biting into my flesh and I said a silent prayer of thanks.

"Let her go, Desmar, and I might not prolong your death."

Oh dear, God, I prayed. *Let him be real.* Slowly, I opened my eyes.

Bastin's head bobbed several feet away. In the dark

room, I could still read the fear in his tightly pressed mouth.

Even with blood trickling down my neck, I breathed a sigh of relief. If I had to die, at least I got to see him one last time.

Desmar smirked. "Not a chance, Bastin. You may be a prince, but *I* hold the girl. That means *I* give the orders."

The green-haired merman popped out of the water next to me and thrust his arm around me possessively. "We've been waiting for you, Bastin. I hope you're prepared to trade."

Bastin's jaw flexed. "You want the nicite, then?"

The merman snorted. "Of course, the nicite! Hand it over or your human dies."

Bastin looked at me. "If I give you the stone, she'll die anyway. You plan to flood the land, do you not?"

Desmar laughed. "Absolutely. But you're a merman, Bastin. Just give her your blood and keep her with you."

His blood! So, that's how they kept humans alive underwater. My mind wandered to the Japanese folktale. How much more of the tale was true?

Bastin's body shook in angry waves that formed ripples the water and licked the blood from my neck. "You know that the humans you keep are in misery, Granton. It's torture."

The merman shrugged. "It's your human. It matters little to me the method of her death. Just know that if you don't give us the stone, we'll choose for you."

As if excited by the idea, Desmar dug the knife deeper into my neck, renewing the stream of blood that had nearly trickled out.

I whimpered as white spots flashed in front of my eyes.

"No!" Bastin started to swim for me but stopped when Granton pushed me behind him.

"Do we have a deal?" Granton asked.

Bastin glared at him, the tendons in his jaw flexing as

he spoke through clenched teeth. “I will give you the stone. But I will need time. I have hidden it on land.”

“Land?” Desmar cried, dropping the knife from my throat. “How can you be so careless?”

I brought my hands to my neck, surprised at how quickly the blood seeped through my fingers.

“Not careless,” Bastin replied. “You hate the land. So I knew it was safe.”

“Go then.” Granton grabbed my bicep hard enough to bruise and yanked me to his side. “We’ll watch your pet for you until you get back.”

He shook his head. “I won’t go without Edith.”

Granton sneered. “Nice try, but the girl stays with us.”

“I cannot retrieve the stone without Edith.” Bastin looked at me for a long time without saying anything. Something flashed across his eyes. Regret? But it was gone as quickly as it came. “The stone is in her house.”

The mers looked at me, but I could only blink. In my house? Bastin had to be lying. Telling them the stone was in my house so they’d let me go. After all, Bastin had only been inside my room long enough to put me in bed. The only way the stone would be at my house is if I had . . . *oh, God.*

I wasn’t sure if it was my revelation or the amount of blood I’d lost, but tremors shook my body. Bastin had told me he’d given me a gift—but he hadn’t. He’d been looking for a hiding place.

He’d lied.

A cold numbness settled across my chest and grew outward. I wasn’t sure if it was from blood loss or the realization that Bastin hadn’t been honest with me. And if he’d lied about the stone, what other things had he lied about?

My mind flooded with more questions, none of which I could deal with at the moment. The only thing that mattered was the fact that the nicite—the key to destroying the world as I knew it—was tied around my ankle between my aunt's pearls.

"Edith . . ." Bastin reached a hand for me but Granton pushed me further away, which was almost a good thing because I didn't know how I would react to Bastin's touch.

"You lied," I whispered.

His eyes locked on mine, pleading. "Yes. But things changed. I never lied about the way I felt about you."

Desmar snorted. "You trusted the *human* with the nicite?"

"No," I answered. "He didn't trust me at all." Hot tears fell from my cheeks where they were swallowed by the ocean. "How can I believe you, Bastin? All those times that you visited me . . . how do I know you weren't just checking on your precious stone?"

"At first, I was. But things changed, Edith. You have to believe me." He brought a fist against the water with enough force that Granton was pelted with droplets from the splash.

Desmar's high-pitched laugh rattled the inside of my head. "If you were smart, human, you wouldn't believe a word he says." She turned away from me and looked at Bastin. "It's good to know that you haven't gone as soft as the rumors say, Bastin. The tribes will be happy to know the only reason you were fooling around with the human was to suit your own purposes. I see you inherited your father's ruthlessness. Maybe we won't have to kill your tribe, after all."

"Edith." Bastin's voice echoed around the cave, surrounding me from every angle.

Had *everything* been a lie? Every word? Every touch? My head fell against my chest and, if it weren't for Granton's grip on my arm, I would have sunk under the weight of my grief.

"Please. I'm sorry for betraying you. But I need you to come with me so I can get the stone."

Bastin's pleading pulled at my heart enough that I

looked at him. Even though his eyes were black, I was able to read the desperation written on them.

Granton grunted and tightened his grip on my arm.

"Or," Bastin said quickly, "Edith can go alone. You can keep me as your prisoner until she returns."

"Agreed." Granton released his hold on me.

I sank for a moment before treading my way back to the surface. But I wouldn't be able to float forever. Even now, my muscles screamed for me to stop.

Bastin swam to me and wrapped his arms around my waist. I wanted so badly to relax my head in the curve of his shoulder and let him carry me into the waves. But this was not the Bastin who said he loved me. This was a stranger, someone who'd used me from day one.

As if reading my thoughts, he spun me around, forcing me to look at him. "Edith, you have to believe me when I say that I love you. I admit, my initial interest in you was selfish. I *was* only looking for a place to keep my stone safe. I didn't plan on falling in love—but it happened. You captured me, Edith. I would die before hurting you."

I bit down on my lip, forcing myself to look away from his eyes before they sucked me in. I didn't know what to believe anymore. I had no way of knowing if he really meant what he said, or if he was just trying to get his stone back.

And I wasn't about to give it to him.

"The stone isn't at my house," I told him.

Desmar hissed and Granton went rigid in the water. "What is this, Human?" he growled.

"Are you deaf?" It took most of my strength, but I managed to tilt my chin and glare at them. My heart was broken and my body was torn and bleeding. Desmar's last cut went deep and the blood still flowed. Every second I grew colder. If I wasn't going to leave this cave alive—what power did they hold? "I *said,* the nicite isn't at my house."

~ ☾ ~

"Stupid, Bastin!" Desmar shrieked, pounding her fists against the water. "I can't believe you trusted a human with something as precious as nicite. I'll kill her now just for the pleasure of hearing her screams."

Bastin moved in front of me, his arms spread. Even in my battered state, as his back pressed against me, my body reacted to his nearness—wanting to pull him closer. Disgusted with myself, I tried to shove him away. "I have the nicite. It's here with me."

The mers froze and the cave went quiet. The only sound was from the droplets of water falling from the ceiling.

Slowly, Bastin turned to face me. "Please tell me you're not serious."

"Yes."

Granton and Desmar said nothing, their chests still, as if they were afraid to breathe.

Bastin's voice held an edge of fear. "No, Edith. Tell me you have it in your pocket. Tell me it's not touching your skin." He gripped my shoulders, almost painfully, and gave me a slight shake. "*Tell me!*"

He was scaring me. I didn't understand what difference it made where I kept the stone and why it should make him so upset. Afraid to answer him, I reached underwater and, with the last bit of energy I could gather, snapped the cord from my ankle. I brought my hand out of the water and slid the green stone off the twine, ignoring the pearls as they fell and sank into the dark water. My gut twisted into a knot of regret as I lost the remaining link to my Aunt Margie. But I had more important things to deal with.

To my surprise, Bastin dropped his hands from my shoulders and backed away. "No. This can't be happening. No. No. No."

Desmar looked just as horrified. "You've been wearing it next to your skin? You have no idea what you've done, do you?"

~ ☾ ~

I glanced at Bastin who was still shaking his head. "I don't understand."

Granton hissed before answering. "The stone you hold in your hand is highly concentrated calcium carbonate. More powerful than anything your kind possess on land. By wearing it next to your skin, you've exposed your body to deadly levels of calcium carbonate."

"Stupid Human," Desmar growled. "Not only have you poisoned yourself, but you've drained our nicite."

First the beating, then the stabbing, and now this? "Bastin?"

He stopped shaking his head and looked at me.

"What do I do?"

He said nothing, he didn't have to. The grief written on his face told me what I needed to know.

There was nothing I could do. But that was okay. It made what I had to do next that much easier. "I'm dying," I said, just to hear the words out loud.

"Damn it, Edith!" Bastin punched the water and sprayed the room in a mist of droplets. "The nicite craves water. Didn't you notice anything unusual?"

Ah. So that explained all the leaky faucets and faulty plumbing. The nicite had been calling to the water.

When I nodded, Bastin turned away, holding a single fist above his head. "This is all my fault." When he turned back around his shoulders shook, either from rage or grief—I couldn't be sure. He continued talking, spitting his words through his clenched teeth. "If only I'd left you alone—or told you about the dangers of keeping the stone close . . . I just never thought you'd *wear* it." His head bowed.

With Bastin distracted, Granton swam toward me. "Maybe your skin didn't absorb it all. There might be some calcium carbonate left." His eyes locked on the stone in my hand. "Enough to flood half your land."

Desmar stopped growling and snapped to attention.

~ ☾ ~

"Yesss," she hissed. "Give us the stone, human."

An inky darkness seeped into the corners of my vision. Whether it was from the blood loss or the poisoning finally taking effect, I couldn't be sure. The only thing I knew for certain was time was running out.

Granton was an arm's length away. He licked his lips.

Slowly, I stretched my hand toward him. I knew if I gave it to them, millions of people would be killed. On one hand, I wouldn't be around to see them die. On the other, I knew I wouldn't be able to rest in peace if I allowed that to happen. There were people—good people like Morgan and my mother—who were worth saving. I wouldn't be selfish. And, besides, I was already dead.

Granton reached for the stone. Such a pretty rock. Even in the dark I could see the flecks of gold glittering under its green surface. It was amazing how something so beautiful could bring about such suffering. Ironic, even. Bastin was just as pretty as the nicite and every bit as dangerous.

Granton's fingers hovered above the stone.

I smiled. He was going to be pissed.

Before he could react, I closed my fist on the rock and brought it to my mouth. I made sure to give the shocked mers my best "Screw you" grin before placing the stone on my tongue and swallowing it whole.

"NO!"

Their screams surrounded me, bouncing off the stone walls and mixing together, until the words were mangled and all that remained was a garbled roar of frustrated rage.

And then there was splashing. And more screaming. But I hardly noticed. I was already falling inside myself . . . or maybe it was outside. Dying was confusing like that. I could hear the fight as it raged around me. I even thought I heard Luna join in, but at the same time, I was someplace else. As I floated along in a river of black velvet, I couldn't help but take some comfort in the fact that Luna had found us. She'd keep Bastin safe. Death had a way of putting things in perspective like that. Because, despite everything that had happened, I loved Bastin.

And I told him so before I floated away, touching the stars with my fingertips along the way.

~ ☾ ~

Chapter 36

There wasn't a whole lot I could remember about William. I'd only been four when he died. And Sir had tried so hard to make us forget. I guess that's what a person does when they kill someone—pretend they never existed in the first place.

What Sir didn't know was that Mom kept a secret photo album stashed away under the china cabinet between a tarnished serving tray and a ceramic gravy boat hand-painted with purple violets. That in itself would be enough to keep Sir away, but Mom had wrapped the scrapbook inside a rose-colored pillowcase as an extra security measure.

Occasionally, while Sir worked and Mom ran errands, I'd pull the album out and thumb through the pictures. Even though I've seen the images a hundred times, I'm still surprised by how much the little boy with the mess of curly brown hair—the same mocha color as my own—was a stranger to me.

I'd learned by reading books about death that people can repress memories of traumatic events. I did the opposite—I could only remember the tragedy. The pictures of us waving sparklers on a Fourth of July afternoon, swimming in a kiddie pool, and, stranger still, sitting together on Sir's lap with a picture book held between us, felt feel as familiar to me as looking through a Sears catalog. Happy faces without the stories to inspire the smiles.

The memory I've kept, however, had been burned into the grey unconsciousness that existed before the sun would pull me from sleep into sweat-soaked sheets.

William, chubby and tan, his shorts sagging slightly under the weight of a diaper that needed changing, smiled at me from the opposite side of the driveway. He'd just arrived around the corner of the house and hadn't seen Sir climb inside his truck. In truth, we were forbidden to play in the front yard, but our game of chase had grown so intense I'd forgotten the rules.

William's cherry lips opened and he spoke to me, but the years have erased the words from my memory. He squealed happily as he darted onto the driveway, throwing his arms wide.

I should have moved, should have screamed, should have done *something*. And because I hadn't, Sir blamed me for the death of his only son.

I'd relived that moment in my mind every day when I covered myself in black. Only sometimes I cheated and tried to spare myself the pain I deserved. Sometimes I changed the ending to the story. And in that fantasy, there was no muscle-tightening paralysis of fear keeping me rooted where I stood. In that fantasy I scream, I run, I scoop William up and we continue our games in the backyard. In my dream, there is no baby boy, lifeless on the concrete with a fistful of dandelions scattered inches from his outstretched fingers.

Years later, I'd learn that on this particular morning Sir had been late for work. He hadn't bothered to check his rearview mirror.

~ ☾ ~

Chapter 37

My first thought upon opening my eyes was that I'd gone back in time. Back to the moment when I'd woken up on the shore after the boating accident. The black eyes that stared down at me reinforced the feeling. Maybe instead of having my life flash before my eyes I was being given the opportunity to relive it. The question was, would I do anything differently?

"Edith, thank God." Bastin exhaled loudly and bent over me, placing cool lips on my forehead.

I frowned. That wasn't right. That wasn't how our first meeting went. Where was Luna? Where was the ache in my shoulder? After blinking the grit and sand from my eyes, I glanced at my shoulder. There was no collarbone glittering in the moonlight. But there was a brand new shiny pink scar. My frown deepened. That couldn't be right, either. Did people have scars in heaven?

I pushed myself into a sitting position, surprised at how easy it was. Shouldn't something hurt? Or maybe death had taken the pain.

Bastin's hands slid around my shoulders. "Easy. Take it slow."

I fell into his eyes all over again. "Are you dead, too? Not that I'm complaining. It wouldn't be heaven without you."

He looked startled. "What?"

The night sky behind him was filled with an endless scattering of stars. But, somehow, Bastin was still brighter, more beautiful. “Where’s my brother?” I asked. “Shouldn’t he be here? I mean, I thought your loved ones came to get you when you died. I need to tell him something.”

Something passed through his eyes—a sadness I’d never seen before. He swallowed several times before answering. “Edith, you’re not dead.”

I frowned at him. That was impossible. Not only had my throat been slit, but I’d swallowed the nicite. I’d died. I’d felt myself slip away from my body. “No. I’m dead. How else do you explain my scar?” I gestured toward the pink line on my shoulder. “It had barely scabbed over before our trip to Disney, and now look at it. It looks like it’s years old.”

“You’re not dead,” he repeated.

I touched my neck, but there was no sign I’d been cut. “But I’m not hurt. What happened? Did you take me underwater with you?”

The sadness returned. “No, Edith. I swore to you I would never do that, and I meant it.”

I rotated my ankle and discovered no sign of the sprain from my fall. There was no way my shoulder, neck, and ankle could have healed in under a day. I ran every type of scenario through my mind, and still, what had happened to me was impossible . . .

Oh God, no.

Suddenly, the memory of Morgan sitting in my back yard with her folded sheet of paper was fresh in my mind.

“The point is, after the girl eats the mermaid, she goes on to live a long healthy life.”

Her words echoed inside of my head, turning my blood to ice. Bastin wouldn’t—he couldn’t.

As if reading my thoughts, his hands slipped from my shoulders. “Edith, I—”

“No!” I screamed. I scuttled away from him, needing the distance, trying to think.

~ ☾ ~

"I'm so sorry," he said. "There was no other way."

"That's a lie." My hands curled into fists. "There was another way. You could have let me die, Bastin."

"How could I do that, Edith?" Bastin's voice cracked with grief. "I held you in my arms, watching you slip away . . . I couldn't let you go."

"Don't you get it?" I pounded the sand with my fists. "That wasn't your choice to make. It was mine! I swallowed the nicite knowing I was infected, knowing I was going to die. I wanted to die, Bastin. If it meant saving the earth and saving you . . ." I choked on my words as I struggled to keep from crying.

He touched my shoulder but I shook his hand off. Bastin brought it to his chest like he'd been burned. "But I did what I did to save you. How is that different?"

I glared at him, shaking with anger. "Because you're leaving out one very big detail, Bastin. What did you do to me?"

He looked away. Tears streamed down his cheeks, glittering like diamonds in the moonlight. Finally, he whispered, "You're right. It was a selfish thing to do. I just hope," he paused to suck in a breath, "you can someday forgive me."

"What did you *do*?" I screamed, not caring if someone heard me.

His body tensed, and I wondered if he might try and make a run for the sea, rather than tell me. But instead, he looked at me. "I gave you my blood."

I hugged my knees to my chest, scared to hear what would come next, but at the same time, desperate to know. "And what did that do?"

"It healed you." He blinked. "It's another one of our secrets. Like how fish oil is good for the human heart, mer blood can heal every human ailment. It's one of the reasons we were once hunted to the brink of extinction by your kind. It's also why we keep our existence a secret now."

~ ☾ ~

I waited for him to continue but he didn't, which only angered me more. If Morgan hadn't told me the story—would Bastin have left out the most crucial side-effect? "But there's something you're not telling me. Mer blood does something else to humans, doesn't it?"

He jerked his head up, surprised, and quickly looked away. If I hadn't already known, would he really not have told me? Just left me to live my life, wondering why I wasn't aging the same way as the people around me? "You extended my life, didn't you?"

He nodded but didn't say anything.

"For how long, Bastin?"

He shrugged. "I'm not sure. The average human slave lives roughly five hundred years. But I only gave you a few drops, so . . . hopefully your life has only been extended three hundred years or so."

My lungs filled with lead and I couldn't breathe. I was drowning in fear.

"Edith." Bastin moved to my side and held out a tentative hand, afraid it seemed, for the first time, to touch me. "I am so sorry."

I couldn't answer him. What do you say to someone you love but who has also cursed you? The time for words was gone. What was done was done and there was no going back. Burying my head into my knees, I broke into sobs. I wasn't sure how long I'd cried, but at one point when my tears had run out but the pain lingered on, Bastin pulled me into his arms. Only, for the first time since meeting him, I felt completely alone.

Finally, when the sobs stopped pouring from my throat, I asked, "If you knew we could never be together, what did it matter if I lived or died?"

He was quite for a moment before answering, "Because I could not live in a world without you in it."

I tilted my head to look at him, to fall one last time into his endless eyes. "And how long is that? What is your average lifespan?"

~ ☾ ~

He swallowed. "About eighty years."

I nodded as if this was to be expected. Of course, Bastin would live to eighty while I would continue on for another two hundred or so years. "Can I end this?"

He shook his head. "If you can, I don't know how. The tribes that keep humans as slaves can be pretty cruel—and still the humans live on."

I didn't ask him to explain because I didn't want to know.

I leaned my head against his chest and whispered into his neck. "I'm cursed."

"*We're* cursed," he corrected. "Each second of each day that goes by without you, Edith, will be torture. But I look forward to my suffering, I will embrace it. I deserve it for what I've done for you. And I promise you something else—I will search for a way to fix this. If there is a remedy for the effects of mermaid blood, I vow I'll find it for you."

"Where does that leave us now?" I asked.

His jaw tightened, and I knew before he said anything that he had more bad news. "What is it, Bastin?"

He cupped my face in his hands, staring at me so intently I wanted to flinch. "I need you to run, Edith. You must go to the mountains, where you will be safe. My kind cannot survive high elevations. The thinner levels of oxygen make it difficult to breathe—even with water. There will be others looking for you. You need to go where other mers won't find you. Even though you live, nicite remains inside of you. Your blood makes you a walking weapon against your own kind."

A walking weapon? It was as if his words had become a tangible force the moment they left his mouth. A fist that repeatedly slammed into my stomach. There was no way to recover. When I could finally talk, several moments later, I asked, "What does that even mean?"

He sighed. "There are mer tribes that will seek you out for the same reason we were attacked today—for the nicite. Only now, it's your blood they would use to flood the earth. You could destroy the world."

There was nowhere for me to go. I wasn't safe in the ocean. I wasn't safe on land. I wanted to curl inside of myself and die—only, now, that wouldn't happen for a very *very* long time. "I can't handle this, Bastin. How could you think I'd be able to?"

He leaned forward and brushed his lips against mine. "Because you are stronger than you think, Edith."

I pulled away from him, and as his fingers fell from my back, I was aware that was the last time I would ever feel them on my skin. "What am I supposed to do? Sir plans to send me to a military school."

Bastin shook his head, silver hair spilling over his shoulders. "No, Edith. You can't allow that to happen. Run if you have to. You're not safe here. You will never be safe by the water again." He turned to the sky. "I hear the mountains are beautiful. You'll be safe there."

I'd experienced a lifetime of hurt and betrayal in a single day. The result had ripped out my heart, stomped on it, and shoved it back inside my chest bleeding and broken. Carefully, I stood. "I guess this is goodbye?"

He nodded. "It will be safer for you if you never see me again."

I didn't know what to say. I loved him. I should have started there. Then, I should have told him that despite everything he'd done to me, despite the lies, the poisoning, and his blood, that I always would. But I didn't say those things. Instead, I turned and walked away. Behind me I heard a splash.

~ ☾ ~

Chapter 38

I walked the path to my house. I couldn't really call it home. When you broke it down, it was nothing more than a wooden frame, vinyl siding, and a room. Love made a house a home, love and family. Neither of those things waited for me.

As I maneuvered through the trees in the dark, I couldn't help but wonder how mad Sir was. Bastin had warned me to run away, but that was impossible. I had no money, no food, and I wasn't even wearing shoes My best bet was to face Sir and accept my punishment. I'd go to military school, then probably attend a military university. And after that? I'd serve my country as a member of the armed forces. As far as I could see, there was no way to break free. It was the beginning of the end.

I paused, just for a moment, enjoying the warm night air as it lifted my hair across my face. This was my last my last moment of freedom, and no matter how much I wanted it to, I couldn't make it last forever. But I could take my time. I had no doubt Sir would be waiting for me when I returned. So I walked, my footsteps getting heavier with each passing step. As if it wasn't underbrush I was pushing through but a marshy swamp thick with sludge.

When I arrived into the clearing of my backyard, every light in the house blazed. I didn't pause. Straightening my shoulders and lifting my chin, I marched forward. I wouldn't cower, or worse, cry. I had spent the day getting ripped apart and put back together, having everything taken from me, including my heart. There was nothing Sir could do to hurt me now. I'd tangled with the gator. Now it was time to tangle with Sir.

My bedroom door slid open before I had a chance to grasp the handle. Sir's eyes blazed, the veins within so enlarged, his eyes held a reddish tint. I heard a crunching sound and it took me a moment to realize it was his teeth being ground together. "Where the hell have you been?" His voice was low, and dangerous.

Despite the overwhelming urge to shrink under his gaze, I took a step forward. "Out." I answered, finding that I no longer cared how pissed off I made him. In fact, I almost took pleasure at the sight of the scarlet that flushed his face.

"Have you forgotten who you are talking to?"

"No." I crossed my arms over my chest. "But you have. Let me remind you—you're my *father*."

His mouth dropped. Never in the thirteen years after William's death had I been allowed to call him anything but Sir. The title felt like his way of distancing us—but I was done with it. I was done with everything.

"Yes," he stammered. "Well, with that title comes a certain level of respect. Obedience. None of which you've shown me as of late."

"That's bullshit. *'Father'* is not a title. It's a duty. And with *that* comes a certain obligation and understanding. None of which you've *ever* shown me."

His eyes looked dangerously close to popping out. "Excuse me?"

I shook my head. "No. There is no excuse. Not for the way you've treated me for the last thirteen years—since William died."

He paled and took a step back.

I took another step forward. "And, it would seem, my father died that day, too. Replaced by this"—I gestured to him—"this drill sergeant. I'm not one of your troops, *sir*. I'm a teenage girl who's spent the last thirteen years trying to live up to your unobtainable standards, trying to gain your approval, trying to win your *love*." I spit out the last word as if it left a bad taste on my tongue. "And what did all that trying get me? That." I pointed to the suitcase of my bed. "So, fuck it all, I just can't do it anymore."

I climbed the steps into my pink room and stood before him clenching my fists. I was dizzy from the release of words I'd kept bottled inside. I was so angry, but so elated. I wasn't sure if I wanted to laugh out loud or cuss at him some more. It no longer mattered that I was going to military school. Sir knew how I felt, he knew I thought he was a terrible father, and with that I could make my peace.

I counted ten eye blinks before the shock melted from Sir's face and was replaced by a viper's steely gaze. "Don't you dare say his name to me."

Now it was my turn to look surprised. After everything that I'd said to him, that was the only thing that had registered? "William?" I asked.

"Yes, William." His eyes bulged from their sockets. "You have no right to say his name. If you'd listened to me, if you'd stayed in the backyard like I directed, he'd still be alive." He grimaced in such a way that I knew he was reliving William's final moments in his mind.

It was true that William would never have been in the driveway if he hadn't been chasing me. But something else was true, too. Keeping my words calm and even, which was the complete opposite of how I felt, I said, "I wasn't the one driving the truck."

I'd expected Sir to get angry. I didn't expect the confused look on his face as he stared at me, as if seeing me for the first time. Then his shoulders slumped.

"He had your eyes," he said.

Stunned, I took a step back. That was not the

response I expected and it scared me more than if he'd yelled.

"And every day," Sir continued, "I have to see him looking at me through your eyes. Always accusing, always reminding me of what I'd done." Small tremors vibrated along his body.

I couldn't move, couldn't breathe. It was as if I'd been hit in the gut. All these years I'd assumed Sir was punishing me because for William's death. But the truth was that Sir was punishing me for his own guilt.

As if sensing my thoughts, Sir's face softened. The transformation of expression from his usual stone-eyed gaze into something almost apologetic was terrifying to watch. "Now you see why you have to go," he said. "It's because I'm weak."

So there it was. He'd more or less admitted his guilt, but at the same time, it didn't change anything between us. And while it hurt to have the finality of our relationship spoken out loud, at the same time I felt the constraints of guilt laced around my heart loosen. Sir had accepted the blame. It was all I was going to get—but it was enough.

With my suitcase in tow, I marched around him and opened my bedroom door, so ready to leave this house with its sliding glass door and tree-lined paths that lead down to a dock on the edge of a bayou. It was time to move on.

The only problem was, Mom stood in the doorway, blocking my path. Surprised, I dropped the suitcase. There was something different about her, something in her eyes, a spark of some kind. She placed her hands on her hips, her lips drawn tight.

"Carol?" Sir's question held the edge of a threat. All traces of vulnerability on his face were gone, replaced with an expression hard enough to cut through stone. "What's the meaning of this?"

Her mouth twitched and she brought her hands

together, as if she might reach for her wedding ring. But before she could grab it, she balled her fingers into fists and shook her head, letting out a frustrated cry.

Sir and I froze in place. For me, it had been mid-breath. We were definitely in unfamiliar territory.

"Michael, I've let you bully this family for far too long. Enough is enough. I've lost one child already because of you . . . I'm not about to lose another."

Sir's mouth opened, but the words wouldn't come. I knew how he felt. Shock jolted through my spine like an electric current. Who was this person and what had she done with my mother?

She reached out and squeezed my shoulder. "Oh, Edi-girl. I'm more sorry than you'll ever know."

Every unfair judgment I'd ever passed off on her flashed through my mind—and I took them all back. Because the woman who stood before me radiated a fierceness that prickled my skin. This woman, the one with her hands balled into fists and her jaw clenched in a determined line, was my mom. Something tight crushed my chest hard enough to spring tears to my eyes. God, I'd missed her so much.

"Carol, you know this isn't working," Sir said, but his voice wavered uncertainly. After years of dictating orders to my mom, arguing with her was definitely new territory for him. "We talked about this. We agreed it was the right thing to do."

"No, Michael." Mom released my shoulder and pushed me behind her. "We didn't talk—*you* talked. And I listened, quiet, like I always did. But I won't be quiet anymore."

Holy hell in a hand-basket. I had to swallow my heart, which had leapt to the back of my throat.

Mom continued. "Edith is right. There is no excuse for the way you've ordered us all around, treating us like your troops instead of your family. For Christ's sake, Michael, this is your daughter standing here with a

~ ☾ ~

suitcase in her hands because you can't come to terms with your own guilt. That's not Edith's problem—it's *yours*. And I won't let you send her to a military academy because of it. I'm not about to let her become you."

Sir did something else I'd never seen him do before this moment—he flinched. "So what do you propose we do, Carol? You can't ignore the fact that Edith has been lying, skipping school, and sneaking out of the house. Who knows what she's been doing with her little freak friend. Drinking? Drugs? Do you really want to sit back and do nothing?"

"No." She looked over her shoulder and locked eyes with me, studying, as if she was really seeing me for the first time. "You're right about one thing—Edith has been acting out. But I hardly think it's all her fault. I've realized something recently . . ." She sighed and shifted her gaze to Sir. "You two are not good for each other. That's why I called my sister."

Aunt Margie? My breath caught in my throat at the mention of her name. And, while I loved her and missed her, I didn't understand how she could help the situation.

Mom turned to me and squeezed me tight, filling my nose with her English rose perfume. "I told Aunt Margie everything, Edi-girl. She wants you to come and stay with her until *your father* and I sort things out."

My head spun in a cloud of roses and sea salt. In a matter of minutes my life had changed course again.

Mom smoothed the hair along my face and tucked it behind my ears like she had ever since I was little. "You're going to love staying with Aunt Margie. I know she's older and a bit . . . *unique*, but I think she can give you the attention you've been craving. Besides," she stuck a finger under my chin and tilted my head to meet her gaze, "you haven't done well here. You seem paler. I don't think the ocean is good for you, Edi. I think the

~ ☾ ~

mountain air is exactly what you need."

"Mountains?" My knees buckled and I leaned against Mom for support. In all of the chaos, I'd completely forgotten that Aunt Margie lived in The Smokies. Way up high.

She smiled. "In Gatlinburg."

I nodded, too stunned to talk. So far, in the course of twenty-four hours, I'd been stabbed, poisoned, almost died, cursed, lost the love of my life, narrowly avoided military school, and now was on my way to Tennessee.

"This is ridiculous." Sir threw his hands in the air. "Your sister has no experience with children—let alone delinquents. Not to mention, I think she's not right in the head. What makes you think she can handle Edith?"

Mom smiled. "Because, Michael, she's not *you*."

~ ☾ ~

Chapter 39

I stepped off the bus at the Gatlinburg station. Mom was right about one thing—the air *was* different here. It smelled wet, but nothing like the ocean. The scent was a mixture of leaves, dew, and the damp underside of a rock.

I weaved my way through the crowd of people swarming the sidewalks of an outdoor mall. Not realizing what a tourist attraction Gatlinburg was, I was initially surprised to see so many people. I wondered how I would ever find Aunt Margie in the crowd of sticky-fingered kids, bikers, and senior citizens wearing socks with their sandals.

My memories of Aunt Margie were faded—like a newspaper left out in the sun. I remembered her warm smile, and I remembered her sweetness. But what if she picked me up and things weren't the same between us as they'd been when I was little? What if Sir's accusations had preceded my arrival and Aunt Margie thought I was some out of control party girl who she had to keep locked in a cellar? I clutched my suitcase tighter to my body. *Stop imaging the worst, Edith,* I mentally scolded myself. Coming here was a good thing. Anywhere was better than military school. And if I couldn't be with Bastin, at least I could be with someone who loved me and let me know it.

And then I saw her. I recognized her immediately, not from any mental recollection, but by her eyes. They held the same bright fire that burned in Mom's eyes when she told Sir I wasn't going to military school. Her hair was pulled back into a braid, but that didn't stop the wiry strands from escaping and haloing around her head, making her look like the patron saint of static electricity.

"Edith!" She shouted, waving her arms wildly, and apparently, not caring who she swatted in the process. Despite the annoyed glances of passersby and despite the fact I was looking right at her, she didn't stop shouting. "It's me, your Aunt Margie!"

She wore a flannel shirt with the sleeves rolled up to her elbows and a pair of rubber muck boots coated in mud. I hadn't known what to expect—but this certainly wasn't it.

I approached her slowly, afraid of what would happen if I made any sudden movements.

"Oh, sweetie. I'm so happy you're here," she said, causing me to gasp when she pulled me into a rib-cracking embrace. She held me tight for a few moments, then released me and held me at arm's length, warmth and love suffusing her face.

My heart clenched—she was looking at me the way Bastin had looked at me the last moment we were together, but without the sadness he'd held in his eyes.

She gave me a friendly shake, then said, "Well, let's get on with it, shall we?"

I allowed her to guide me into a full parking lot, where we stopped in front of a rusted-out pickup truck. She pointed to the bed. "Just throw your bag back there."

I did what I was told. After several good yanks on the handle, the passenger door finally opened with a squeal. Despite the obvious cosmetic issues, the truck's engine roared to life on the first turn of the key.

The drive up the mountain was beautiful and I didn't want to be distracted from the view. It was just like Bastin had said—magical. Having left the ocean for the mountains, it'd felt like I'd been transported to a different planet. Especially since I knew this was a world Bastin could never be a part of. It made his absence more real. Tonight would be the first night since I'd met Bastin that I wouldn't hear the familiar tapping on my door.

And that was when it hit me. There would be no more talking by the dock, no more kisses in the ocean, and no more nights spent in his arms. My heart ached and a heaviness inside my chest threatened to sink me down into the ripped cushion on which I sat.

It was then I was glad Aunt Margie had the radio so loud. With her music blaring and her attention on the road, she couldn't hear me cry.

~ ☾ ~

Chapter 40

We drove away from the tourist areas with their outdoor malls, kettle corn stands, crowds, and indoor skydiving. We sped up the highway until the cars became fewer and tunnels made of evergreen and oak tree branches towered over the road, making the day go dark. Again, I was struck by the difference between here and Valparaiso. Next to the ocean, the world from the sky to the water is bathed in blue. But here, where the trees blocked out the sky and moss covered the ground, green covered everything.

We continued to climb as the road became steeper and narrower. When the concrete gave way to gravel, I noticed a painful pressure building inside of my ears.

Right on cue, Aunt Margie pulled a stick of gum from her jeans pocket. "Here ya go. We're headed up the mountain. Elevation change will get you. If you chew on this, it will pop your ears and you'll feel loads better."

When I only stared at the gum, ripped in some places and covered with pocket lint in others, she thrust it in my face. "It won't kill you."

I swallowed past the wedge of sorrow that rose in my throat. No, it wouldn't kill me—thanks to Bastin—there wasn't anything that could. I took the fuzzy blue gum, stuck it in my mouth, and chewed. Almost immediately, both of my ears popped and the tension in my head eased.

We climbed higher and at a steeper angle until the truck groaned and trembled. Margie shifted the four-wheel-drive lever and the truck stopped shaking, but grunted unhappily. I was half wondering if we'd make it before the truck fell to pieces, but luckily, a cabin came into view.

"There she is," Aunt Margie said.

It was like a picture on a bottle of maple syrup. A small log cabin waited for us, complete with a wisp of smoke swirling from the chimney. I half-expected a witch to open the door to try and convince us the logs were actually rolled gingerbread.

There wasn't much outside; a small charcoal grill, an ax wedged into a tree stump, and a bird house on the porch made from a hollowed out gourd. Dangling from the tree branches were over two dozen wind chimes made from everything from aluminum cans to ceramic glass, all clanging and chiming together in a welcoming chorus.

"Welcome to your new home, Edith." Margie jerked the gear into park and shut the truck off, which in turn gave one final grunt of protest. She hopped out of the cab and went to the bed to pull out my bag.

I took my time getting out. It wasn't that I didn't like Aunt Margie or her gingerbread cabin, but I knew that the moment the gravel crunched under my feet, it would make everything real. It would prove that I really was thousands of miles away from the ocean—away from Bastin.

But it wasn't like I could stay in the truck forever. I let out the breath I'd been holding, in a giant whoosh, and heaved open the door.

The mountain air enveloped me. Lighter and more crisp than heavy ocean air. I felt dizzy. Could you get high on fresh air? I took one cautious step to make sure I wouldn't fall on my face, when I heard a whimper.

Margie, who was in front of me on the path, froze. "What in the name of Tom Sawyer do you suppose that is?" She took another step forward then stopped. "Oh, dear!"

I rushed down the walk as she kneeled down to look at something. "What is it, Aunt Margie?"

She stood. "Apparently, we have another roommate. This is going to be one full cabin—but the more the merrier, I always say."

I peered around her and what I found took my breath away. A small brown puppy whined at us; a leash tied him from his collar to the cabin's doorknob. I rushed to him. When I unclasped his leash and picked him up, the little guy stopped his crying and yipped in excitement. His long tail spun like a boat propeller as he licked my face. He was the most beautiful shade of brown with a reddish hue, the same color one would find under a piece of bark freshly torn from a tree. His coat was short, yet wavy, and felt waxy when I ran my fingers through it.

I giggled as he tried chewing on my nose. At long last, I had a dog of my very own. The most perfect dog there was. It almost seemed too good to be true.

Aunt Margie came up beside me and put her hands on her hips. "I can't believe someone would dump a poor innocent puppy way out here in the mountains. There are bears out here for cripe's sake. It really does take all kinds."

I nodded. And while I had no idea how this puppy got here, I knew this was no random dump.

Aunt Margie leaned in close and squinted her eyes. "What a strange looking dog—like a Labrador, but with curly hair. Do you suppose he's a mix?"

I shook my head. Even though I'd never seen one in real life before, I knew exactly what kind of dog he was by the description Bastin had given me so many nights ago on the beach. "He's a Chesapeake Bay Retriever."

Aunt Margie looked surprised, but then nodded her head in understanding. "I forgot your Mom said you knew a lot about dogs. Well, it looks like you finally got one. Do you have any ideas on what you want to name him?"

"Tide," I answered, hugging the little guy to my chest. It seemed fitting because of all the changes I'd undergone. I snuggled Tide, nuzzling my nose into the soft fur behind his ear—that's when I noticed it. At first I thought it was my imagination, so I took another deep breath to be sure. And then there was no denying it. Emanating from Tide's coat was the faintest scent of sea salt. Something inside me stirred.

~ ☾ ~

Chapter 41

Like how pressure had build up behind my ears on the way up the mountain, pressure now built up under my skin. “Aunt Margie, can I borrow your truck?” I handed her the squirming puppy who happily licked her cheek. “I need to, uh, go buy some puppy chow for Tide.” Which was true, but I also needed to find the nearest body of water. The nicite made my bones ache with need.

“Not at all.” She laughed as she shook her head from side-to-side, trying and failing to avoid the puppy’s enthusiastic kisses. “The keys are in the ignition.”

“Thanks.” I turned away from the cabin I had yet to step foot in, and concentrated on keeping my feet from bolting into a sprint.

“Oh, and Edith?”

I froze, worried that she’d either changed her mind or she’d decided to come with me.

“Pick up a gallon of milk while you’re out, would you?”

I released the breath I’d hadn’t realized I’d been holding. “Sure thing.” I forced myself to walk the rest of the way to the truck, despite the fact my heart bounced inside of my chest like a hornet trapped in a jar.

Inside the truck, I adjusted the bench seat forward so I could reach the pedals, and started the ignition. Even though I’d had my driver’s license since I was sixteen, I felt a little out of my league with the thought of maneuvering down the winding mountain roads in a truck as big as a tank. But despite its size and age, it responded to me as if it was just as eager as I was to get where we were going.

The only problem was, I didn't know where that was.

But I had an idea.

I found a crank on the side of the door and manually rolled the window down. Now that there was no glass between me and the forest, I could feel the call to water like the strings on a marionette doll pulling me forward. Apparently, even though it flowed in my blood, the nicite still longed to be near water. I knew exactly where to go.

I drove about a quarter mile until the pull became so strong that I wondered if my bones might break free from my body. I found a small clearing with a patch of gravel that was large enough to park several cars. I pulled the truck in, turned off the ignition, and climbed out. It only took me a moment, but I located a path too wide and trodden to have been created by animals. As I walked along the trail, my suspicions that this was a human-made path were confirmed by the multitude of empty beer and liquor bottles discarded in the brush. It hurt my heart to see them there.

I sighed and pushed further until I could hear the faint rumble of thunder. But that didn't make sense. Tendrils of waning sunlight pushed through the overhead canopy of leaves in whatever cracks they could find. How could there be thunder if the sun was out? The nicite in my blood didn't wait for a response. Instead, it urged me forward until I stumbled out of the brush and into a clearing, where I discovered the source of the noise.

A ten-foot-wide creek cut through the forest floor in front of me, its water white and churning where it parted for a scattering of large boulders. I took another step and faltered. What the hell was I doing? Something inside of me continued to press me forward, and I wondered if it wasn't the water I was drawn to . . .

~ ☾ ~

"Bastin?" My voice left my throat only to be swallowed by the sound of rushing water. I pressed my palms against my chest to keep my heart from beating through my ribs.

No one answered. Disappointment burned my heart like fire-hot branding iron, followed by anger that I'd wished he were here in the first place. Bastin had lied to me, after all. But another part of me couldn't help but remember all the nights we'd spent alone on the dock pouring our hearts out to each other, and the moment he told me he loved me. And that part of me knew, deep down to the marrow of my bones, that Bastin hadn't lied about that.

My body craved water.

My heart craved Bastin.

The shadows on the forest floor grew longer, saturating the ground like spilled ink. I should leave now if I wanted to get back to the truck before night fell. I hugged my arms to my body and crouched down so I could peer one last time into the crystal blue water. The creek flowed too quickly for me to make out anything beyond the lines of color from the overhead trees reflected on the water's surface.

"I'm still angry at you, you know," I said, hoping against hope that my words would somehow be carried through the water to him. "You lied to me . . . but I guess I understand why you had to do it. You were only trying to do what was right for your people." I sighed. "And while you've basically cursed me, I have to wonder if I wouldn't have done the same thing to you if our situations were reversed. I don't know how I could have let you die, either."

I stood and dusted my hands off on my jeans, feeling a little silly that I was having an intense conversation with a creek. "Anyway, I have to go now . . . I just wanted you to know how much I miss you." I turned to leave the opening to trail that would lead me back to the truck, then threw over my shoulder, “And that I do love you.”

“I love you, too.”

I froze, too scared to move out of fear that I’d imagined the voice. Surely my mind was only playing tricks on me. Without turning around I asked, “Bastin?”

His voice answered. “Edith.”

I gasped and swiveled on my feet. He was in the middle of the creek, exposed from the waist up. Without thinking about what I was doing, I ran forward. Bastin pushed against the creek’s current until we met at the edge of the bank, an arm’s length away from each other.

Bastin eyed the ground at my feet with longing before he looked up and met my eyes. “I can’t leave the water here, Edith. The elevation is too high. I’m already weak enough just being here.” He gestured to the creek around him.

That wasn’t a problem for me. Before he could say anything else, I launched myself into his arms. He caught me around the waist so my legs were only submerged from the knees down. Even though it was spring, the water was cold enough to bite at my toes—but I didn’t care. What was a little hypothermia when you were practically invincible?

I wrapped my arms around his neck. “What are you doing here? Don’t get me wrong, I’m happy to see you, but I didn’t think we’d ever be together again.”

Bastin’s never-ending onyx eyes searched my face. “I couldn’t let you leave with things they way they were. It was eating me up inside.”

“So you swam to Tennessee and brought me a puppy?”

He smiled. “I wish I could take all the credit, but I had some help finding out where you were going and getting the puppy to your door.”

Morgan. I bet she’d found out my new address from my mom. The question of how she’d arranged to get

Tide to Aunt Margie's could wait for another day. This moment was all about Bastin. "So, what does this mean? Are you staying?"

The smile faded from Bastin's lips. "No. I wish I could but there's too much land and not enough water. If I stayed, I'd get weaker and weaker until—" He didn't finish, only gripped me tighter against him.

I suppressed a shiver and buried my head against his neck. "Will you be able to visit?"

"As much as I can."

I didn't ask how often that would be—I didn't want to know. For the first time in my life, I couldn't work up the energy to worry about what might happen or what was to come. All I cared about was living in this moment with Bastin's arms around my waist and our hearts pressed together, echoing each others' beat.

And for now, that was enough.

~ ☾ ~

Aknowledgements

First and foremost, this book wouldn't be possible if it weren't for the brain power and input from my amazing crit partners T.W. Fendley, Brad R. Cook, Sarah Bromley, Shawntelle Madison, and Michelle McLean. Thank you for your amazing advice and for convincing me to forego my timeshare in the pit.

Amanda Bonilla and Windy Aphayrath, thank you for answering my frantic emails and getting me to laugh at times when all I wanted to do was cry.

Special thanks to the wonderful CMP super duo, Steph Murray and Marlene Castricato. Thanks for welcoming me into the fold and making me feel like part of the family.

And super duper thanks to my amazing editor, Rochelle French. If she weren't an editor, I'm sure she'd have a career in gems. That lady knows how to make diamonds out of coal.

And, as always, thank you to the Hubs and Bubs, who never complain about the amount of dog hair on the floor or if we're having frozen pizza again. Love to you both.

COLE GIBSEN

When Cole Gibsen isn't writing fiction for young adults she can be found shaking her booty in a zumba class, picking off her nail polish, or drinking straight from the jug (when no one is looking). Cole currently resides in the Greater St. Louis area with her husband, daughter, and one very cranky border collie.

Visit her page at www.colegibsen.com !

CPSIA information can be obtained at www.ICGtesting.com
Printed in the USA
LVOW131554140512

281684LV00001B/141/P

9 781937 254278